# GUNFIGHT AT GOWER GULCH

# GUNFIGHT AT GOWER GULCH

# PAUL DELLINGER

FP

FuturesPast Publishing

Interior design and formatting by

E.M.
TIPPETTS
BOOK DESIGNS

www.emtippettsbookdesigns.com

Futures Past Publishing
ISBN 978-0-9907530-2-5

First edition

*To Mack Houston, Craig Allison and Richard B. Smith III,*
*long-time western movie boosters, and to some sadly no longer with us:*
*John Rutherford, Bobby J. Copeland and Ron Downey.*

Looking back from Hollywood in 1950, it seems like yesterday, but it was more like eighty years ago...

The wooden stairs creaked as I came down into the saloon, and three pairs of eyes jerked up. One of the gunmen kind of resembled Republic Pictures' perennial bad man, Roy Barcroft. Another looked a little like actor John Carradine. The third was just ugly.

All that saved me, I guess, is that they were as surprised as I was. That, and their mistaken idea that I knew how to use the pistols I was packing.

They thought I was my brother, whose clothes I was wearing as he lay upstairs with a bullet in him. He would know how to use the two guns I had borrowed from him. Me, my idea had been simply to make it outside onto a horse and lead them away. I was certainly no match for them in a gunfight.

The thing was, they didn't know that...

# GUNFIGHT AT GOWER GULCH

By Paul Dellinger

# PREFACE

For young people growing up in parts of the United States between the 1930s and the 1950s, western movies provided more than entertainment. They often carried with them moral values that molded several generations. One movie historian summarized it this way:

"Even when there was no message, these films had a long term, subtle and unconscious effect. To today's audiences they are transparent, wide-eyed, unrealistic, and naïve. To the immature, defenseless and more innocent audience in those darkened theaters waiting to be entertained, a total life style or at least ethical system was often pieced together from countless B films which, unrealized by them, influenced the way they conducted the rest of their lives."

From: *Republic Studios: Between Poverty Row and the Majors,*
by Richard Maurice Hurst, Scarecrow Press, 1979, quoted by permission

"Another fight at Hollywood and Gower! Backup needed. This thing's practically a riot... Shots fired! Shots fired!"

Given the number of uniformed police responding, it was amazing how thoroughly the incident at Gower Gulch was hushed up. Most of the actors and stunt men involved had been from minor studios, and practically all of them had been associated with B-westerns. Studio representatives moved quickly to kill any publicity.

There had been one gunshot injury, and Rick Martin, reluctant detective with the Los Angeles Police Department, had just completed a preliminary interview with the victim. Now Rick wondered how he was going to explain it to his boss.

"It's an evil threatening the entire country," the injured man had said. "It's been going on for nearly a hundred years. This movie thing is just a small corner of it. Please, detective, take this seriously!"

I ought to be in Korea, Rick thought, not for the first time. I know what's happening there is a threat. Since the North Koreans crossed the 38th parallel last summer, he had wanted to re-enlist. It had been Nazis during last time, now it was the commies. But Rick had been deemed "essential personnel" here in L.A., so here he stayed.

When word came in about the fight, he'd figured it was just another squabble among the usual rowdies. That wouldn't be uncommon over there, where Poverty Row studio extras hung out most days hoping for a movie call, even if just to fall off a horse. But, no, as it turned out, it really had almost been a riot, and even a shooting before it got stopped. It all happened near the corner of Sunset Boulevard and Gower Street, a part of Hollywood once known as the Watering Hole and these days as Gower Gulch. That corner had been a gathering place for out-of-work cowboys hunting film jobs since the days of silent pictures. Even now, right smack in the middle of the twentieth century, they still came.

Rick remembered hearing that actor Tim McCoy, a working cowboy himself before his expertise about Indians got him into movies, claimed that nearly as many men had been killed in or around those Gower Gulch bars and back-alleys as had been buried in Dodge City's Boot Hill during its cattle-shipping heyday. But those bits of mayhem mostly sprang from scraps between some of the Gower Gulch regulars. Not this time. This melee drew in some of the busiest cowboy stars ever to grace a movie poster. And now Rick had to try and sort it all out to his captain, who was leaning back behind his desk frowning with growing impatience.

"Come on, tell me," Captain Brown said in his deep rumble of a voice. "You saying it wasn't just another brawl among drunks with knives or guns?"

"A little more than that," Rick said.

Brown gave Rick his Broderick Crawford stare. He had never taken his resemblance to Crawford as a compliment when the beefy actor was appearing in pictures like When the Daltons Rode and Bad Men of Tombstone, but, since Crawford had won an Oscar for All the King's Men last March, Brown no longer seemed to mind. Although he would never say so, Rick preferred the earlier movies. He enjoyed westerns.

"Well," he said, "it involved a bunch of movie people—and I mean some stars, even if they are mostly from second-tier studios. I'm talking about your cowboy hero types—people you'd never connect with anything like this. Real straight arrows, at least in public. Well, I guess they have to be. Over at Republic, their contracts even forbid them to smoke or drink in front of their fans. Might ruin their image with the kids."

"Skip the trivia, Martin. And get rid of that chewing gum! Just who are we talking about?"

Rick dropped his wad of Doublemint into the wastebasket by the desk. If Doublemint was good enough for Gene Autry, on his radio show, it was good enough for Rick.

"About all of them!" he answered. "Everyone from the king of the cowboys to the king of the bullwhip and the king of the wild west, three or four Red Ryders, action heroes, villains, singing cowboys, sidekicks, stunt men..."

"Okay, all right, let's not go overboard." Brown released a long, loud sigh. "Wonderful. Just wonderful. Any of them injured or dead?"

"Just some bruises and black eyes. It'd be interesting to see how they cover them up when they go back to work. When you're shooting pictures in six days or so, you can't just wait for them to fade. But you'd be surprised at who actually did get hospitalized. Does the name Johnathan Six ring a bell?"

Brown's heavy brow furrowed. "The script doctor?" He shook his head. "Tell you the truth, I thought he was one of those Hollywood folk tales, something like those 'Kilroy was here' scrawls all over Europe during the war."

"Well, he just had a bullet removed at city hospital, Captain. He's real."

"Huh! So he's actually surfaced."

"Apparently, all those actors already knew him, worked with him, liked him. When word got around that someone was laying for him, they showed up."

"Have you interviewed him?"

"A little," Rick said. He hesitated, then took the plunge. "He was in and out, still under sedation. According to him, Captain, the men shooting at him belong to some cabal that's supposedly been active for decades, some subversive group..."

"Subversive? Come on, Martin. A western movie writer making like a member of the House Un-American Activities Committee?" He looked steadily at Rick, who remained silent. "Don't tell me you think there's something to it?"

Rick had his own misgivings about HUAC. The so-called Hollywood Ten were on their way to prison for contempt of Congress, refusing to answer the committee's questions about previous communist party memberships or to name others in that category. Rick was as worried about the commies as anyone, but he didn't think a bunch of movie people were going to subvert the country. And it was the communists in North Korea who had invaded another country this year.

"I don't know what to make of the guy, Captain," he said. "He's got to be 'way up in his eighties, maybe older, if half the rumors about him are true. I mean, he actually lived through some of the stuff he ghost-writes about. He's a tough old bird, but he seems lucid enough."

"Just what we need. A script sweetener making like Gabby Hayes."

"At least the newspapers haven't picked it up, or connected the name. And those studios have managed to keep the lid on the involvement by their folks. The afternoon papers have it as another Gower Gulch scrap. Captain, I'd like to get his whole story, before some reporter tumbles to who all was really there. Even if it never gets into an official report, it might be something we should know about."

"Yeah. It might also be the ramblings of a senile old man who makes up stuff for a living."

"Yes, sir, it might. But, well, look what's going on these days. The police action in Korea. Truman authorizing production of the hydrogen bomb this year, since the Russians detonated their atom bomb. Then there was that federal indictment a couple of months ago of the Rosenbergs..."

"What does any of that have to do with a bunch of movie cowboys getting into a rhubarb?" Brown demanded.

Rick hesitated. "I don't really know," he admitted. "The old boy has just dropped hints. But I think it's worth pursuing," he said, realizing how weak that sounded even as he said it. To be honest, he wondered himself if his curiosity was whetted by his addiction to cowboy movies. But...naah.

Brown gave Rick the glare again. Rick, who had worked his way up to staff sergeant during the last two years of World War II, remembered how Brown had deep-sixed his re-enlistment, with the department already losing men to the draft. He didn't want to lose Rick's four years of investigative experience.

Rick could almost read those thoughts on Brown's broad face. He knew the captain figured he owed him one, and would cut him some slack. Brown sighed again, then started shuffling through one of the piles of paperwork on his desk. "All right. Just let me know what you get." When Rick didn't stand up to leave, Brown looked up again. "Something else?"

"Well, I'd like to borrow Miss Hamilton from the secretarial pool..."

"I'm sure you would. So would all the males in this building."

"I mean, to take down the victim's statement," Rick continued, needlessly running a hand over his G.I. haircut. "In his condition, it might take a number of visits to get the whole story. It would just go faster if..."

"All right, all right, I get it. Like I said, let me know if you hear anything that seems worth following up, and we'll decide how to proceed from there."

"Thanks, Captain."

Nancy Hamilton gave Rick a bright smile when he approached her desk. It went well with her light brown hair, slim figure and glowing complexion. A Lux girl, he thought. But when he told her what he wanted, she wasn't sure she liked the idea of a task that could last days, or weeks, sitting beside a hospital bed taking dictation.

She changed her mind when Rick told her the name of the injured man. "He's real? I thought he was some Hollywood legend," she said.

Rick couldn't help grinning. "You and the captain, both."

"So there really is this ancient western movie mastermind that all these writers consult to perk up their scripts? And we'll get to interview him?"

It hadn't occurred to Rick that even Nancy Hamilton could be star-struck. "Haven't you ever wondered why westerns are so much alike?" he joked. "He's real enough, Nancy. I don't know if what he tells us will be true, or something out of another script he's making up, but I do have to interview him. We still have no idea what was behind that fight over at Gower, but he's the one who ended up getting shot."

"You mean that rumor was true? Wow. Okay, Detective Martin, you've got yourself a girl." Rick was tempted to ask if there was a double meaning there, but decided not to press his luck. Nancy called him by his first name the few times they'd dated, but he was strictly "Detective Martin" during working hours. He had stolen a perfunctory kiss at their last goodnight outside her door. Nancy hadn't resisted, or encouraged, but it warmed him during the entire drive to his own little apartment—more than kisses much more ardent with previous girls ever had.

At the hospital, a busy doctor agreed to let them talk to the patient but warned against tiring him. "He's older than he looks," the doctor said. "He could still have a relapse."

Even at his age, even in a hospital bed, Jonathan Six impressed Rick. His darkly-tanned face could have been carved out of mahogany, he still had his hair although it was salt-and-pepper now, and there was a wiry musculature beneath the hospital gown. An occasional tightening of his lips was the only evidence of pain he showed. But, whatever his age, his dark eyes brightened at the sight of Nancy when Rick introduced her. Still some juice in the old man, Rick decided.

"Yep. I can tell you exactly what it was about, detective," said the man in the bed, in a voice almost as deep as that of Brace Beemer, radio's Lone Ranger since 1941. "In fact, like I told you before, it has a lot to do with bad stuff going on around the country. But it started a long time ago. Almost a century ago." He chuckled, then grimaced in pain. "Seems like I can remember what happened back then better than what happened last week."

Rick glanced at Nancy, but her full attention was fixed on the man in the bed. "That's…intriguing," he finally said.

"But you have to let me tell it my own way. I've spent so many years crafting stories that I just naturally have to start with a hook." He winked at Nancy. "Besides, for you to understand everything, I'll have to go back a while." He smiled, as though at a private joke. "Quite a while."

"Tell it any way you want to, Mr. Six."

"Okay, then." Six shifted his gaze to where Nancy sat, her shorthand pad on one shapely knee and her pencil poised above it. "Miss Hamilton, you might want to label this as chapter one…"

# ONE

The wooden stairs creaked as I put my weight on them, and three pairs of eyes in the room below jerked up to where I stood—and froze when they saw me. I figured I was a goner right then. Any second now, they would start shooting, and these three wouldn't miss. My skin felt like it was trying to shrink away from the borrowed clothing I wore, like I could already feel those impacts, and a cold drop of sweat inched its way down the middle of my spine.

All that saved me, I guess, is that they were as surprised as I was. That, and their mistaken idea that I knew how to use the pistols I was packing.

Even with the rainstorm outside, I hadn't counted on them strolling into this isolated crossroads saloon so casually. Didn't they have enough sense to realize I could have been waiting to pot them, one by one, as they came through its swinging doors? Which is maybe what I would have done, if I'd been who they thought I was.

My plan had been to slip outside into the gathering dusk before they spotted me, climb aboard one of their horses and gallop away like a scalded dog, drawing them after me. Sure, they knew this country better than I did, but this Nebraska downpour just might have given me enough of an edge to lose them.

Instead, here I was, frozen on that rickety stairway, facing all three of them and knowing I had about as much chance as a bluebelly serenading Quantrill's late little band with a rendition of "Yankee Doodle." I mean, these men were professional gunfighters; they made their livings killing people. And even though I was packing a matched pair of heavy forty-fives belted around my waist, I had never fired a six-shooter at anyone in my life.

The thing was, they didn't know that.

They thought I was one Jackson Six, better known as Double-Six because of the two fancy pistols he—or, at the moment, I—carried. Jack had packed two pistols ever since he'd ridden with Quantrill back during the war. He probably carried more, back then. Quantrill's men kept saddlebags full of six-guns, grabbing a fresh one whenever a gun clicked empty instead of bothering to reload. The James boys and the Youngers still equipped themselves that way when they made their banking withdrawals.

Well, I'd wanted them to think I was Jack and apparently I'd done it. But what I'd wanted them to see was my east side heading west, not me standing here on this rickety narrow stairway looking down at them, with them between me and the way out. I tried to keep from swallowing, figuring they'd recognize it as fear.

The only shooting I'd ever done with someone firing back had been three years ago, not far from my home—my former home—back in Virginia. That had been with a cast-off single-shot powder-and-ball rifle, in what became known as the Battle of New Market, where I was among those who joined ranks with a bunch of Virginia Military Institute cadets who charged the Yankees and turned things around that day. I might have been the youngest kid there. We went into the fight full of vinegar, but their classroom instruction and my thoughts of glory hadn't covered things like how you were supposed to stop the bleeding when someone's ear got shot off, or what to do for a boy using both his arms to try and keep his insides from spilling out of his stomach. General Breckinridge and us, we won the battle. Too bad we lost the war. Although it turned out I was probably fighting on the wrong side, but I didn't know it then.

A rifle was one thing, a short gun was another. Sure, I knew how to fire one—I was even pretty good at hitting stationary targets. But I was no match for men who made their living with one.

"I must be slippin'," said the biggest of the three, a genial grin on his whiskered face. He was a good-size man. Think of Roy Barcroft, the burly bad guy you see in all those Republic films. He actually did resemble Barcroft in one of his crusty heavy roles. "I figured, where I put that bullet, you wouldn't be up to no walkin' around."

This would be Ben Quinn. Jack had told me it must've been Quinn who fired the bullet into his back—but for no reason he knew. They were never close friends, but there was no bad blood between them. If there had been, Jack had told me, he would never have turned his back on Quinn.

Besides the trio I was facing, there were a couple of evening loungers in the place—herders, most likely. At Quinn's words, they both eased casually off the cracker boxes that served as chairs and ambled out of the line of fire. The bartender stepped behind one of the barrels that held up the makeshift bar, and looked ready to drop to the dirt floor at the first move by any of us.

One of the men behind Quinn was a tall, gaunt-looking character in a black coat, buttoned up so you'd think he'd have trouble getting at any gun inside it. I decided he was probably the least dangerous of the three. It would be months before I learned better. This man—he would be reminiscent of John Carradine if you'd seen him in *Stagecoach*—was actually the most cold-blooded killer of them all.

The remaining gunman looked almost my own age, a blondish buck-toothed kid wearing a rain-soaked white shirt under a silver-studded vest, with chaps and a gun belt and a brace of pistols even more ornate than those I'd borrowed from Jack. His mouth hung open, and his pale blue eyes were wide. He hadn't gotten over the shock of seeing me upright and seemingly ready to give them a fight.

"Yeah, I reckon you're tougher than I thought, Mister Double-Six," Quinn went on jovially. "But I'm bettin' that hunk of lead you're carryin' will slow you down considerable, when we get around to it."

That seemed to perk up the kid. His eyes narrowed to ugly slits, and his mouth turned up in the kind of grin I remembered seeing once on a man beating a slave for no reason other than the slave owner probably enjoyed it. I decided then and there that, if I had a chance of taking down any of the three before I hit the floor, it would be him.

Something of my decision may have shown. "C'mon, Double-Six," the kid hissed at me. "C'mon, let's see if you're as good as they say."

They had no way of knowing that the real Double-Six was lying in a cramped little room upstairs, maybe near death, and that I'd switched my eastern clothes for his trademark black outfit, guns and all, hoping to lead them away from him and that knockout of a young woman who was his nursemaid at the moment.

Well, it had seemed like a good idea at the time.

Me, I was Jackson's younger brother, Jonathan, and I'd come west from Virginia to find him before some of Aaron Sutherland's hired guns did. Unfortunately for him and me both, it looked like the race had ended in a tie.

The last we'd heard of Jack when I was back home, he'd been moving around the Nebraska Territory—well, it was the state of Nebraska now, since the previous March. Jack, or Double-Six, had become just well-known enough for us to read about him in sporadic newspaper writings from frontier correspondents, although you had to take their accounts with a grain of salt. At least they hadn't made him out to be some kind of Robin Hood, as they'd done with some of the other rowdies, like Jesse and Frank James. In fact, Jack had actually been a peace officer a time or two—and a gambler, and a stagecoach shotgun guard, and a lot of other things that sometimes encouraged gunplay and increased his notoriety. When I started out, I didn't think I'd have much trouble tracking him down—but neither would others. And there was no way he could know those others were coming after him.

I'd traveled west by train until the rails ran out at Omaha. A few more years and the Union Pacific would extend them. It was in Omaha where I picked up rumors about Double-Six having been in another shooting scrape, this one in Jefferson County. Allowing for exaggeration, it seemed he'd suggested that a couple of cowpokes in a card game had been working in unison to give Lady Luck a little help, and they'd invited him outside to discuss the matter. In the street, Jack had simply kept on back-pedaling until he was beyond their pistol accuracy range, then put a couple bullets from one of his long-barreled Colts right by their booted toes. They got the message. They'd probably never studied the classics, but they took Shakespeare's advice about discretion and valor.

Back home, a nickname like my brother had acquired struck me as a silly affectation. It would take me a little longer to realize that out here such tags were commonplace, and Double-Six was no more outlandish than, say, the Sundance Kid, Mysterious Dave Mather, Shanghai Pierce, Dog Kelly, Big Foot Wallace, Red River Johnny, Calamity Jane, Big Nose Kate, Bat Masterson, Buffalo Bill, Wild Bill, Curly Bill or Billy the Kid, to name a few. It was a colorful time and place, and so were its characters.

The stagecoach on which I'd booked passage took the road, if you could call it that, to Kansas City but would pass through much of Jefferson County on the way. I'd been the last of six passengers to climb aboard. I eased myself onto as much seat as was available on my side, while my eyes adjusted from dazzling sunlight to the dark interior.

She was the first thing I saw when I took a look at the passengers sitting opposite and, lordy, she was worth seeing.

You noticed her eyes first, dark brown. Her hair was long, also dark and framed her oval face nicely. Even seated, you could tell her figure was notable. Picture Linda Stirling, the model-turned-serial queen. Those were the kind of looks she had.

Her name, I learned as we got to talking among ourselves, was Callie St. Clair. And that was about all we learned, despite obvious interest from all five of us male passengers. Oh, she was polite enough, but her friendly small talk never revealed as much about her as you might have thought when you mentally played back what she said.

On the other hand, all five of us fell over ourselves to tell her our life stories—even me, up to a point. I said where I was from, that I was trying to locate my brother to tell him our father had died and there was an estate to be divided up. Beyond that I dared not go since, for all I knew, one of the other passengers might be taking pay from the Sutherlands, keeping an eye on me in hopes I'd lead him to Jack. My being last into the coach should have eluded any followers, but who knew?

I needn't have worried. As it turned out, Jack would lead the trouble to me.

Several times, I thought I caught Callie St. Clair studying me uncertainly, as though she expected me to say something more, but then looking quickly away when I caught her eye. I put it down to wishful thinking.

Heavy rain clouds darkened the evening skies even before nightfall, but our driver seemed to know where he was going. At least he never slackened speed until, with no warning whatsoever, we heard him push his foot on his brake and felt the coach swerve and tilt alarmingly before it bumped to a stop.

"What the hell?" "What's going on?" "Is there trouble?" The questions spewed out all around me and, knowing no better at the time, I leaned across another passenger and stuck my head out a window. It wasn't bandits, Indians or a natural disaster, but a man on horseback, swaying alarmingly in the saddle.

"Get back in there, kid!" the grizzled driver yelled down at me, as the shotgun guard swung his two barrels toward the horseman.

"But he's hurt," I protested.

"Maybe he is, maybe he ain't. You stay put 'til we find out, hear?"

The driver was right, of course. I was a greenhorn, and the price of my ticket included letting him and the guard handle stuff like this. Anyway, it was none of my business. I just wished the driver hadn't made a point of it in front of Miss St. Clair. Maybe that was why I got stubborn and kept my head poked outside for longer than common sense dictated.

It was just long enough for the rider to raise up in the saddle so I glimpsed his face. Then his head drooped again, and this time he did slide down onto the road, falling the last little distance as his foot dropped free of the stirrup.

Even in the dimming twilight, I recognized the face as a near mirror-image of my own. It was Jackson, appearing out of the blue even as I'd been seeking him. I think the driver yelled at me again when I opened the door and jumped down, but I was beyond listening.

Jack's eyes fluttered open as I knelt beside him. "Johnny," he said weakly. "Where...where'd you drop from, kid?"

Sure enough, he was dressed all in black just like the dime novel magazines described—hat, coat, boots, even the gun belt with the long-barreled forty-fives. The bandana around his neck was a contrasting red. So was the monogram sewed into the upper part of his shirt, depicting two number sixes, just like his nickname. So was the blood I felt on his back when I reached under to lift him up.

It scared me, every bit as much as when the V.M.I. cadets had been dropping around me in New Market. All this way, and I'd been lucky enough to stumble onto him—maybe only to lose him.

I realized the driver was standing over me and, to my surprise, so was Callie St. Clair. The blood on my hand didn't seem to affect her. To the driver, who was built sort of squat like cowboy-turned-actor Bud Osborne, one of the few actors who actually could handle a team of horses, it was confirmation that the man in the road wasn't faking. If either of them noticed in the dimming light that his looks resembled mine, they didn't comment.

"There's a crossroads saloon about a dozen miles ahead," the driver said. "We could drop him there. If he lasts that long."

My reaction to the statement must have shown in my face. "Drop him? He needs a doctor!"

"Might be someone there who could do him some good. Anyhow, that's closest. They got a couple upstairs rooms for passers-by. He'd have a bed, food, time to heal up if he's not too bad off."

Of course, I had no idea of the many functions a crossroads saloon served in this wide-open territory—how it not only catered to a traveler's thirst, but also served as a supply depot, an information center on things like what trails were flooded or where hostiles might be on the prod, or just as a place to rest up. These were all things I would learn eventually.

The driver and guard laid Jack out between the pieces of luggage tied to the top of the coach, since there was no room inside. I joined them on top, thinking I could at least volunteer to help hold onto him. Actually, I was lucky just to hang on myself.

Those twelve miles seemed like a hundred, but we finally pulled to a stop outside a square-shaped two-story sod building. They carried Jack to one of those upstairs rooms, me trailing along and glad someone else had taken charge. The gladness evaporated when I realized our driver meant to resume our journey immediately.

"But we can't just go off and leave him here with a bullet in him," I said.

Even now, standing in the dark hallway outside the room, the driver seemed not to have looked closely enough at either of us to catch our resemblance. Or maybe he just didn't care. "Can't do nothin' else, son," he told me. "They can take care of him here, better than we can. I ain't no doctor. My job's to deliver goods and passengers on schedule, or as close to as possible. You comin'?"

"No," I said. "No, I'm not. I'll get my bag before you go."

"You're paid up through to Kansas City..."

"I said no." I was in no mood to explain. "I'm getting off here."

He shrugged and started back down the stairs. "Suit yourself. I'll leave your bag."

The man who ran the place, a big bruiser with a bald spot on the back of his bullet-shaped head, helped me strip Jack down to his underwear and I saw two ugly wounds on his lower left side. That surprised me. During his occasional periods of consciousness, Jack had managed to tell me about a man named Ben Quinn having shot him, once. He'd been hit too hard to fight back, but managed to stay in the saddle and gallop off before Ben and the two men with him could get to their horses.

I tried to tell Jack who might have paid Quinn for that. But I wasn't sure how much he understood.

"You gonna stay with him?" the proprietor asked, after we'd loaded Jack on the couch-like bunk. "Good. See if you can stop the bleedin'. I got to get back downstairs before that helper of mine sells someone the wrong kind of whiskey and gets us both in trouble. Check his pockets, see if he has any money to pay for his keep."

His leaving me on my own didn't bother me as much as hearing the coach pull out down below. I must have been getting accustomed to the casual attitude toward whether a wounded man lived or died. That's why I was doubly surprised when, a few minutes later, the door squeaked open and Callie St. Clair walked briskly inside.

"How is he?" she asked, her pretty face creased with worry.

It didn't even occur to me to wonder why a young woman traveling alone would dare leave her transportation as I'd done, out here in the middle of nowhere. I was all too glad to take any help I could get.

"I don't know. He hasn't come around again since they carried him in here. He's still bleeding. I thought he said he'd only been hit once, but..."

She lifted the blanket off him. If his lack of clothing bothered her, she gave no sign of it. "Just once," she said. "This wound in front would be where the bullet came out. That's good, actually. It means he's not carrying it around. But it's hard to tell what damage it did. Do you have any clean shirts in your gear?"

"Yes..."

"Get one and tear it into strips. No, wait. Have you got any money?"

"Yes, as a matter of fact..."

"Go downstairs and buy a bottle of something that still has the top on it. We can sterilize the wounds and, if he comes around, maybe get some of it inside him. Go on, get moving. You were looking for your brother, right? Now that you've found him, we need to keep him alive."

I was stunned, but I didn't argue. She seemed to know more about this sort of thing than I did. And she'd been more observant than I'd thought, I realized, about our likeness.

When the light from the room's tiny window had totally gone, we worked by lantern. The rain was pouring outside now, punctuated by occasional flashes of lightning. Jack remained unconscious, and there came a time when all we could do was sit and wait. I suggested that she might want to go downstairs and get something to eat. She said it would be better for me to go buy something for both of us and bring it up. I did that, and we were washing the last of it down with coffee when we heard the sound outside of horses clopping slowly up to the front of the building.

I turned down the lantern and crept to the window. Three horsemen, all wearing slickers. The guard had tied Jack's horse to the coach, and left it under a lean-to where some of the customers downstairs had parked their animals. Suppose one of these newcomers was Ben Quinn? He might recognize Jack's animal. That was when I got my brilliant decoy idea.

No, I was not trying to impress Callie. I didn't feel a bit brave. I just plain couldn't think of anything else, short of waiting in the room until they found us and finished the job they'd started. If it was them, I wanted them far away from here.

I asked Callie to turn her back while I put on Jack's clothing. She ignored that, and asked me if I could ride a horse. As it happened, I could. We'd raised horses back home, and Jack and I had often raced one another over the grassy meadows of the Shenandoah Valley.

I was big for my age, and Jack's outfit fit me pretty well, even if he had a few years and pounds on me. I tried to ignore the scratchy hardness of his caked blood inside the shirt, and pulled the coat on over it.

"In case I don't...I mean, if things don't go right, there's some money in those clothes I'm leaving. Use it for food, board, a doctor if you can find one—whatever you think best. I don't know how to thank you for what you've done already..."

"If you really can ride," she said, cutting me off, "your best chance would be to follow the way the coach went. As soon as you're out of sight, cut to the east. You'll run into a creek. It may be up, with all this rain, but, if you can get across it, they'd have a hard time picking up your trail at night on the other side."

I found myself holding Jack's heavy gun belt. "Maybe I should leave these, in case they come up. I could ride better without them, anyway."

"Don't be silly. You'd never pass for him without them. Besides," she said, producing something small and silvery in the dull lamplight, "I'm not unarmed."

Like I said, Callie St. Clair was full of surprises.

And so, decked out to look like the Double-Six I'd read about back home but who still seemed to me somebody foreign to the brother I remembered, I stepped into the hallway, started downstairs and ran right smack into Quinn and company.

"Keep comin', mister," Quinn said. "Keep comin'." Little did I know that one day I'd help put that dialog into the mouth of the actor who so resembled him, only Barcroft would be talking to "Rocky" Lane, playing a role more competent than I was.

I forced myself to keep moving down the steps, ignoring the hissed challenges from the big-mouthed kid and keeping my eyes firmly on Quinn. If he was the leader of this jolly little band, maybe the other two would wait for him to make the first move. I reached the bottom of the stairway and kept walking toward him.

Jack had referred to Quinn by his first name in his halting account of what happened, so I did that, too. "Why'd you try it, Ben?" I said, surprised that my voice didn't crack.

He threw back his head and laughed. "Try, hell. You can't tell me you ain't hurtin'."

"Come on, Ben. Since when have we got trouble between us?"

"To tell the truth, I'm kind of sorry about it myself, Jack. But business is business. Someone paid right handsome to get you out of the way."

I kept hoping some of the bystanders would step in and help. I hadn't yet realized the value folks out here put on minding their own business. Quinn wasn't telling me anything I hadn't already guessed, but I tried to keep him talking, anyway. "Who paid you, Ben?"

"An old friend of the family, he said he was. Come on, Jack, what's it matter?" His hand touched the wooden handle of his pistol in its well-worn holster, and I noticed his companions spreading to either side of me. "That wound ought to have stiffened you up pretty good by now, so I guess it'll be safe for me to take you from the front this time..."

I hit him.

It was the last thing he expected. I'd kept my hands away from Jack's guns, hoping Quinn would take his time. But if they thought I was hurt too badly to grab a pistol, they certainly wouldn't be ready for me to wade into them with fists.

Both Jack and I had had our share of scraps back home, part of the ritual of growing up in those days, so I knew a little about what worked. My right fist struck the side of Quinn's whiskered jaw with all my weight behind it. He stumbled back into the lean figure in the undertaker's coat. I turned and swung my left straight into the buck teeth of the kid wearing all the finery. It gashed my knuckles, but seeing one of his teeth fly across the room was worth it.

Neither man went all the way down, but both were staggered. That gave me time to dash through the swinging doors into the pouring rain.

They hadn't bothered to put their horses in the lean-to, but had left all three at a hitch-rack to my right. I lurched toward them. As I moved, I heard what sounded like another clap of thunder, only it came from behind me and I saw that one of the swinging doors where I'd been standing had been blown away. It looked like someone had touched off a small cannon.

I hit the stirrup of the nearest horse, a bay, and caught up its reins, yelling in hopes the other two would bolt. No such luck. They bucked a time or two, but their reins held to the rack and I wasn't about to waste time loosening them—not with whatever was being fired at me from the saloon. I jerked the head of my confiscated horse toward the stage road and dug in my heels.

The horse went straight up in the air, and came down snapping at one of my legs. I guessed its owner must have treated it with less than tender loving care, but he obviously hadn't broken its spirit. I grabbed its mane with one hand and kicked its sides again, and this time it took off.

This was no smoothly-gaited horse like those I'd been used to in Virginia, but it could move. I heard more gunfire behind me, pistol shots this time. I crouched low, trying to encourage the horse to pick up more speed as I heard hoof-beats starting up back where I'd been. Instead of the horse speeding up, it gave me a feisty snort. Apparently I'd picked the meanest horse instead of the fastest.

To make matters worse, flashes of lightning kept making things bright as day. I'd counted on the darkness and the storm for concealment, but it wasn't working out that way. I thought about trying to shoot back at my pursuers, but doubted I'd be able to hit anyone, so I just concentrated on riding.

I couldn't shake off the two horses pounding along behind me. When the lightning flashed again, I glimpsed what looked like a raging river paralleling the road to my left and a bank of trees beyond that. If this was the creek Callie had mentioned, it was up, all right. Still, if I could get across, I figured I could lose the would-be killers in those trees.

It took some powerful pulling to guide the horse off the trail. He didn't slacken his speed at all as we headed for a jump-off point above the water—but, just as we hit the edge of the bank, he slid to a stop that must have left furrows in the ground a foot long.

The horse stopped, but I didn't. I went sailing over his head and, before I knew it, I was deep in water and being dragged along by a strong current. Above the roaring of the water, I heard more pistol shots, but I didn't think any of the bullets came anywhere close.

Something else did, though—the trunk of a tree, a log-like piece of debris, big enough to deal me a solid whack on the side of the head. Fireflies exploded in front of my eyes. I grabbed blindly at whatever had struck me, and held on as it pulled me along in the water. It kept turning in my grasp, leaving me swallowing water and coughing it up each time I battled back to the surface.

I tried to wrestle myself onto it, but it was a lot bigger than I was. The blackish water rushed over me, and my only comfort was that, at least, Jack and Callie St. Clair should be safe. The killers would believe they'd finished their job on Double-Six.

*Jonathan Six laid his head back on the pillow and closed his eyes. Nancy finished her shorthand version of the last sentence, and looked at Rick expectantly, pencil still poised. "Well?" said Rick. "What happened? I don't guess you drowned, did you?"*

*"Too tired," the old man said. "Come back tomorrow."*

*"Now, wait a minute, Mr. Six. I know you've been working with screenplays probably since* The Great Train Robbery, *but this isn't some movie serial, it's a police investigation. When are we going to get to what happened over at Gower Gulch?"*

*The man on the bed managed a small smile, but kept his eyes shut. "If it was a serial, I'd tell you to come back next week. And it will be some time yet before we get to what happened down at Gower. I told you I'd have to explain in my own way."*

*Outside in the hospital corridor, Rick touched Nancy's arm. "What do you think? Is he just making all this up?"*

*"I have no idea," Nancy said, her eyes bright. "But I'm certainly looking forward to the next installment."*

# TWO

*Eddie Dean: "Where there's so much stew, there's bound to be a little gravy."*
Wild West *(1946)*

I'd always been a little afraid of my father. Well, not afraid, exactly—more in awe of him. He was an awesome character, I realize now, with a deceptively quiet manner which could explode whenever he was prodded. Jack and I both had memories of blistered backsides to prove that. Maybe that was why Jack had decided it was safer to go west and even into Bleeding Kansas than to stay in Virginia and face Dad's wrath.

Looking back, I'm not so sure Dad wouldn't have let Jack off the hook, maybe just admonished him to be more careful next time. Dad never had gotten along with Sally Louise's old man anyway, even before Colonel Sutherland caught Jack and Sally Louise in the loft of his stable, communing with nature and one another.

Dad seemed smaller somehow, as he lay in the coffin with his large hands folded in a pious attitude he would never have assumed in life. His eyes were closed, his iron-gray hair combed with uncharacteristic neatness, and I kept expecting him to sit up and kick off the sides the box which held him.

But he didn't, and the burial proceeded on schedule. The headstone was simple, as he would have wished, listing only his name—Samuel Six—and his dates, 1801 to 1867. A long life for some back then, but not for him. Not from some fool thing like a cold, which went into pneumonia and got worse until the raspy breathing finally stopped one night and the silence jerked me awake in the chair where I'd dozed off next to his bed.

There had been no time to reach Jack, even if I'd known where to try. But he would have hated the funeral ceremony as much as I did—as much as Dad would have, if he could've expressed an opinion. Our father never pretended to be more than he was, the son of a German immigrant named Sixt, before the family altered the spelling.

Dad had been a sailing man, and became something of a legend in the slave trade, given that importation of slaves into the United States became illegal in 1808 and a capital offense in 1820, although only one man was ever executed for it. Dad apparently was luckier, or his clipper ship was faster, as he was never caught.

And then, something caused him to give it up and scuttle his ship when he returned from his last voyage to the Dark Continent.

All that happened about the time Jack and I were born, and he never explained it to us. When war came, he wouldn't let us enlist in the ranks of the Confederacy, because of slavery, he said, which made no sense to us given his earlier profession. He hadn't been able to keep Jack from running off and joining a guerilla band out west supposedly affiliated with the South, not after the Sally Louise incident, or to keep me from my one and only combat experience when the war came to us in Virginia. But neither action pleased him.

I figured it had to have been our mother who wrought the change in him, but I wasn't sure why I thought that. Jack and I had never known her, aside from some occasional bit of information Dad would drop on occasion, in that brooding way of his. He would make some remark about her beauty, her gentleness, especially her ability to forgive, even her stubbornness, with great affection. I built up a mental picture of her over the years. I was twelve years old when it struck me that I didn't even know what her name had been.

The mystery of our mother never seemed to gnaw at Jack as it did me, close as we were. He took it as simply another fact of life. I'd tried to sound out some of my father's acquaintances in the towns around our farm, only to find out that they knew no more than I, or wouldn't admit to more. Dad had returned after being gone for an unprecedented three years on a slaver trip. But this time he'd brought back no human cargo—just an empty ship which he had the crew sink despite how well it had served him, and a pair of squalling brats, us.

I would often daydream about who our mother might have been. My favorite scenario had her as an English noblewoman, whose values would not condone the ownership of one human being by another. Or he could have met a woman in France, or more likely Spain, I thought, since both Jack and I had darker hair, eyes and complexions than the Scotch-Irish and German families that made up much of our county's population.

In retrospect, I wonder how I could have missed something so obvious. But no one else seemed to have realized it, either. Or, if they did, they didn't say anything where Dad could hear them.

I learned the truth within hours of the funeral, when I was summoned into the august presence of Colonel Sutherland. Well, Aaron Sutherland wasn't actually a colonel in the military sense. He'd never served in any army. It was purely a courtesy title for our most prominent citizen. Maybe that's why I generally have the major bad guy in my little movie scripts turn out to be the town's most prominent citizen.

But then, people also continued to refer to our father as "Captain" long after he had no ship.

What happened between my brother and Sally Louise quickly became common knowledge after the colonel raised such a fuss, and made it clear that he blamed Jack entirely. Jack hadn't waited around for the colonel to come charging over to our farm on his snow-white horse to brace Dad about it. He packed a few things, left a note apologizing for any trouble he might have brought on Dad, and expressed the hope that his departure from Virginia might alleviate it. He didn't even tell me goodbye, which kind of hurt. He was probably right, though. Had he stayed, I could see our father and Colonel Sutherland meeting with dueling pistols over Sally Louise's honor, or lack thereof.

But Jack was no longer around to be under Dad's protection. All that happened was that the colonel, his wife, Sally Louise and her brother, Sean, avoided Dad and me as much as possible. If one of us came into a store where any of them were, they would silently stalk out. If we came face to face in the street, they would look past us. I could only remember the colonel speaking to me once up to then. And that had not been a pleasurable experience at all.

It had been on a day when Dad and I were in Woodstock, the county seat, to record a deed on some acreage Dad had bought to add to our farm. That farm and my school work had kept me busy since Jack's abrupt departure. But I actually had hopes of getting into the Virginia Military Institute one day, having fought beside its cadets that one time, however briefly and ineffectually. Looking back, that had been a silly dream. But I was still a kid.

Dad's legal work was taking a long time, or so it seemed to my boyhood self on that warm, summer day, so I slipped out of the law office to walk around the town. The war hadn't been over long, not long enough for most of us to realize what Lee's surrender would mean to the South. I wondered if Jack would come home now, with the nation's hostilities ended, even if the local ones had not. And so I was thinking about the colonel when I all but bumped into him, rounding a corner where he and another man stood talking in low tones.

They had been partly concealed behind a pillar on the porch of a local doctor's home. When he spotted me, the colonel stopped talking in mid-sentence. His eyes widened and his nostrils flared. He seized a heavy-looking cane from the hand of the haggard-looking man with him. I think he was ready to brain me with it, when he was distracted by a cry of pain from its owner, who had been leaning on it. The stranger grabbed at the pillar to keep from falling. His anguish gave me a chance to back off and run back to the courthouse, wondering how my mere appearance could provoke such wrath. Maybe it was because Jack and I looked so much alike.

So the memory of that incident left me confused, when one of the colonel's newly-freed servants handed me a note as I was leaving the cemetery: Would I do Colonel Sutherland the honor of calling upon him at his home after dinner that evening, on a matter of business?

The colonel was all smiles when another of his ex-slaves ushered me into his living room. Sean was there, too, and he wasn't smiling—but then I never remembered seeing the colonel's spoiled son smile. When we'd been kids in school, I don't think a single year passed without Sean and Jack having at least one good fight. Sean was older now, and cut quite a dashing figure in his white shirt, red sash and tan riding britches, but the habitual sneer he wore kind of ruined the image.

I nodded to him, but he simply turned away without acknowledgement. Well, it was his father I'd been called to see. Actually, I'd been a little glad not to have to return so soon to the empty home where Dad had so recently breathed his last.

"Sit down, boy, sit down," the colonel said, with a smile so tight it seemed more of a grimace. His hair and beard, trimmed in a manner reminiscent of pictures I'd seen of General Lee, were as white as his hair. I wondered if it had ever been the rich chestnut-brown color or Sean's and Sally Louise's.

"I'll come right to the point, boy," he said when I was seated. "We've lost a war, here, and we're going to have to put up with what amounts to a Yankee occupation, at least for a time. Much of our beloved South is suffering food shortages, as you must know."

"Yes, sir," I agreed, wondering what he was getting at.

"I'm in a position to buy and work croplands, and I want to purchase yours. You certainly can't work it all by yourself, and our labor supply..." He permitted himself a dry chuckle. "Well, it's not what it was, is it? I can give you five thousand dollars, in cash, this very night, for the buildings, the livestock and the rest of the property."

It was all coming at me too fast. I hadn't even though ahead far enough to realize that I would, with Jack, inherit our farm. The offer seemed more than fair, and by now I doubted that my slightly-older brother ever expected to come home again. All the same, I felt I needed to contact him about it, and wondered if I dared bring up his name to the colonel.

"It's a fine offer, sir," I said. "I'd like to say yes, but I can't just yet. Dad's will hasn't even been read..."

"Oh yes it has," Sean put in.

The colonel waved him to silence. "What the lad means is that the captain's attorney knew of my interest, and confided your father's intent to leave the property to you. Since you are not yet of age, I offered to act as executor to protect your interests..."

"What?" Abruptly, I lost all reverence for the Colonel. "What right did that lawyer have coming to you?"

"Mind your tone, boy." The colonel picked up some papers from his elegant mahogany roll-top desk and handed them to me. "This agreement needs only your signature to make the sale official. And, as I said, I will make you an immediate cash payment. That money could take you a lot of places, you know."

He was too smooth, too rushed, and I wasn't even sure what he proposed was legal. I tried to buy time. "I'd need to consult my brother..."

"That's no good," the colonel interrupted. "We either complete the transaction right now, or forget it. Your choice, boy. It's a matter of take it or leave it."

I was still numb from Dad's death, I suppose, but I saw no reason to turn down his offer. I'd have to locate Jack, and get his half of the money to him. The colonel was right about me not being able to run the place alone. With Jack, I might have hung on. He was the more practical of us, more attuned to tilling the soil than I was. I took a deep breath, and hoped I was doing the right thing. "All right, sir."

"Very wise. Just sign here, and here. And then you can count this," he said, reaching into his desk and coming up with a sheaf of bills which looked big enough to choke that big white horse of his.

I signed, and counted, and still saw no disadvantage to Jack or myself in the deal—until I pocketed the wad of bills, and realized the colonel was no longer smiling. In fact, he was now regarding me with much the same expression as when I'd run into him in Woodstock a year ago.

I stood up, suddenly uneasy. "Well, I'll go directly to the farm, sir, and pack my stuff. You'll be able to move in..."

"Hold on, boy," Sean said. "We're not through with you, yet."

"No, we're not," the colonel agreed. "There was more in your father's papers than his will, boy. There was a letter to you and that filthy brother of yours."

I stared at him, now more angry than concerned about politeness. "A letter? And you read it? Who do you think...?"

Sean's fist slammed into my stomach. The breath whooshed out of me, as I sank to my knees on the carpeted floor, taken completely by surprise.

"Don't dirty your hands, son," the colonel said. "Use the whip."

As I knelt there fighting for air, Sean took a long black whip from where it hung on the wall. It had probably been there to keep the Sutherland slaves in line. Now it was going to be used on me.

The colonel was holding up another paper. Even with my eyes still watering from the effect of Sean's blow, I recognized the long bold strokes of Dad's handwriting. And then I felt the bite of the whip across my back.

"Know what it says, boy?" The colonel's voice seemed to come from some distance away. I could only concentrate on the cracking sounds of the whip, cutting through my shirt and leaving it in ribbons. "It says your father actually married, legally married, one of those African blacks on that last trip of his. A Christian ceremony, he says here, performed by some missionary. He'd have stayed over there with her, he says, but she died in childbirth—having you! Didn't you ever figure out that both you and that brother of yours are half nigger?"

His words burned into my brain as Sean's whip burned into my back. It wasn't possible! Jack and I half black? The colonel had to be making it up.

"And your half-breed brother, putting his hands on my daughter..."

Just like that, I knew it was true. The colonel couldn't have faked the anger which now left him momentarily speechless. The wonder was how he'd held himself in check long enough to complete the transaction. It wasn't just our land he wanted, I realized. It was us without a home anywhere near him. And now that he had my signature, all bets were off.

I must have reached out for the letter, reached for my father's last words to me, despite the whip. "You want this, boy?" the colonel rasped. "This romantic account of how he got injured, how she nursed him back to health, even knowing what he did for a living?" And then he began ripping it methodically into smaller and smaller shreds. "Nobody will see this, ever. All right, Sean. That'll do. Have some of the servants drag him out of the house."

Sean dealt me one final whiplash, anyway, as I tried to bottle up the pain in some remote corner of my mind. Flat on the floor, barely able to move, I did get a miniscule satisfaction at seeing some of my blood seeping into the colonel's expensive carpeting. I stifled an involuntary laugh at the thought.

Sean saw it, and his boot caught me in the ribs. "Think it's funny, do you? You and that brother of yours, going to school with us, acting like you were as good as the rest of us." He kicked me again.

It sank into my mind that I could actually die here. I felt like I should be more worried about that. But I couldn't afford to take away from any of that concentrated mental barrier against the pain.

The same thing must have occurred to the colonel. "That's enough, Sean. We don't want a corpse on our hands. He's got no place to go now but away."

I found myself wishing he'd thought of that a little sooner. Sean didn't need any help from servants. He grabbed me by my hair and the back of my trousers—there wasn't any shirt left for him to use—and dragged me to the front of the house, where he shoved me into the cool night air outside. I tumbled down the stone steps in front of the home, dropping onto the grass at the bottom.

Sean was breathing heavily from his exertions, and maybe from something else. He bent down to where I lay, grabbed my hair again and twisted my face so I was looking into his.

"I want you to know something, boy. You're going to die, and soon. Not here and now, where my family would be involved, but as soon as I catch you off by yourself, wherever you go. And that shouldn't be hard to do, now that you've got no home to run to." He reached into my trousers pocket and pulled out the wad of bills his father had just paid me. "And no money to buy more property, either."

"Give it back," I managed to croak. "Give it back, or I'll tell..."

"Who? The sheriff? The judge? Think they'd take your word against mine?"

"I'll tell your father," I gasped.

His grip tightened on my hair. "If my father ever sees you again, he'll probably kill you himself. You don't think so, boy? You wouldn't know it, but he's helped get rid of people bigger than you could ever guess."

Anger drove me to keep talking. "Maybe the sheriff or the judge would be interested in that. Maybe you'd better ask your father if he'd like me to talk about that to them."

He let me go and, maybe thirty seconds later, the lump of bills smacked me in the face as he threw it. "Keep your damned money," he said, in a somewhat different tone, somehow less sure of himself. I didn't know how I'd reached him, but something I'd blurted out had worked. "But what I said will still happen to you if you stay around here, understand? And your brother, too. Oh, I know what you're thinking. He's out west somewhere, and we can't get to him. Well, someone can, and my father can find just the ones to do it."

I managed to get to my knees, and Sean took a few steps back. Maybe it occurred to him that it was just him and me out here now, and I might still have some fight left in me.

"You said it yourself, Sean," I managed to say, glaring at him. "Maybe your father's hands aren't all that clean. And maybe I know more about what he did to other big people than you think." I was bluffing, pure and simple, but a simmering rage made me plunge ahead. "If anything happens to my brother, don't think your family will get off."

"We'll see," he said, but he sounded even more unsure as he turned and stomped quickly back up the steps to his door. "We'll just see," he shouted again over his shoulder as the door slammed behind him.

By then I'd managed to stagger to my feet, with some half-formed notions of saying something more to discourage him from going after Jack. But he was gone, and I wasn't even sure I could make it up the steps after him, much less open the door.

My back felt like it was on fire. But I had to know how serious Sean's threats against Jack might be. Instead of dragging myself away, I worked my way around the big house in the growing darkness, to where I remembered seeing a window in the living room where I'd just been. I also remembered that it had been open.

Sure enough, as I crept toward it, I could hear voices—Sean's, protesting and angry, and his father's, low and dispassionate. Yet it was the colonel's softer words that chilled me more, as I knelt below the window and listened.

"...no choice in the matter. You're right, Sean. It could ruin a lot more than our family reputation."

And then Sean's voice: "But can we do it? Without anybody finding out, I mean?"

"Do it, or get it done. One way or another, from what you've told me, that Six boy has got to die."

# THREE

*Fuzzy Knight: "And then that redskin appears from out of nowhere*
*on top of the stage and clunks me over the head with a tommy-hawk!"*
*Kirby Grant: "Maybe he flew on. Could've been a Crow Indian."*
Gun Town *(1946)*

I woke up on dry land, wondering how I'd gotten there. The sun was just starting to light up the distant horizon, the sky was clear of storm clouds, and the man kneeling at the campfire had his back to me.

Squinting through my nearly-closed eyes, I studied his silhouette. A wide-brimmed hat and a colorful blanket around his shoulders obscured most of him. A similar blanket lay spread over me, and I realized it was all that I was wearing. The blanket felt scratchy, and smelled of recent acquaintance with a horse. Had he stolen my clothes? But, then, why was he still hanging around?

The man at the fire shifted slightly, and I could see he was holding a blackened pan over the flames. A sizzling sound and the smell of frying bacon caused my empty stomach to growl.

Moving my head to look around as carefully as I could, I verified that we were by ourselves. Our only company was a couple of horses grazing nearby. As I peered further at my surroundings, I spotted my clothes—or rather Jack's—folded neatly over a flat rock next to their boots, hat, gun belt and Jack's twin Colts lying there beside their holsters.

So near, and yet so far. It would be really good, I decided, to have one of those weapons in my hand before the man realized I was awake. I decided to give it a try, and slipped from beneath the blanket as I crept toward them.

I was almost there when the man spun around and something flashed in my direction. An impressive-looking knife buried half of its shiny blade in the ground not three inches from my bare right foot.

"Be careful, senor," a mild voice with a trace of Spanish accent warned me. "Next time, I might hit something more important."

His teeth gleamed white as he turned fully around and smiled. A handsome man, dark eyes and hair and a complexion darker than Jack's and mine despite what I'd recently learned. I felt more than a little foolish, crouched on my hands and knees there in the altogether with a knife handle quivering in the ground beside me.

"Maybe that was your only knife," I suggested.

"Si. On the other hand, perhaps I have a dozen more. In your position, I believe I would choose caution." I took it as a good omen that he was still smiling. "Would you not rather wrap yourself up again, and join me for breakfast?"

He had a point—besides the ones on however many knives he might still have.

"That is better. You can probably use some coffee, also," he said, handing me some in a battered tin cup. "After your fight with the water, you should rest before seeking out another conflict, no?"

"Did you fish me out of there?" I asked sheepishly.

"You were clinging to a piece of timber with an admirable stubbornness, considering that you were all but unconscious at the time," he said. "I would not have seen you in the darkness if I had not been watching, but I heard gunshots upstream and became curious. You came floating by shortly afterward."

I glanced over my shoulder at the knife, still upright in the ground near my drying clothing.

"How'd you throw that so fast?" I asked. "I didn't think you'd even heard me move."

He inclined his head in a mock bow, his dark eyes dancing with amusement. "It was not so fast as it might have appeared. I heard the change in your breathing when you awoke, so I had time to prepare. I also heard your belly gurgling."

"I owe you an apology," I said. "Heck, I guess I owe you my life."

"May I ask how you came to be in such a situation?"

I almost laughed. "It's a little complicated. What it boils down to is three men mistook me for someone else and started shooting at me. I got thrown off my horse—or, rather, one of theirs—and ended up in the water."

"You stole one of their horses?" It was obvious he did not approve.

"It was the only way I could keep from being shot," I said.

He shook his head. "You must be new to this country. Taking another man's horse is serious business, senor. It is like taking a man's canteen in the desert, or his gun in hostile country. A man on foot is as helpless as..." He looked at me. "Well, as you, amigo."

"For what it's worth, the horse and I didn't spend much time together. It didn't like me any better than its owner did."

"I am a curious man, senor. Perhaps you can tell me how a man can be shot in the back, and yet have no bullet wound on his body." He gestured toward the shirt on the rock. If he had checked my back, he couldn't have missed the scars that Sean's whip had left but, if so, he didn't mention them.

"Yeah," I said. "I'll have to sew up that hole." He refilled the tin cup I had drained of coffee and, after another few sips, I introduced myself.

"Johnny Six," he repeated. "Not the one they call Double-Six? I could not help noticing the embroidery on the shirt."

"No, I'm not Double-Six. That's just it. Those men thought I was."

He shrugged, not pressing the matter. "Well, I am pleased to know you, Johnny. My name is Warbonnet Pedro Alfonso Jose Gonzales." I must have looked dubious as we shook hands. "An Indian mother and a Mexican father," he explained. "The mix has occasional benefits."

I would remember Gonzales many years later, when I saw Richard Martin playing a bombardier of Spanish and Irish ancestry in a World War II movie, and suggested to some folks at RKO lifting the character out of that picture and dropping him into a western. It turned out pretty well. His character, Chito Jose Gonzales Bustamonte Rafferty, did sidekick chores for Bob Mitchum, James Warren, and now with Tim Holt—probably the only time the comic sidekick has been taller, darker and maybe more handsome than the hero.

I was tempted to tell him everything about myself and Jack—it would have been nice to be able to unburden myself to someone—but, after all, I didn't know him. And I had learned caution, if nothing else, in these past weeks since I had crept away from that window at the Sutherlands' mansion, grabbed a few things at the home which was no longer mine, and began a series of trips toward Kansas in hopes of locating Jack before the colonel's hired killers did.

There was no way to know how far that swollen stream had carried me from where I'd left Jack, or how soon it might be safe for me to go back there. Quinn and his friends might still be hanging around, unless they felt certain they'd finished me. Of course, there was no reason why they shouldn't. It was by pure chance they hadn't succeeded.

Gonzales sat up a little straighter and cocked his head to one side. "How many men did you say were chasing you?" he asked.

"Three."

"Only three? You're sure?"

"Real sure. Why?"

"Because there are more than three riders approaching us from the southwest at this moment. Given their numbers, I don't suppose they are the ones who were after you…"

I jumped up and turned in the direction he'd indicated. There was a cloud of dust, but I couldn't tell if it represented three riders or thirty. Whoever they were, they were moving toward us fast and I didn't see any place to conceal myself before they'd be on us.

Warbonnet eased himself to his feet, slung one end of his blanket across his shoulder, walked slowly to his knife and retrieved it. The blade disappeared somewhere under the blanket. I didn't know what kind of preparations I should make. There wasn't even time for me to have pulled my still-wet clothes back on.

"Indians," Warbonnet told me. "Sioux."

I took his word for it. "Friends of yours?" I asked hopefully.

"As I said, I am half Indian. They trust me perhaps halfway. They have been letting me hunt and trap on their land. So far."

"I'm glad to hear that," I said.

"That does not mean they will take kindly to you," he said. "Although they do tend to avoid interfering with someone whose wits seem to have left him. I suppose running around stark naked in the middle of the prairie might qualify."

The riders were getting close enough now so that even I could identify them as Indians. "Some of them look pretty near naked themselves," I observed.

"You have a point. We must think of something else," he said, moving casually around the campsite, stowing Jack's gun belt and weapons into some well-used leather saddlebags and throwing his blanket over where the clothes lay. "Pull that blanket over your head," he said. "Squat down by the fire. Say nothing, and keep yourself covered as best you can."

"What? You think they're not going to notice me?"

"Hush!"

By the time the half-dozen horses pulled up around us, he was back crouching by the fire, too, and it seemed to me he was taking his sweet time about acknowledging our visitors. From what little I could see, peering out from the blanket, they looked pretty impassive about seeing him, too.

Finally, he stood up once more and greeted them in some guttural language I couldn't understand. They responded in kind. I sat very still as the strange conversation went on around me. I heard a few of them laugh when Warbonnet gestured toward me. One lean warrior who looked about twenty years old, with a scar across his face, seemed to be the most vocal in their party.

He gestured at me and said something which made all of them laugh this time, even Warbonnet. The Indian with the scar must have liked the response he got, because he repeated whatever he'd said several times. Then, the Indians turned their ponies and rode sedately away. I breathed again, thinking our problems must be over.

Wrong.

Warbonnet shook his head, and began gathering up his utensils. He stopped to pour the rest of the coffee on the campfire. "It has not worked out exactly as I had hoped," he said in a low voice.

"Why not? They're gone, aren't they?"

"Not so loud!" he hissed. "It would not do for them to hear your voice, after what I just got through telling them."

"What was that?"

He ignored my question. "My horses are tethered near a small pool of water over there," he said, gesturing toward the animals. "We have been invited to spend some time in a Sioux village within riding distance from here. It would be an insult to refuse their hospitality. You can ride along on my pack horse..."

"Warbonnet, exactly what did you tell them?"

"Keep your voice down!" He still wouldn't look at me. "I told them you were my squaw."

"*What?*"

"Well, I thought they would leave to give us some privacy, Johnny," he said. "But instead, they have invited us to enjoy ourselves in the privacy of a wigwam."

"Now, look here, Warbonnet..."

"Do not worry, Johnny. You are definitely not my type," he assured me.

"But I've got someplace I've got to go. I have a brother who's hurt, maybe dead. I can't hang around some Indian village pretending to be your...your..."

"I understand how you feel," he said. "But I think you must reconcile yourself to a few days of rest and recovery, Johnny. I cannot change my story now. They would not take kindly to having been tricked."

"Why couldn't you have just told them who I was?" I demanded.

"Because they would also not have taken kindly to your impersonating Senor Double-Six."

"Impersonating? But I...no!"

"Calm yourself, Johnny. I believe you when you say you are not the man whose clothes you were wearing. The real Double-Six would have cleaned and oiled his weapons, first thing, even before eating. I take it he is the brother you spoke of?"

"Well...yeah."

"If they realized you had his possessions, they could only assume that you took them from him, probably by ambushing him—and that, they would not like. Especially Curly, the one with the scar."

"I noticed him."

"He noticed you, too." Warbonnet chuckled, then became serious. "I have never met your brother, Johnny, but I have been told that he once saved Curly's life, or at least saved him from getting a bad mauling. Curly had put all his arrows into a large bear which was not taking kindly to such treatment, and your brother happened along in time to finish off the animal with some well-placed bullets."

The Indians had pulled up some distance away. It was obvious to me, after what Warbonnet had said, that they were waiting for us to mount up and follow. I guessed I had no choice but to go along. Even if I committed the unpardonable sin of swiping one of Warbonnet's horses, I could never outride them.

"Okay," I said reluctantly. "But this is going to make for an uncomfortable ride, wearing just this blanket. By the way, what was it the one with the scar kept saying when he pointed to me?"

"Oh, well, your feet were sticking out a bit from under the blanket."

"Yeah, but what was it he said?"

"You do not want to know."

"Warbonnet..."

"Oh, very well. He said you had nice legs."

# FOUR

"Gabby" Hayes: "Well, Bill, looks like we gotta cherchez la femmy...That's Indian.
It means 'Locate the squaw.'"
Hidden Valley Outlaws *(1944)*

The deception, over the next week, proved surprisingly easy. Warbonnet's acquaintances among the Sioux did indeed seem to respect his privacy, and his tent-like quarters were off to one side of their main encampment. By the time we got there, with me riding the pack horse still wearing just the blanket, I ached in places too embarrassing to mention.

I could tell when Warbonnet finally noticed the scars on my back, by an abrupt change in his expression, but he didn't pursue the subject and I offered no explanation. He was fastidious about his own looks, shaving almost every day, which nowadays still makes me think of Richard Martin and his Chito character at RKO, always decked out in a fancy Mexican coat which he referred to privately as a monkey suit. It hadn't been quite the same when John Laurenz substituted in the Chito role for two of the three James Warren pictures, and I was glad when the studio decided to pay Dick enough for him to return to the role. Of course, Dick's character was half-Irish instead of half-Indian. As it turned out, though, Warbonnet's Spanish half was just as romantic as Dick's character on the screen.

I'd told Warbonnet about my own mixed heritage. "Half-black? In the

South?" he said. "Well, you should try being half-Mexican in Texas. There, they are still angry about Santa Ana. And then half-Indian, around the Dakota and Montana territories? With a name like mine, I can deny neither one."

My time in the water must've taken more out of me than I realized, because I found out I really could use the time in hiding for recuperation. I hadn't started on my journey in the best of shape, anyway, after the beating I'd taken. Then the cut on my left hand, where I'd knocked out one of the teeth of that two-gun kid, got infected and the entire hand swelled up. I soaked it for two days in a pan of water which Warbonnet kindly provided.

But the worst aches—well, you'd have to ride a horse bare-back and bare-skinned for as long as I did to really understand. Every strap and buckle from Warbonnet's saddlebags felt etched into my ass—beg your pardon, Miss Hamilton.

Warbonnet kept me supplied with food and water, but otherwise left me pretty much alone. I didn't ask him how he was spending his time, although maybe I should have. I spent mine thinking things over, pondering my next move if I ever got out of here, fixing the bullet hole in Jack's shirt, and examining his pistols. They looked to be fine weapons, as Warbonnet had said, and marked with fancy scroll work. Today's Texan Jr. cap pistols remind me of them.

All that made me wonder anew just how Jack had been making a living since we'd been apart. We'd only gotten the briefest of letters from him during the years after he fled Virginia, usually weeks old by the time they reached us, and never with a return address. He would mention the occasional job such as shotgun guard on a stagecoach run, or deputy to a peace officer. More often, we read accounts of his involvement in shooting scrapes in the rare news stories that we found in some of the more popular publications about the Wild West.

The pistol in the belt's left-hand holster was carried butt-forward, unlike its mate. I supposed that was to allow Jack to draw the pistol with either hand. The other was holstered in the traditional fashion. I was probably recalling that when I suggested Tim Holt wear his pistols that way in the first four movies he made at RKO after he got back from the war, when he was teamed up with Warbonnet, I mean, Chito. I'd kind of promoted the idea of that particular gun belt so certain people, who would see the movies, might recognize it and know I was still out there watching them from behind the scenes. I'd done much the same thing by suggesting black outfits, instead of the more traditional light clothing and white hats, for occasional leading men like Hoppy, George O'Brien, McCoy and Starrett over at Columbia, and Lash LaRue, of course— again as a reminder or even a warning to certain people I knew would see those films, since Jack had traditionally worn black—to let them know that someone associated with him was still around. But I'm getting ahead of myself.

Warbonnet was unusually quiet during one of the meals we shared during our stay. I wondered if something was wrong. When he finally spoke, it confirmed my worst fears.

"Johnny, my friend, I am sorry to bring you this news," he said. "It seems that your brother is dead."

I clung to a tiny bit of hope. "You mean, they thought they were chasing him, and that I must have drowned..."

"No, that is not what I mean. This news came from a trapper who has a Sioux wife—a squaw man, as such are called, like my own father—and he heard it at a trading post. The story is that Double-Six was shot and killed by a man named Quinn."

"Ben Quinn," I said. That could mean that Jack had died of his wound. It could mean that Quinn hadn't been fooled by my impersonation, and had found Jack and finished him off. But it could also mean that Quinn and his friends had indeed mistaken me for Jack, and simply hadn't spread around the rest of the story, about my taking one of their horses and being pitched into the stream. If Quinn did think I'd drowned, he wouldn't want to make his own role less heroic by admitting a wounded man had slugged him and almost gotten away.

Besides, unless Quinn could make that story stick, he wouldn't be able to collect his bounty money from the Sutherlands.

It made sense. But it was a slim hope. I had to find out for sure, one way or the other. And the only way to do that seemed to be to make my way back to that crossroads saloon, to find out what had happened there after I'd escaped. But I was stuck here until I could ride out under Warbonnet's blanket disguise.

"Quinn would be wise not to remain in this territory now," Warbonnet said. "Curly still feels that he owes your brother a life, and I am sure he would happily make it Quinn's."

I was beginning to chafe with the inactivity. Even eavesdropping on the conversations that took place around our wigwam, and even picking up a rudimentary knowledge of the local Sioux dialect with occasional tutoring from Warbonnet, didn't keep my mind fully occupied. I was tempted to try to slip away on my own, but Warbonnet kept assuring me we'd leave in just a few more days and I could then continue on my way. I couldn't figure out what was keeping him here—until the start of the second week.

Her name translated as Shining Star, and she was quite good-looking in a buxom way. If Jane Russell had brown eyes instead of blue, she'd have been somewhat reminiscent of Shining Star in those buckskins they had her wear in *The Paleface*. Warbonnet was proud enough of Shining Star to take her walking nearby enough so I could get a glimpse, once he'd broken down and told me about her. Apparently she had no misgivings about Warbonnet having another squaw in his wigwam with him. Or maybe Warbonnet had confided his little deception to her.

Warbonnet had tutored me how to properly clean and oil Jack's pistols. "They are indeed fine weapons," he told me. "Too fine for you to dishonor the man who carried them, by letting them rust and deteriorate." He provided me with some oil from his saddlebags, which he used on his array of hunting weapons, and had me practice handling the empty pistols, when I admitted my lack of skill, until I at least gained some familiarity with them.

So I got used to the balance of the long-barreled Colts, and with the feel of their carved bone handles in my palms, the weight of them belted around my waist. I still had a hope of being able to give them back to Jack one day. Or, failing that, to use one of them on Ben Quinn.

Along with my getting acquainted with my brother's pistols, I developed strong kidneys. I didn't want to foul my own nest, so to speak, and so waited until nightfall to attend to calls of nature. Warbonnet had scrounged a modest wardrobe of Sioux clothing for me, snatching a buckskin vest here and a pair of fringed trousers there, so I might pass for one of the Indians, from a distance. The buckskin fringe was much longer than what you see in the movies. Indians used it to tie on various tools they needed to carry with them.

I was carefully making my way back to the wigwam from one of my nocturnal excursions when I came uncomfortably close to walking into a gathering of braves, conferring in low tones beside the wooded path just ahead of me. I froze and listened, thankful for what little bits of the language I'd picked up.

One particular brave was doing most of the talking, complaining that Warbonnet already had a woman of his own, and was abusing the hospitality of the village by courting another. Warbonnet's attitude was that of whites with whom he associated, the brave argued, who killed more buffalo than they could eat.

That was a rough translation, but you get the idea. If Warbonnet could behave that way toward Shining Star, the Indian was saying, then it should be all right for the brave to help himself that very night to the squaw that Warbonnet was ignoring in his own wigwam.

I didn't need to hear any more. I slipped back into the trees, and made my way back to the wigwam by a more roundabout route, to warn Warbonnet about what was coming our way.

But he wasn't there. I could guess what he was probably doing, and was quite sure he was enjoying himself, but it left me in a spot. I thought about loading one of Jack's pistols, and filling that amorous brave full of holes the moment he poked his head inside. I also thought about simply grabbing my stuff and trying to escape on my own. While I was still thinking over those options, the Indian appeared.

Even knowing that he would be pushing his way inside any minute, I hadn't heard him approach. I acted on pure instinct, grabbing the blanket on which I habitually slept and throwing it over his head. He grunted in surprise and I could feel his hands trying to throw it off, but not before I grabbed up the nearest object I could find—which happened to be Warbonnet's serviceable frying pan—and banged it against where I thought the brave's head would be. It connected with a satisfying thunk. The blanket floated to the ground, as did the brave beneath it, both of them equally limp. I finished his job of pulling the blanket off, grabbed him by the scruff of his neck and seat of his pants, and heaved him out the way he'd come in.

I heard some surprised yelps from his companions, who were apparently gathered all around to eavesdrop. He must have flopped into their midst.

Luckily, he had not gotten a look at me, and I don't know what he told them about Warbonnet's squaw, but none of them ever bothered me again. Warbonnet came near collapsing with laughter when I related what had happened. I was still too shaken to see the humor in it, myself.

And neither did he when, the following afternoon, a brave with a bluish lump on his forehead and some of his friends jumped Warbonnet on his way back to our wigwam from one of his trysts. I could hear it all from where I cowered inside. I rationalized that Warbonnet probably had a beating coming to him, that he'd known what he was getting into and the chances he was taking. But when Lump Head and two of the others drew their knives and challenged Warbonnet to settle things with them on a more permanent basis, I knew I couldn't stay out of it.

Warbonnet was good with a knife, I knew that from experience, but I didn't think he could last indefinitely against odds of three to one. He'd nicked Lump Head—maybe that blow from the pan had slowed his reflexes—but one of the others managed to cut him in return, along one side. Several other braves, including Curly, had apparently heard the commotion because I saw them gathering as I peered through the flap. None of them seemed inclined to stop what was going on.

I'd been dressing in the only real clothes I had, the ones belonging to Jack. I didn't kid myself about what was likely to happen when I stepped out there. It would probably only delay the outcome as far as Warbonnet was concerned, and add me to the fatalities, but what else could I do? Warbonnet had saved my life. At least, I could help him take some of his attackers with him, if my shooting turned out to be any good at all.

So I jumped out, my pistols holstered but my hands within grabbing distance when the braves turned my way. I'd expected them to be surprised, counted on it, even, since they couldn't know I'd been there all the time and would have to wonder where I'd popped up from.

But their surprise went beyond anything I had anticipated. One by one, they caught sight of me, and the fight stopped dead. Warbonnet pushed himself free of an Indian who'd had him in a bear hug, and the Indian just stood there, open-mouthed, staring at me.

Warbonnet staggered, and I grabbed him instinctively, realizing, even as I did it, what a stupid move it was, occupying my hands as it did. But nobody took advantage of it. The Indians continued staring at me for what seemed a long time, and then, with uneasy glances at one another, started backing off. In another minute, Warbonnet and I were standing alone in the little clearing around the wigwam.

The cut along Warbonnet's ribs was ugly, but he insisted it wasn't serious. "It is past time to follow your wish to get out of here, Johnny," he told me. "Let us pack up quickly and get out, before they catch on."

"Catch on?" I said. "To what?"

"To the fact that you are not a ghost," he said. "Do you not understand? Some of them have seen Double-Six, whom they have been told is dead. You must look very much like your brother, Johnny. Very much indeed."

# FIVE

Paul Hurst: "Ted, I gotta know, I just gotta know.
Who are you figurin' on pryin' out of Santa Dolores?"
Monte Hale: "Well, if you just gotta know..."
Paul Hurst: "No, no, don't tell me! I changed my mind.
What I don't know can't hurt me—I hope!"
Pioneer Marshal (1949)

"It's been four days, Rick. Whatever you're going to get from him, you should have gotten by now."

Rick didn't really disagree with the captain of detectives. He'd had the same misgivings himself about the daily trips to Jonathan Six's hospital bed.

"He's not a young man," Rick said. "And the wound was a serious one. He claims to be worn out after a certain amount of talking each day, and he just stops at some point."

"Claims to be. So you do think he's just stringing you along?"

Actually, Rick didn't think that. But he did think that Six was into his screen-writing mode when he was giving his account of what happened. And, just like in a movie serial, he tended to end a segment right at the point where his audience would want to come back for more.

"I just think it's going to take some time," Rick said. "It seems to be a pretty complicated story."

"Well, the fact is we can't afford to tie up one of our robbery-homicide people *for an hour or so a day, just taking one statement. I think you're going to have to tell our mysterious script-writer to cut to the chase."*

*And if he did that, Rick worried, Six might simply clam up. And if his injury actually did prove fatal, no one would ever know what had led up to the incident over at Gower Gulch. Rick had known it would come to this, sooner or later. It was just a little sooner than he'd hoped. Well, there was still one approach he might try.*

*Later, he had to try it on Nancy, too. He was driving her to the hospital for their next session when he brought it up.*

*"The captain agreed that I didn't have to be there every day while Six is telling his story," he said. "It's not as if I'm interviewing him, it hasn't been a question-and-answer thing. He just more or less dictates, probably like he did his writing at various movie studios where he helped with scripts. I could read your notes each night when I finished up, you know, to keep up with his account and see if it raises anything I'd need to ask the next day. And I told the captain I'd do that on my own time."*

*He glanced over at Nancy, but couldn't tell what her reaction was going to be. She was looking at him in an uncomfortably serious fashion.*

*Was he pushing too much? Rick still felt like he should be in Korea, along with some of the friends he'd served with during the last war. That option had been taken from him, but now he was intrigued by the old man's hints that there was more behind this than an attempt at murder.*

*Finally, Nancy spoke. "Rick," she said slowly, "that would mean I'd have to transcribe my notes every day, in time to get them for you before quitting time. I haven't even caught up with transcribing everything up to now. They have me doing other things, you know."*

*"Yeah." He couldn't argue with that. "Of course. The thing is, I feel like this could be really important. Just a hunch, but I really do think there's more to it than we've gotten so far. And if we don't get it from him now, we never will."*

*Nancy nodded, still frowning. "To tell the truth, I don't think we've scratched* the surface, either. But there are only so many hours in a day, Rick." He noticed that she was sometimes calling him by his first name now during office hours.

Rick pulled into the hospital parking lot and found a parking space. But he didn't get out immediately to open Nancy's door.

"Look, couldn't we get together after work hours? You wouldn't have to transcribe everything right then. You could just read your shorthand to me, then transcribe the notes normally as your work schedule allows."

She shook her head and sighed. "Okay," she finally answered. "But you really know how to mess up a girl's social life, don't you, Detective Martin?"

# SIX

*Wild Bill Elliott: "Now, Tex, you know I'm a peaceable man."*
*Tex Ritter: "Yeah. I been noticin' that."*
King of Dodge City *(1941)*

It was months later, clear into December, before I got back to that crossroads saloon. I didn't know the territory, and I'd had no idea how far that flood had carried me after I'd made my mad dash away from Quinn and his friends. After my little side trip to the Sioux encampment, I was thoroughly confused.

Warbonnet Gonzales helped me out, though. Within a week after we'd put the encampment behind us, he seemed to have fully recovered from his knife wound. I tagged along with him as far as one of those little settlements that dotted the routes to Kansas City, and on the way he drew me a crude map showing roughly where we'd been and what landmarks he knew around that area. All that, at least, gave me a starting point.

In Kansas City, I found a job at a livery stable—about the only thing for which I had the skills, at that point in my life—shoveling manure, forking hay, grooming horses, and even helping the owner put up a new corral fence.

I stayed there for several weeks, sleeping in the stable and taking care of the occasional night customers, until I'd accumulated enough pay to buy some essentials like extra clothing, boots, a second-hand saddle and bridle and, finally, my own horse. He was a bay, dark brown with a black mane, tail and stockings, a part-Tennessee walker with a white mark on his forehead which gave him his name, Star. He was also a cribber, which was one reason I could afford him; left to his own devices, he would chew on anything he could reach from the wood of his stall to any hitch-rail he could reach. The man from whom I bought him said he was tired of having to tie his halter to both sides of a stall to keep him from eating it.

Star was also feisty, maybe because he was slightly smaller than the average horse and felt the need to bite or kick at bigger ones before they thought of doing it to him. Another reason I got him cheap.

Until I bought myself some everyday work clothes, I'd had to wear the buckskins Warbonnet had filched for me from the encampment. It was either that or Jack's distinctive clothing, which could have raised questions I didn't want to answer. And that outfit was certainly not suitable for my stable work.

I still had the money Colonel Sutherland paid for our home and lands in Virginia but it was banked back home. Except for what I'd taken out at the start for travel money, I didn't have ready access to it. And I'd left most of what I'd been carrying with Callie St. Clair, to cover whatever Jack's needs might be. I wasn't ready to send for the rest. I wanted it intact until Jack and I could decide what to do with it—if, indeed, Jack was still able to help with that decision. Anyway, it didn't hurt me to work for some walking-around money, and I figured it was good cover from the Sutherlands' hired guns.

If Star could've talked, he'd have had some choice words for all the wild goose chases I took him on once we rode out. Not only that, but he had to pack my gear as well as me; I hadn't saved up enough for a pack horse. But he got me to wherever I wanted to go. It wasn't his fault that none of the places turned out to be the right one.

Finally, I had to travel all the way back to the place in Jefferson County where I'd caught the stage to start the trip. That was an easier place to find. Even then, since I'd only been a passenger and hadn't been watching our route all that closely (truth to tell, I'd mostly been watching Callie St. Clair), I got on a number of false trails before I finally hit the right one.

Jack's duds were rolled up in my saddle blanket, and his weapons stayed in my saddlebags. I debated whether I should strap them on, or at least stick one in my belt, in case I ran into Quinn or one of his partners. But I decided I'd have a better chance of going unrecognized without them. Anyway, I didn't feel as though I would stand a chance with any of those three in a gunfight. They were more adept with firearms than I ever would be.

With my store-bought hat pulled down as far as practical, and the rest of me covered in a used coat I'd bought from a traveler who stopped at the stable where I'd worked, I strolled into that crossroads saloon with as much nonchalance as I could muster. It looked different, but only because now it had more occupants. Nearly a dozen loungers were scattered around the place, a lot more than had been here when I was the first time. They sat around on crudely-fashioned wooden chairs or barrels like those that supported the plank bar on one side of the room.

The man behind the bar was not the fellow who had helped me with Jack on that long-ago night. This one had a bushy beard. Maybe the place had changed hands, or had more than one bartender.

I didn't recognize anybody else in the place, either, which was a relief. That meant they wouldn't know me. Some of them glanced my way as I walked in. Seeing nothing of much interest, they quickly went back to their drinks, or meals, or conversations, or all three.

I still hadn't gained back all the weight I'd lost during my meager meals with the Sioux. Checking the price to make sure I could cover it, I ordered a steak, bread and coffee, and seated myself at the bar so I could talk to the bearded proprietor while he was getting all that together.

"Were you here when they brought in Double-Six?" I asked, knowing he hadn't been, but hoping for some information.

"Who?" he asked.

"Double-Six. You know, the gunfighter. A friend of mine was on the stagecoach that picked him up on the road, wounded." I gave him the approximate date.

"Oh, yeah. Yeah, I did hear about that," he said. "They tell me it was Ben Quinn who did for Double-Six. Him and the Silver Dollar Kid and Cord McCluer. A little bit one-sided, them three to his one."

It was the first time I had heard names put to the two men who had been with Quinn that night. The Silver Dollar Kid—it sounded like something from one of the dime novels I used to read back home. I'd never heard of him or McCluer, and said as much.

The man behind the bar was surprised. "Not heard of McCluer? Huh! He's the worst of the three, most dangerous man in the territory, maybe. Carries a sawed-off shotgun 'neath that black coat of his. Sure can make a mess of a man."

I remembered the blast which had ripped apart the saloon door after I'd gone through it. A chill went up my spine as I realized how close I'd been to becoming one of those messes.

A man in working clothes like mine standing next to me decided to take an interest in our conversation. "Yeah, it don't pay to cross McCluer," he informed me. "You'd best just go through life hopin' McCluer don't notice you. He takes a dislike to you, you're as good as gone."

The speaker seemed to take a perverse pleasure in imparting this bit of information. At least he was grinning as he said it. He was one of four men, all herders from the look of them, standing along my end of the bar. And all four of them were looking at me with a kind of smirking amusement that I didn't care for at all.

"McCluer's a gunman?" I asked. Back in Virginia, I'd read a lot of the stories—both fictional and, supposedly, factual—about various pistol artists who lived in the west. If this McCluer was as deadly as the herder and the bartender seemed to think, I wondered why his name hadn't cropped up in any of the literature.

"Kid," the herder said, stepping toward me as his three companions maintained their derisive grins, "you really don't know who McCluer is? That's downright ignorant," he said, glancing at his friends to make sure he had their affirmation. "You must be pretty stupid, huh?"

I wasn't stupid enough to miss the fact that I was being baited. These four were in a mood to have some unpleasant fun, ganging up on anyone they could by himself. I'd seen their type before, in school. Sean Sutherland had been a prime example. That was one reason he and Jack had gotten into their fights. Well, I wasn't interested in a fight, and I didn't much care what they thought of me. I was never going to see them again.

I turned back to the man at the bar and spoke directly to him. "Tell me about McCluer," I requested.

Before one of the foursome could interrupt again, the bartender answered. "A paid killer, so they say. Nobody's ever proved it, 'cause whenever the law turns up a witness to a killin' that might have been his, the witness ends up dead, too. Shot from ambush. Makes it hard for any lawman to find anyone to testify against him."

I half-expected one of the four men to interrupt again, to try and stir something up. But apparently they decided I wasn't worth the effort. They went back to conversing among themselves, and I happily ignored the occasional comment I overheard questioning my courage or my ancestry.

The man behind the bar finished preparing my meal, and put it in front of me. I passed over some coins, and started eating.

"Friend of mine," the bartender continued, seeming to get into his story-telling now that he'd started, "told me about McCluer actually bragging to a judge what was gonna happen to a man who testified against him. The testimony hadn't been enough to convict him, and he told this judge to watch the newspapers 'cause the witness wasn't gonna be long for this world. Sure 'nough, four weeks later, the man turned up dead. Next time McCluer saw the judge, he flat-out told him about riding a long ways away from where the man had been shot and sending a telegram to establish an alibi for himself. What was the judge gonna do? Him and McCluer were the only witnesses to that conversation, and that judge wasn't about to take any action on his own hook. I mean, hell, would you?"

"I guess not," I admitted, concentrating on my chewing since it was becoming obvious my meal would require a lot of that. "But the judge must've told somebody. I mean, you heard the story, right?"

"McCluer didn't give no never-mind who heard the story. Fact is, he probably wanted it spread around, to discourage legal problems like that. I guess it worked. I ain't heard of him being hauled into any court since."

"What about the third man? The Silver Dollar Kid?"

The bartender turned and spit on the floor behind the bar—not close to the area where he'd prepared the food, I hoped. "Him, he's just plain mean. Hooked up with Quinn somewhere, runnin' errands for him, fetchin' his drinks, and finally backin' him up in his shootings. Got his name from wearin' silver dollars on his vest and belt. Shoots a hole in the middle of 'em, then ties 'em on. Showy little bastard, and I guess he fancies himself a two-gun terror. Can't recall I ever heard his real name. But he ain't as smart as Quinn, and he sure ain't as deadly as McCluer."

"And you're sure they killed Double-Six?" I asked, dreading the answer.

"Why, it happened right here. Well, at least it started here," the barman said. "It finished down the road a piece, by the river."

Hope flared anew. "They didn't kill him here, then?"

"Nah, but Quinn and the others, they been back a few times. I've heard 'em talk about how they chased down Double-Six and finished him."

"Chased him down," I repeated, trying not to smile. "At a river, you say?"

"Well, I didn't ask 'em for details. I just listened. I got the idea they caught up with him, finished the job they'd started earlier, and threw him in the water. Ain't heard of his body washing up anywhere, though."

The barman was distracted by another customer, and I finished my meal in silence. Now that I'd finally found the place where I'd left Jack, I wasn't much better off than before, except I did know they hadn't found him helpless in that bed upstairs. They really had mistaken me for him, and probably did think I'd drowned. But, assuming Jack survived his wound and had managed to get out of here, I didn't know what my next step should be in trying to find him.

When I finished eating, I asked the barman if I could look over the rooms upstairs. "You lookin' for a room?" he inquired.

"Maybe. I won't bother anything."

He waved a hand. "Nothin' in 'em to bother. Go ahead and look. Nobody's used either one since I been workin' here."

The stairway still creaked, as I remembered all too well. The room in which I'd left Jack and Callie appeared to be unchanged from the way I'd seen it last. When I dropped my hand on the covers on the bunk, dust rose into the air. They hadn't been changed in a good while.

I looked under the bunk, in every corner, even under the blankets, hoping to find something, anything, that might give me a clue as to what happened in this room after I'd left it. Nothing. My bags from the coach were nowhere to be found, either. I hadn't expected them to be, after all this time.

As I came back downstairs, fighting down the uneasiness remembering my last trip down them, I saw that a newcomer had taken my place at the bar. If I had been a target for that fun-seeking foursome, this man would be irresistible to them. In the clothing I'd bought, I didn't think I looked too out of place among the occupants of the place. But this man did.

He wore a wide-brimmed hat, a beaded buckskin jacket, and had brown hair all the way down to his shoulders, like a girl's, plus a mustache covering his upper lip. And I'd thought Jack's outfit stood out. This fellow had all the marks of a well-to-do easterner trying to masquerade as a frontiersman, I thought.

Sure enough, even as I reached the bottom of the stairs, it had started. I could hear the four already heckling him. I was torn between a desire to just walk out, and a morbid fascination with what was about to happen. The dude, I knew, was in for a rough initiation. The men at the bar seemed, if anything, more eager to spite him than they had me.

I heard him order a drink in a low voice, as the foursome continued their derogatory remarks about his immaculate attire and their guesses at his ancestry.

He seemed to be trying to avoid trouble the same way I had, by ignoring their comments, refusing to rise to the bait. But, in his case, it wasn't working.

"Sure has pretty hair, ain't he, boys?" said the man who'd been picking at me. "Hey, you reckon we got us a gal disguised underneath all those braids and buckles?"

The other three found that hilarious. They roared with laughter, while the stranger continued to ignore them. This time, ignoring them didn't work. He had just lifted his glass when the man who'd been doing the talking shoved him roughly. The liquid splashed in the newcomer's face. His head struck the flat bar, knocking his hat off.

Without even thinking about it, I found myself moving across the room. Four to one was bad enough, but against this helpless-looking dandy, it was pitiful. I didn't know what I was going to do when I reached them, but I figured it would probably end with both of us getting thrown out of the place a little the worse for wear. Or maybe a lot.

But before I'd taken three steps, the man in the beaded buckskins swung the back of his hand into the face of the man who'd pushed him. The man had been totally unprepared for that response—I think everybody in the room was unprepared for it—and an abrupt silence followed the hollow sound of the smack. The bully staggered back, his eyes wide in shock, against one of the sod walls.

"Now back off," the stranger said, "before this gets serious."

The bartender dropped to the floor, realizing before I did what was about to happen. Others in the room scurried behind barrels or tables. Stupidly, I just stood there.

One of the four men uttered a curse and grabbed for his holstered pistol. I still stood and watched, not yet having accepted the idea that one man would actually try to kill another over a little jostling. Maybe it was in my mind that they were still just trying to scare the dude.

He didn't scare worth two cents. From somewhere, a pistol appeared in his hand and exploded before the other man got his own weapon raised. I glimpsed blood smearing his face as the would-be bully fell back and dropped onto the floor, one hand to his face.

As fast as the stranger had acted, one of the remaining three near where I was standing moved nearly as quickly. His pistol was out and pointing at the newcomer almost before I realized it. Purely by instinct, I shoved him from the side. He still got off his shot, but I had deflected it.

Not enough, though. The stranger staggered, and I could see blackness from the powder burn sear the right shoulder of the otherwise-spotless jacket. He fell back against the bar. He stayed on his feet and kept hold of his pistol, but seemed unable to raise it. And now all three of the others were throwing down on him.

A second pistol flashed up in the stranger's left hand. It thundered three times, each shot coming so quickly one after the other that they almost sounded like a single boom. The room filled with the smell of powder smoke. One of the other men fired once, but his bullet went into the floor. Another got off a second wild shot, and I never did know where it went. Then all three of them were wobbling, falling, leaving only myself and the injured stranger standing in a room with all the other spectators were crouched or lying as low as they could.

I'd never realized a pistol could be fired that fast. It was obvious, even to me, that the three downed men were dead. The fourth, the one that had started all the trouble, lay on the floor groaning as blood poured down his cheek. My stomach turned over as I looked down at him, just as it had in the battle of New Market all those years ago.

"Anybody else want some?" the stranger asked, in the sudden silence.

The smoking pistol in his left hand swept the room as he spoke. Even with a bleeding shoulder, he seemed to be daring anybody to pick up the fight. It didn't surprise me when there were no takers.

Nodding, he stuck the pistol into his belt, reached across to where the other dangled from his limp right hand and sheathed that one as well. Then, cool as could be, he picked up his glass with his good hand and swallowed what little was left in it before starting to the door. Yeah, he was an easterner, all right, a dude completely at the mercy of the rough element out here. And I was Queen Victoria.

He was attempting to pull himself up onto a big black mare outside when I caught up with him. I don't know to this day why I followed him out there. It was obvious he didn't need my help to take care of himself. But I wasn't sure how badly he was hurt, and it didn't seem right to let a wounded man ride off alone in that cold Nebraska winter.

Neither of us said anything as I helped him up onto his horse. I walked over and fetched Star, mounted, and rode along by his side, letting him pick the direction. We must have ridden a good mile before he spoke.

"You don't even have a gun," he said, a trace of disgust in his voice. "Why'd you mix in?"

I'd been asking myself the same question. "Four to one," I said, finally. "Didn't seem right."

"You don't know who I am, do you?" he said. The disgust seemed to be replaced by mild surprise, and maybe a hint of amusement. "Well, I don't suppose those boys back there did, either."

"No sir, I'm afraid I don't," I admitted.

"Well, then, I guess I owe you my thanks. The name's Hickok, Jim Hickok."

"Hickok..." Recognition clicked from some of those dime novels I'd read back in Virginia. "Not the one they call 'Wild Bill?'" I blurted.

Despite the pain he must have been feeling, he managed a chuckle. "Yeah, I guess that's me," he said. "Hell of a name for a peaceable man, ain't it?"

# SEVEN

*William Boyd: "Well, Hammond, it looks like no one wants to earn that price*
*you put on my head... You'll leave, all right. Riding, walking, or feet first."*
Forty Thieves *(1944)*

It took us about a week of riding with occasional stops for rest, refreshment and food along the way to get to Kansas City. Once there, I arranged for a hotel room and helped my still-weakened companion up the stairs. "You really should let a doctor look at that wound, Mr. Hickok," I said for probably the twentieth time. "I'm sure I could find one here."

"Naw." With some grimacing, he managed to get out of his jacket slowly and carefully, and then slumped in the room's only chair. "Bullet went clean through. It's just gonna take time to heal, that's all. Tell you what you can do, Johnny, is hunt me up a store shirt something like this one I'm wearing. It's not much good to me anymore, with these holes and powder burns all over it."

I'd been on the verge of saying my goodbyes, now that my injured companion was back to what passed out here for civilization, and renewing my detoured hunt for Jack. But I really had no idea where to start. The saloon where I'd last seen him had proved a dead end, almost in more ways than one.

So, over the next few weeks, I drifted into running errands for Bill—having meals brought up to the room, hauling up buckets of bathwater on occasion, and just generally fetching and carrying. I couldn't complain. After all, he was paying for everything, including my own meals which tasted great after our meager trail fare, and I had to do something so as not to feel like a freeloader.

Often, when he wasn't using copious amounts of whiskey to dull the pain of his wound, he would chat with me about himself. It seemed to be a favorite subject and, right now, I was his only available audience, because he didn't want to show himself around publicly until both hands were in working order. It's like that new movie with Gregory Peck, *The Gunfighter*—there would always be some punk who'd try to take advantage.

Bill told me about how he'd run off from his hometown of Troy Grove, Illinois, because he thought he'd killed a man in a fight. By the time he learned the man he'd knocked into a canal had not drowned, he was already making a life for himself in his new surroundings out here. He'd been a teamster with a freight caravan, a stage driver along the Santa Fe and Oregon Trails (he could probably handle a team back then as well as actor Bud Osborne does now in the movies where he's the default stagecoach driver), and got into his first shooting scrape at a place called Rock Creek Station where he'd killed a man he thought was about to attack him. A jury apparently thought so, too; as he was found not guilty by reason of self-defense.

When I heard the same story later from others, and read accounts of it in dime novels, it had somehow grown in the telling to where he'd wiped out a whole gang of ruffians at Rock Creek.

The same way I'd read tales about him, he'd grown up reading about the exploits of scouts like Kit Carson, he said. Those stories were among the reasons he came to enjoy hunting and outdoors shooting as a youth, and he'd done enough of it even back then to become pretty proficient. About a decade earlier in Santa Fe, he'd actually gotten to meet Carson, near the same time as he got his first taste of saloon life. He liked that, especially the gambling tables, and became proficient there as well.

After traveling with a government wagon train from Fort Leavenworth, Kansas, to Sedalia, Missouri, he'd worked as a Union scout during the Civil

War. It was after that when he took up with another gentleman who apparently enjoyed hearing about his own exploits, real or imagined, by the name of William F. Cody.

The two Bills, Buffalo and Wild, ran across a crooked gambler during what started out as a friendly game in Springfield, Missouri. But Hickok told me he'd spotted the man switching cards under the table, supplying himself from some new ones and dropping the ones he'd been dealt into his hat, out of sight. He hadn't been very adept at it, though. When the time came for everyone to show his cards, Hickok produced a pistol and laid it carefully on the table between them. "I'm calling the hand," he told the man, "that's in your hat."

Hickok walked away with the pot. And, of course, I've helped work that bit into movies and even the *Deadwood Dick* movie serial. Wish he could have known about those celluloid exploits of his. I think he'd have enjoyed that.

Just last summer, Hickok had been working as a dispatch rider for the Seventh Cavalry at Fort Hayes. He had been impressed with the lieutenant colonel who was in charge, a man named Custer. Naturally, I had no way of realizing at the time that Hickok was telling me about yet another westerner who was destined to become a legend in stories real and exaggerated.

Although he never came out and said it, I gathered that Hickok was also impressed with Custer's wife, Elizabeth. At least he was smiling whenever he spoke of being a frequent guest in their household. Maybe he and Custer recognized an ambition in each other to achieve fame, something done more easily out here on a frontier which was already spinning off tales of its people by the wagon-load. But when he described Custer, with his long hair and extravagant manner of dress, he really didn't seem to realize what was obvious to me, that he could as well have been describing himself.

Back in school in Virginia, I'd been a good listener and, when I was in groups of talkers, I guess I still was. I had no inkling that this would pay me dividends years down the road, when I would draw on those stories as a technical consultant and script doctor for pictures at Republic and Monogram and Columbia and PRC and Universal and so on. What was more practical at the time, I also picked up some survival skills which, as it turned out, I would need even sooner. Hickok gave me lots of pistol-handling advice.

Once, and only once, Hickok let me to handle his custom-made pair of ivory-handled Army .44s with which he'd been presented just that past summer. They had been a gift to him from a United States senator from Massachusetts, Henry Wilson, after Hickok had conducted Wilson's party on a five-week sightseeing tour of the west. He also had another pair of less-fancy double-action .44s, and even a couple of hideaway derringers. Some gunfighters, as I would learn, believed in taking their time and scoring with their first shot. Bill believed in firepower. He'd filed off the trigger action on his guns so all he had to do was thumb their hammers to fire them. And he had extremely agile thumbs.

When he was finally up and around once more, and felt more like his old self, he would carry his "white-handled" Colts butts-forward stuck in his waistband when he went out. So there really was some truth behind the recommendations I gave for pictures like *The Plainsman* over at Paramount, and that serial about Hickok over at Columbia, where they had Gary Cooper and Gordon Elliott wearing their pistols butts-forward. But I couldn't persuade the props folks to use ivory handles. For some reason, they liked those stag handles. You can usually recognize a cowboy movie's hero by his stag-handled or pearl-handled hardware and ornate gun belt.

Elliott made such an impression in that serial that he's been known as "Wild Bill" ever since, and of course he played Hickok a few more times before he went from Columbia to Republic. It's kind of funny—neither Elliott, the actor, or Hickok, in real life, was actually named Bill, but neither one could ever shake that "Wild Bill" nickname. Even when he played "Red Ryder" at Republic, Elliott was still billed as Wild Bill in the opening credits, just as George Hayes was always "Gabby" after he went to Republic.

According to Hickok—the original one—some woman hung that tag on him, back in Independence when a bartender friend of his was being threatened by a lynch mob over a shooting. The mob's ringleaders were ready to storm the jail when they found themselves facing Hickok's grim visage. Hickok calmly told them to get lost, "or there'll be more dead men around here than this town can bury"—another line the movies appropriated here and there. They took him at his word, and that anonymous woman shouted out, "Good for you, Wild Bill!" After that, James Butler Hickok would never be known by his proper name again.

Of course, I was never sure just how much to believe of what Bill told me, or even how much he believed himself. Years later, I read an interview conducted by none other than Henry Stanley, the reporter who would locate "Dr. Livingstone, I presume" in Africa. But Stanley's piece on Hickok told some rather tall tales, including a claim that Bill had killed more than a hundred men. Actually, I don't think Bill's toll ever reached twenty, although I guess that's plenty. The number has easily topped a hundred by now in all the movies about him, if you count the villains dispatched by Coop, Elliott, and all the other Wild Bill impersonators from Bill Hart and Tim McCoy to Bruce Cabot, Lane Chandler and George Houston. Heck, Roy Rogers even played him once.

After Bill had recovered to the point where the stiffness in his wounded shoulder no longer slowed his right arm, he stopped holing up in the room and began making the rounds of the local saloons. Everywhere he went, there would be admirers who would buy him drinks and ask him for stories, and he told some of the same ones he'd told me. But he also enjoyed poking fun at his image at times.

He had one particular story he'd tell every time there was a new group, about when he'd been scouting for Custer and was trapped in a dead-end canyon by a couple of dozen Indians. He emptied his guns at them, he said, but they kept coming. Then he took out his knife and killed more of them, and they still kept coming.

Then he'd stop, take a drink, and wouldn't say anything more until, finally, someone who couldn't stand it any longer would say, "Well, tell us, Bill, what happened?"

"Hell, boys, they killed me!" And Bill would slap his knee and laugh uproariously.

I accompanied him sometimes to Kansas City's Market Square, where wagon guides, buffalo hunters, stage drivers and even gunfighters congregated to exchange information on trails, floods, hostiles and other travel stuff. Kansas City seemed to be a neutral zone, of sorts, among the gunfighters. I never saw a single one of them challenge another. In fact, some would often gather periodically at a place known as Tom Speers' bench, Speers being the city police chief, and compare shooting techniques, weapons and other fine points of pistolry. It was there that I had my first glimpses of men like Wyatt Earp, Bat Masterson, Doc Holliday, Luke Short, Dave Mather, Clay Allison and more others than I can remember. I watched them from a distance, naturally. Speers invited only the elite to his bench.

Bill didn't need my help anymore, so I moved out of the hotel and started looking for odd jobs again, to fatten my pocketbook until I could decide what my next step would be. One such job was sweeping out some of the city's many saloons. That may sound like a lowly job to you folks, and I guess it was, but saloons in those days were wellsprings of information. Like the one where I took Jack, that was where travelers learned what trails were open, where there was Indian trouble, where the buffalo herds were, all those things. If I was going to hear anything about Jack, I figured it would be in a place like that.

Most of those saloons were fancier than the ones you see in the movies. Many provided meals as well as drinks. The one we fixed up last year for that Monte Hale picture, *Pioneer Marshal*, which was supposed to resemble an establishment in Chicago, well, that was actually closer to the norm in the west. Of course, there were always tables of card players. And some of the bigger places had floor shows, actors or singers to help draw crowds away from the competition.

This particular singer had danced on down from the raised stage area where she'd started, and was moving around the room, belting out a playful little tune about showing a lady a good time. Naturally, it struck a responsive chord with her audience, sort of like Linda Stirling's number in *Santa Fe Saddlemates*, the picture where Sunset Carson had three fights in the first five minutes. I wasn't paying any attention to her, though. Since I'd been in any number of saloons since hitting Kansas City, I'd seen lots of singers and few of them genuinely rated a second look unless you'd had enough booze.

But this one did, when I finally glanced her way. I recognized her as soon as I had a close look at her: Callie St. Clair.

She wasn't looking toward me, and I figured I was probably just another face in the crowd to her. Nobody tended to look closely at the saloon swamper. But I had to talk to her. She could tell me what had happened to Jack, whether he lived, died or whatever. My hands gripped the broom I was holding as I began thinking my search might finally be ending.

I'd have to wait until her number was over, naturally, and probably until she was finished for the afternoon. The customers in the place weren't going to wait in line for someone of my station to engage her in conversation, when they would like nothing better than to make her closer acquaintance themselves. I'd have to be patient.

And then I saw another face, and this one was looking back directly at me, with an ugly grin of recognition. It was none other than the Silver Dollar Kid.

# EIGHT

Bud Geary: *"Hello, Cutie."*
Linda Stirling: *"Right back at you, big boy."*
Bud Geary: *"What's your hurry?"*
Linda Stirling: *"Go roll your hoop, Casanova!"*
Santa Fe Saddlemates *(1945)*

The kid had two pistols hanging from his gun belt. I was armed only with a broomstick. He looked quite pleased about that, as his gaze traveled over me.

"So you got out of the water, after all," he said, his grin showing the gap I'd left in his front teeth. "Now that's good, real good. Now I can finish the job Ben started."

"It'll be murder if you do," I said, trying to keep my voice steady. " I don't have a gun."

I took a step toward him, along the bar where he was standing when we'd first spotted each other. Customers standing between us backed off hastily, and he took a quick step back as well.

"No you don't," he said. "You don't sucker me like you did Ben. This time we settle it with guns."

You've seen it dozens of times—Henry Brandon sliding a spare gun down the bar to George O'Brien in *Marshal of Mesa City* or Eddie Dean to David Sharpe in *Colorado Serenade*—but it was a new thing to me then. That's just what he did, though. He drew his left-hand pistol, laid it on the bar and gave it a push. It came spinning down to where I stood as it slid to a stop.

"Now we're even," he said. "Go on. Pick it up."

Kansas City might have been a neutral ground for the premiere gunslingers of the day when they encountered one another, but the Silver Dollar Kid wasn't in their league, and probably wouldn't have cared about such an unwritten rule if he had been. People who had been standing in our vicinity, who saw what was going on, kept edging away. I was dimly aware of Callie's song fading out, first the piano player and then her voice, as the realization spread throughout the place and everyone's focus began shifting to the two of us.

Despite what you've seen in the movies, Miss Hamilton, there was hardly any of that face-to-face fast-draw stuff back in those days. Maybe the O.K, Corral shootout came close to it, but that was still thirteen years in the future. Most of the time, it was more a matter of one man getting the drop on another, like Dollar had on me. I didn't kid myself that I could grab up that gun and even cock it before he could draw and shoot. My only chance would be if he missed the first time, or if I wasn't hit badly enough for it to stop me from shooting back.

It looked like I wouldn't have any choice but to try.

Before I could move, I heard a gruff voice from behind me. "Not in here, boys," it said. "Take it outside."

I saw Dollar look toward the source of the voice and flinch. He slowly moved his hand away from his remaining gun. I turned and saw the bartender, covering both of us with a sawed-off shotgun he apparently kept behind the bar. The customers remaining in the path where he swung it back and forth between Dollar and me scattered even more.

The Kid swallowed. "Inside or out," he said, "don't make no difference to me." He straightened up. "I'll we waiting whenever you work up the spit to come outside."

"I'm not interested, Kid," I told him.

"Now, ain't that too bad? 'Cause I'm real interested. Just remember, I'll be waiting whenever you come out. And you'll have to come out sometime."

He walked past me and the bartender, toward the swinging doors.

"You forgot your gun," I called after him.

He didn't even slow down. "I'll pick that one up off your dead body," he said. Then he was through the doors, and I was watching them swing back behind him.

The shotgun disappeared back beneath the bar, and the bartender was offering me the Kid's spare gun, butt first. "Guess you'll be needing it when you go out there," he said, not unkindly. "You do a pretty good job around this place. I'll hate to lose you."

"Thanks," I said, taking it from him, trying to control a tremor from the realization of how close I'd just been to dying. The fact that I was still uncomfortably close to it couldn't stop the feeling of relief that, contrary to all my expectations less than a minute ago, I was still breathing. Of course, the fact that one of my employers had already written me off wasn't much encouragement.

I looked around the place, and found all eyes on me, including those of Callie St. Clair. I stuck the Kid's pistol in my belt, and walked over to her. "May I buy you a drink, Miss St. Clair?" I asked her, hoping my voice wouldn't crack.

She continued to stare at me for a moment. Finally, she turned and walked to a corner table, indicating that I should follow with a slight jerk of her head. We never got around to ordering a drink, but my sudden notoriety in that saloon turned out to be my ticket to some uninterrupted time with her.

"What the hell are you doing here?" she whispered, eyes wide, once we were seated. "You were supposed to disappear until we were sure they were off your trail!"

As keyed up as I was, knowing what was waiting for me on the other side of those swinging doors, I didn't realize what she meant at first. Then, the light dawned: she thought I was Jack.

"So Jack is alive!" I said. And then she caught on.

"You're his brother! The kid on the stage." She shook her head. "Except for the way you're dressed, you sure look like him. Even on the stage, I wasn't sure..." She shook her head, continuing to stare at me. "It's amazing."

"Miss St. Clair, what happened after I took out of there? I've been trying to find out for months now. I even went back to that place to see if anybody knew." I could hear the desperation in my own voice, but I couldn't help it.

She glanced around as though making sure nobody was close enough to overhear. "Well, after they rode out after you, I was able to rent a wagon from the man who ran the place. I used some of the money you left with us. The man at the station and I managed to get Jack into the wagon, and I got him to a doctor in one of those little towns along the stage route."

"Then he's all right?" I asked, scarcely daring to believe it. "Where is he?"

"I hope he's all right. He wasn't all that well when I had to leave him. He was the one who insisted that we split up, in case Quinn and his men caught up with us." She took a deep breath and, to my surprise, looked very close to tears. "I hope he's all right," she repeated, and her voice broke a little.

"Callie..." I didn't know what to say. No wonder she'd been looking at me so strangely on that stagecoach. And no wonder she'd volunteered so readily to take care of my brother when I'd decoyed his pursuers away. They knew each other. And pretty well, I was guessing.

"I'm sorry," she said, and then confirmed my thoughts. "You see, Jack and I were going to be married. That's why I was on that coach. We didn't know anybody had it in for him. We'd thought all that was behind him."

"There was no way he could have known about these particular hirelings," I said. I gave her an abbreviated account of what I'd overheard outside Colonel Sutherland's window back in Virginia. I was vague about why the colonel had such a hate for Jack, deciding it would not be a good idea to mention Sally Louise to the girl I'd just learned was Jack's fiancée. Nor did I mention our mother's race as part of the colonel's rage. I was just glad Callie didn't press for further details.

I asked how she and Jack met. She had been performing in Abilene, she said, after the Kansas Pacific Railroad reached there early last year and turned it into a shipping point for Texas cattle. Jack had been a deputy sheriff there at the time, she said, and supplemented his salary with card games in the place she was working. He'd generated enough of a reputation for gunplay for us to have read about it as far away as Virginia, but he wanted to get away from all that, Callie said, once the two of them had become serious. He turned in his badge, and joined the Kansas Pacific buffalo hunters, who had been hired to feed the rail workers, saving his pay so they'd have a stake to start their new lives together. He might not have equaled Bill Cody's kill record, but he was still setting aside hundreds of dollars a month, and they had decided not to wait any longer.

From what Jack told her, she said, he had shed his buffalo hunting garb, spent most of a day cleaning up and getting rid of the buffalo stench, put on his trademark garb for what he thought would be the last time, and was riding to meet her stage when he ran into Quinn and the others.

He'd told her that he had no reason to expect trouble from them, and he got careless. He'd let Quinn get behind him. When he heard the click of a pistol being cocked, it was too late.

As to where he might be now, she couldn't say. She'd told him she would find a singing job in Kansas City and wait to hear from him. So far, she'd heard nothing.

"I wonder if the Silver Dollar Kid being here means something?" I said. "You think he might be keeping an eye on you, thinking Jack might get in touch?"

"I don't know. I don't think so. Apparently, he thinks you're Jack," she reminded me.

"Yeah. I guess so." The Kid had said he would finish the job Ben Quinn started.

From the comments I'd heard about the Kid in that crossroads saloon, he wasn't in Quinn's class as a gunman. And yet he had challenged someone he thought was Double-Six, who was classed as pretty good with guns. He had to think he had an edge of some kind.

Might Quinn or McCluer be waiting out there, along with him? But surely I'd have picked up rumors if one of them had been around, since I'd been keeping my ears open in all the saloons where I'd been working.

And then another possibility struck me. I took the Kid's six-shooter from my belt, and looked it over. It was a single-action Navy Colt with ostentatious pearl grips, and looked to have been converted from a percussion firearm to a .38 caliber. Even as I was thinking about all this, some part of my mind observed that I'd have understood none of these things about firearms a few short months ago. I guessed I learned more about them from Hickok then I realized.

I shook the bullets out of the cylinder, one at a time. I wasn't surprised to find an empty chamber under the hammer—as Bill had explained to me, that was standard procedure to keep someone from shooting himself if the weapon should fall on the ground, or be impacted some way so it discharged accidentally. But the next two chambers which would have come up when I cocked the hammer were also empty. There were only three bullets in the gun, and I'd have had to click it twice to get to them.

That was the edge he'd been counting on.

I carefully replaced the bullets, but I moved the three rounds to where they would roll under the hammer the first time the weapon was cocked. Then I slowly stood up, and stuck the pistol back in my belt.

"You're going out there?" Callie asked. She hadn't been watching me play with the bullets, so she had no idea how things had almost been rigged.

"Have to, sooner or later," I said. "I can't sit here forever."

"There's a back door," she said.

The prospect was tempting, all right. "Thanks," I said. "But I'd just be postponing it."

She started to say more, but I pushed my chair back from the table and started toward the swinging doors, conscious that most of the people in the place were watching me out of the corners of their eyes while pretending not to. I wanted to ask more questions about Jack, but I couldn't concentrate on what I wanted to know with this other hanging over me. It was strange. As much as I was dreading it, more than anything else, I just wanted it to be over one way or the other.

Besides, I was just plain mad at this bullying little gunsel who'd been in on the plot to kill my brother, and who now was intent on killing me, thinking I was Jack. It was a cold, wary kind of anger, and I knew it could escalate any time into the kind of rage which might leave my hand unsteady. I couldn't afford that, so it was better to go now. And I went.

# NINE

*Rod Cameron: "You're takin' up a lot of street, Floyd."*
*Blake Edwards: "I'm plannin' on givin' you six feet of it."*
Panhandle *(1948)*

There were people standing along the street as I eased through the doors. The ones who saw me faded back into doorways, alleys or into stores. Word had gotten around fast—but not fast enough for the city police to step in and stop this foolishness.

I looked up, down and across the street but didn't see Dollar. I debated whether to stay put or start walking and, if I walked, in which direction. I figured he'd find me sooner or later, whatever I did. In the movies, you sometimes see a character throw away an empty gun. But reliable firearms were not so easy to come by that Dollar would fling one of his pair at me without some certainty of being able to recover it.

I was sure the Kid had done this trick before. That's probably how he'd come out on top of whatever gunfights he'd been in. He hadn't had to fiddle with the gun he'd pushed at me; it had already been set to click on the first two attempts to shoot it, so he'd had it ready—or maybe he'd spotted me earlier and made the adjustment in his spare gun before facing me. No wonder he packed two guns.

I finally decided I'd be better off moving than standing as a stationary target. I had sense enough to keep the afternoon sun behind me, as I edged along the front of the saloon and then the various stores and other buildings on their common wooden walkway. The first time I could, I turned a corner and moved down a narrow alley. Let him find me, I thought.

At the other end of the alley, on a different street not as wide as the one I'd left, I still saw no sign of him. This was probably about where I would have emerged if I'd come out the back way Callie had suggested. And if the Kid wasn't laying for me here, he must have been someplace where he could see the main entrance when I had come out—in which case, he was probably getting worried that I'd slip away from him now that I was out of his sight.

I moved quickly back up the parallel street, toward the sun this time, for several blocks until I saw another alley leading back to the street I'd started from. I eased my way into that one, coming out some distance up from the saloon this time. I'd been watching my back carefully during all these maneuvers, worried that Dollar might get behind me. So far, he hadn't.

Since he hadn't come chasing me down that first alley, he might still be keeping his eye on it, figuring I'd come back out of it eventually. Where I did come out several blocks away, people seemed to be going about their business blissfully unaware of my situation, so I'd reached a safe zone of sorts. I crossed the street as part of the general pedestrian movement and hoped the Kid didn't spot me doing it. If he was somewhere closer to the saloon, he might still be focusing on the other side of this street.

After I crossed, I began walking back toward the saloon, again staying close to the buildings and carefully checking every corner before moving past it. Maybe the Kid was doing the same kind of moving around, looking for me. We probably resembled Joel McCrea and Brian Donlevy stalking one another in those final scenes from *The Virginian*.

And then I saw him.

Or, rather, I saw the pistol in his hand, down by his side. Sure enough, he was standing directly across from that alley I'd slipped into, watching it from the same side of the street I was now on, partly concealed by one of three wooden columns in front of an office building of some kind. I eased closer to him, sliding his spare pistol out of my belt and imitating him by holding it down by my side. It didn't take long for those around us to notice two men, both with pistols out, one closing in on the other, and I knew I now had only a few seconds before their reactions gave me away.

His partial concealment behind that wooden column gave him an advantage, something to duck behind. Probably that's why I hadn't seen him when I first stepped outside. Unless I could get close enough to come up behind him, I might not be able to shoot accurately enough to stop him from shooting me.

He was still intent on that alley. I kept moving, closer, behind him, then past him, until I was on his side of the column.

"I'm right here, Kid," I said, and was mildly surprised that my voice didn't waver.

He jumped at the sound, spun around and still managed to get off the first shot. He probably had his pistol cocked and ready. But it worked against him, because he was still turning when he fired, and he missed. He didn't seem in any hurry to get off his second shot, taking time to aim more carefully. I knew why, and I knew that's why he was going to lose.

I cocked and fired, cocked and fired, then held the last bullet in reserve. I didn't need it. The first shot rocked him back into the street and, as he tried again to bring up his own weapon again, the second knocked him flat on his back. He had managed to get off a second shot, but his bullet only kicked up dust near his own feet before he fell.

I stood there, looking at the crumpled heap that had been a living man only an instant ago. I could see the shocked expression on his face, remaining even in death. Both my shots had taken him in the chest. One of them had taken a corner off one of the silver dollars on his vest.

"Here's your gun back, Kid," I said quietly, letting it fall on the ground beside him.

Then my stomach heaved, and I moved over to the closest hitching rail, gripped it in both hands, and retched violently as the realization of what had just happened caught up with me.

# TEN

Bob Steele: *"I'm gonna sneak in on that bushwhacker from behind.*
*You draw his fire and keep his attention."*
Don Barclay: *"I don't want his attention!"*
Border Phantom *(1937)*

Over at PRC studios, they could end *Stagecoach Outlaws* with Buster Crabbe spotting Stan Jolley aiming a gun through a window, plugging him and then riding out of town with Fuzzy while the heroine and townspeople waved goodbye. You seldom see the hero on trial for gunning down the villain. In truth, even if a lawman shot someone in the course of his duty, there would be a trial.

In my case, there were plenty of witnesses to testify that I'd been pushed into the fight, that I'd had no choice but to defend myself. So, yes, I had a trial, but it didn't last long. But it was long enough for me to lose Callie St. Clair.

"She checked out yesterday, cowboy," the man at the hotel told me. It had taken me a while to track down which hotel she'd been using. I didn't tell the clerk I'd been a mere saloon swamper, not a cowboy. I figured "cowboy" was a step up.

"Did she say where she was going from here?" He shook his head, which somehow conveyed both no and that he felt sorry for someone he thought was a love-struck admirer. I would learn, in the process of trying to track her down, that she often left a swath of men from her audiences drooling in her wake.

I tried to figure it out. Had she left because of the shootout, fearful that it would attract the attention of others who might be trying to find Jack through her? Had she learned something of Jack's whereabouts that she hadn't told me? For that matter, had she told me the truth about the relationship between herself and my brother? I had only her word and, charming as she was, my trust quotient had grown progressively smaller in recent months.

Even if I could find out where she'd gone, I'd have to tap some more of Colonel Sutherland's money now banked in Virginia to finance any long-term pursuit of her. By the time I'd completed the necessary transactions, there was no telling how far she would have gone. The Pony Express had lasted from early 1860 until the completion of the transcontinental telegraph line put it out of business a mere nineteen months later. Its relay riders had taken ten days to carry a sack of mail from St. Joseph to Sacramento. The telegraph had sped up communications mightily now, but a long-distance bank transaction still took time.

Besides, I didn't want to deplete the payment I'd gotten for our farm any further while there was still a chance of finding Jack. But my wages from the various odd jobs I'd been doing, even living as frugally as I had been, hardly represented traveling money.

While I was pondering all this, a man who was about to change the course of my life stood waiting for me in the stable where, currently, I was sharing accommodations with Star.

"Excuse me. Young man, I'd like to speak with you," he said, walking quickly toward me as I began forking some hay into Star's stall and some horse droppings out. I turned around and looked at him—and then I looked again. He was shorter than I and a tad portly, sporting a black mustache which all but covered his mouth, and a suit topped by a bowler hat. Even in cosmopolitan Kansas City, he stood out from most occupants. His red-rimmed eyes spoke of recent acquaintance with a bottle, as did his breath.

"My name is Colonel Judson, sir," he said, offering his hand. "I'd consider it an honor to have you as my guest for lunch."

In time, I would learn that Edward Zane Carroll Judson's military title was as phony as Colonel Sutherland's, but a free lunch was not something to turn down in my circumstances.

"How do you do, Colonel?" I said, shaking his hand. "My name's Johnny Six."

"Johnny? Johnny Six? I was told it was Jack. Oh well, never mind such trivialities. We can straighten all that out over lunch. I would like to interview you about the details of your gunfight last month with the Yellow-Haired Kid."

I pulled my hand back. "You mean the Silver Dollar Kid?" It struck me for the first time that I never did, and never would, know the real name of the man whose life I'd taken.

Judson waved a hand dismissively. "Well, Silver Dollar Kid, then. I can't keep them all straight. It's not him I'm interested in, but yourself, Mr. Double-Six."

"Double-Six? Where did you get that?" I was starting to develop an uneasy feeling about this garrulous stranger.

"Oh, I have my sources. People have told me about how this man and two others thought they'd killed you, and now there's speculation that you've gotten revenge from beyond the grave." He chuckled and patted me on the shoulder. "All grist for the mill, grist for the mill. You seem solid for a ghost, though."

A free lunch was seeming less and less like a good idea. "Look, Colonel Judson..."

"Perhaps I should have introduced myself by my nom de plume," he said. "Ned Buntline. You may even have seen some of my humble writings here and there, perhaps?"

As a matter of fact, I had. Dime novels had been around since the early 1860s, and Buntline just might have been the king of the dime novelists. The newly-developed rotary steam press made it possible to turn out these little books in great numbers, and they'd been as popular back in Virginia as they were out here. I probably honed my reading skills more on those than on the literature I was taught in school. My teachers would no doubt have considered them as trash, but that hadn't stopped Jack or me from hiding them inside our textbooks to read when classes got boring. There would even be congressional investigations into whether they were ruining the country's moral fiber, something like what you hear these days about comic books.

"You've got me confused with another person, Colonel," I said. "I'm not Double-Six. So you'd be paying out your meal money to no purpose."

"Suppose you let me worry about that, young man?" he said, throwing an arm over my shoulder and moving us toward one of the city's better restaurants a little way up the street. "You're the one to whom I was directed, when I inquired about the survivor of that shooting incident. And Double-Six is the name I'd heard associated with the shooting when I made my way here. Now, you tell me who that makes you."

I tried to tell him, but he kept up a line of chatter I couldn't break through. Besides, I decided, I could use a good meal. Before I knew it, we were both digging into steaks, potatoes and coffee—I noticed that Judson fortified his coffee with something from a little flask—and apple pie, with him continuing to talk all the while. I never did figure exactly how he managed to do all that talking and still clean his plate.

"You see, Jack..."

"Johnny," I said for probably the third time.

"Jack, Johnny...you see, this Double-Six is a natural character for the kinds of stories I write. The fancy guns, the black clothing, the supposed death, the return from the grave, the tracking down of the would-be killers one by one. Just the thing to carry on a series of books."

I sighed. He hadn't listened to a word I'd said, or tried to say. "I guess you don't worry about letting the truth stand in the way of a good story," I suggested.

"Well, no," he agreed, totally unabashed. "I mean, I'd written dozens of tales about Buffalo Bill—well, I suppose several of us have—before I even met him. We finally got together last year at Fort McPherson, out in Colorado. I was giving a temperance lecture at the time."

I couldn't keep a look of surprise from showing, but he didn't seem to notice.

"Mr. Cody cussed a blue streak at me over some of the stuff I'd made up about him. But, you know, really, it was all bluster. He didn't mind. In fact, he proceeded to give me some actual accounts of things that had happened to him so I could work them into future stories. So, you see, the subjects of my tales don't get upset about them."

He leaned back and beamed at me before going on.

"And that's what I want from you, Mr. Six. I'd heard of you here and there in my travels, but you hear things about all sorts of people and don't necessarily find material in them for stories. However, when I learned of your street gunfight with the Two-Gun Kid..."

"Silver Dollar Kid," I corrected automatically. It was the only name by which he would ever be known; at least Buntline should get that much right.

But, of course, the last thing I wanted was any kind of publicity linking me to Johnny Six, or Double-Six. I couldn't have Buntline tagging along after me, announcing to the world who he thought I was and, more importantly, where I was. Not with the Sutherlands' hired guns still out there somewhere looking for Jack.

"Now, if you'd tell me a little bit of the circumstances leading up to your little disagreement with this Silver Dollar Kid—you know, it is a pretty good name for a character, at that—it will add verisimilitude to my account, and bring you a measure of fame, as well. I'm sure Mr. Cody would tell you that the stories I've written about him have opened many bottles...I mean, many doors, for him..."

He went on like that at some length, while I was trying to figure out how to get away from him, since I'd digested his meal and was under some obligation to be polite. Gradually, however, as he yammered on, I began to ponder something else altogether, and I started asking some questions of my own. How did someone become an author of dime novels? Who published them? How much did the writers get paid? How did he get his material to the publisher? As Colonel Judson downed a few more cups of his doctored coffee, he became increasingly voluble in answering all those questions. And I was suddenly a very willing listener.

It took more than two hours before we got back to his reason for tracking me down in the first place. "Now, what led up to that gunfight, young man? Just how did it come about?"

When in doubt, I decided, just tell the truth.

"It was nothing but a case of mistaken identity," I said. "Maybe the Kid was looking for Double-Six, I don't know. There seems to be a slight resemblance between Double-Six and me. Or maybe it was because we have the same last name," I added, getting into the spirit of the story as I made it up. "Anyway, I got in a lucky shot when he came after me, and that's really all there is to it."

Even after all his liquid refreshment, Buntline seemed to recognize the truth when he heard it. He looked so disappointed that I actually felt sorry for him.

"Well," he said, finally. "Not exactly the material from which good stories are fashioned."

I had a sudden inspiration. "No, but you may not have wasted your trip, Colonel. Suppose I could introduce you to Wild Bill Hickok? Would you be interested in interviewing him for some story material?"

He was almost panting with anticipation by the time I got him to the hotel where Hickok was staying. Bill, after all, had already figured in any number of exaggerated magazine and newspaper articles. I was pretty sure he wouldn't mind seeing his name in print some more, as the hero of some Ned Buntline stories.

And I was right. Hickok and Judson spent large parts of the next several days as drinking companions, with Hickok telling some of the same stories I'd already heard and Judson drinking them in along with his other liquid refreshment. With Judson so thoroughly occupied, I could get back to my own problems.

Which is what I was doing several nights later when, by the light from one of the busy saloons, I spotted a cadaverous figure in a long black coat riding leisurely into town.

The weather had been glum all day, with just enough rain to keep the streets muddy and enough thunder to put people on edge. I was that way myself when I'd rolled out my blanket over some hay, in Star's stable where I was earning a few coins watching out for late customers.

Ball lightning had been rolling across the sky all night long. I hadn't been able to sleep much, so I'd wrapped the blanket around myself and walked over to the door for some fresh air. It was pure blind luck that I was still standing in the shadows, and that I saw McCluer before he saw me.

He had his hat pulled down and his collar up against the blowing rain, but I recognized him. He drew rein in the middle of the near-empty street, looking around. Then he turned his horse and walked it straight toward where I was standing.

I almost panicked. Then I realized that he was not coming after me, he was just heading for the lantern inside the stable door which would have let him know the place was open for business. I stood there in my pants, socks and with a blanket wrapped around me, torn between whether I should just back out of sight or run for Jack's pistols in my saddlebags.

Then he was at the door, and it was too late for me to do either one.

"Hey, anybody here?" he called, stepping down from his saddle. His voice was as thin and dry as he was. It was the first time I'd heard him speak.

I had managed to grab my hat, which I pulled down low before I stepped into the light. "Si, senor," I said, attempting to mimic Warbonnet Gonzales. "You wish to stable your animal?"

"Yeah," he said, leading his horse inside without giving me a second look. He pulled the horse around and backed it into a vacant stall. He pulled a long rifle from a scabbard in back of the saddle with one hand, and dug into his trouser pocket with the other. He came up with some coins, and handed them to me.

"Here. You unsaddle him and feed him. Where's the nearest hotel that's still open tonight?"

I slouched as I accepted the coins, hoping it would make me look shorter than I was. I mumbled the names of two hotels within walking distance of the stable, hoping that would end our conversation and give me time to decide what to do about my whereabouts before he returned the next day. Unfortunately, he wasn't out of questions.

"You know where an hombre named Six might be found?" he asked, and this time he was looking directly at me as he spoke. I shook my head and made a shrugging motion. "Whatever he calls himself, I'm talking about the gent who shot it out here with the Silver Dollar Kid. Any of that refresh your memory?"

"Oh, si, now I know who you mean," I said, improvising desperately. "He left the city shortly after the fight. No one knows where he is, now."

"Is that right?" He seemed to be peering at me even more intently. "Funny. That's not the way I heard it." He took a step toward me and, in one flick of his hand, knocked my hat off my head. Then the long gun in his other hand started to come up.

He recognized me!

I grabbed the barrel with a strength born of sheer desperation, and twisted it. He hadn't seemed to expect that, and I found that he wasn't a very strong man. His power lay in intimidation, I guess. I almost got the weapon away from him, and did manage enough to slam it back hard against the side of his head. Then I did it a second time, and a third, until he finally did let it go and staggered backwards. Still acting on adrenalin, I rammed the stock of the gun into his stomach. He doubled up with a groan, and I clipped him on the jaw with its barrel. This time, he went down to a kneeling position.

I stood over him, holding his gun. It was a single-shot Sharps breech-loader, I saw, the same kind I'd picked up from someone during the Battle of New Market, back when it was almost longer than I was. Luckily, I'd grown enough to handle it now.

McCluer was groaning as though hurting badly, but I noticed he was stealthily undoing the buttons along the front of his big black coat. Without pausing to think, I hauled off and kicked at the side of his head. This time, he dropped all the way to the floor. If he'd been faking before, he wasn't now.

I put the Sharps aside and jerked his coat open, snapping off the buttons he hadn't yet freed. Sure enough, his skinny frame had left plenty of room to conceal the sawed-off shotgun I'd heard about, hanging by a leather strap around his neck. I pulled it roughly over his head, broke it open and shook out the two shells. Then I searched through the rest of his clothing and came up with a small pocket pistol, with no trigger guard, and an even smaller .32 rimfire in one of his boots. I wouldn't have recognized it but for my tutorial with Hickok.

I was shaking with reaction, but also with anger—the same kind of anger I'd had at the Silver Dollar Kid, when he'd been so ready to kill me, or my brother, for pay. It seemed to me that anyone who took money to kill another person deserved whatever he got. The fact that I was physically stronger than this emaciated specimen didn't bother me at all. If we hadn't been close enough that I could get my hands on him, I'd be dead now.

I pointed the pocket pistol at his head. But, I found, it wasn't in me to kill him—not in cold blood, not like this. It would have been the logical thing to do. He would be right back on my trail, or Jack's, if I let him live. But, even as I picked up the Sharps he'd probably used many times to gun down men from ambush, I couldn't bring myself to use any of his weapons to finish him.

I did do some quick work on the sights of that old gun, though—enough to throw off his aim at any distance, I hoped, but not enough so he'd notice I'd bent the tiny bit of metal out of place. Maybe that would give his next potential victim a break and a chance to get away, or, better yet, to shoot back.

I threw the Sharps aside, took the rope off his saddle and tied his hands behind him. Then I wrapped the rest of it around his feet, climbed up on a stall and looped it over a rafter. I pulled on it, hauling him into the air so his body hung upside down, about five feet above the stable floor.

He came around while I was doing that, and began to struggle, but I'd done a good job with the knots. "Cut me down! What d'you think you're doing?" He called me several names you don't hear in Sunday school. "Take this rope off me, you…"

I ignored him, having started to work on his pistols by then, taking them slowly and deliberately apart and throwing their cylinders and whatever else I could pry loose as far as I could into the muddy street outside.

Right then, I decided Callie St. Clair had had the right idea. I would have to leave town, too, and the quicker, the better. I realized that McCluer had tracked me here, just the way that Ned Buntline had, and, as soon as he got loose, he would be after me again. At least he wouldn't be able to guess where I might go, because, at that point, I didn't know myself.

"Are you listening to me, you young whelp?" he said, his voice rising even higher than normal, sounding almost hysterical now. His face was bruised and battered where I'd hit and kicked him, but I didn't feel sorry. "Nobody treats me like this. Nobody! You've signed your death warrant, you hear? If you don't cut me down right now…"

I actually laughed, and he broke off, staring at me. Apparently he was so used to inspiring fear and awe that anything else shocked him. "You'll what? Try to kill me? What have you been trying to do all this time?" I leaned closer and backhanded him across the mouth as hard as I could. Blood spurted from a cut lip.

It was a cowardly act, hitting a helpless man that way. But I wouldn't have been afraid, at this point, of having a physical confrontation with him even if he was free, as long as we were both unarmed. I was much the bigger and stronger of the two of us; his strength lay in striking from ambush, or with allies to protect him.

And I wasn't being brutal for the fun of it. I was hoping to make him even angrier than he was already, and maybe warp that cold, calculating judgment of his, so he'd make mistakes when dealing with me, driven by rage. Maybe even a little fear. That would be a change for him.

He cursed me some more, so I smacked him again. The lesson got through that time, and he shut up.

I went about dressing, packing up my stuff, and being glad I'd kept it nearby all this time. I saddled Star, who'd been busy nibbling at one of his halter cords. Then I went into the stall where McCluer's horse stood, and did some work on its saddle girth, where he couldn't see me.

While I was at it, I went through his saddlebags. I didn't bother to count the wad of money I found. I left it alone, hoping to find something else—and I did.

The handwriting on the letter was that of Colonel Sutherland, the same writing I remembered from the sales document he'd given me. I tucked the letter inside my shirt, to read later. I found still another pistol, this one a shiny factory-converted Army revolver, with walnut grips and a shiny finish. Knowing McCluer's trade, I was certain that the weapon had been treated well. I saw no reason not to appropriate it. Taking his money would have seemed wrong, but taking a tool of his trade, one that he would have gladly used on me, seemed more like the spoils of war. I helped myself to a box of .44 Remington cartridges nestled in there with it.

When I finished, I still had a few hours before sunrise when the stable owner would come in and find McCluer hanging there. Of course, the owner would free him. I left the owner a note on the door where he'd see it before he would see McCluer. In it, I apologized for leaving so abruptly. But, I figured, once he found out who McCluer was and realized he'd been after me, that would be explanation enough.

I didn't want McCluer to start yelling and bring someone who might free him before morning, so I searched through his pockets and came up with a handkerchief to gag him. If looks alone could have killed, McCluer wouldn't have needed any of his arsenal to take care of me.

Then I blew out the lamp which advertised the stable as being open, led Star into the still-dark street, mounted up and took my leave of Kansas City.

# ELEVEN

Charles Starrett: *"I sure hope you catch him, Mace,*
*'cause that Durango Kid's cost me a lot of sleep."*
The Durango Kid *(1940)*

The sun had been up for several hours before the stable owner arrived for the day, and found my farewell note. The dirt street in front wasn't what you'd call busy, but there were a number of early risers making their way up and down both sides on foot. It must've been three or four more minutes before my ex-boss spotted the trussed-up figure of Clay McCluer, deeper inside, swinging like a pendulum and making inarticulate noises behind the gag I'd tied on him.

The stable man undid the gag first, and McCluer began screaming curses like I'd never heard, at least not all at one time. The racket began drawing the interest of passers-by, who drifted toward the stable entrance and began gawking at what they saw.

Apparently, the owner had not been able to lift McCluer and untie him at the same time. He called for assistance to boost the man up high enough to take the stress off the knots I'd tied, so he could undo them. A handful of men responded, some of them shaking their heads in bewilderment over how this stranger had come to be in such a fix.

They finally got McCluer untied and on his feet. He staggered outside, obviously still recovering from the effects of hanging upside down for so long.

It was then that someone recognized who he was, and a buzz began to sweep through the growing crowd.

After he could walk normally once more, McCluer stalked back into the stable and recovered his sawed-off shotgun and his Sharps, shoving the latter into the scabbard on his still-saddled horse. He ignored inquiries from some of the bolder onlookers, who risked his wrath by asking what happened. His only reaction was a cold glare at each questioner, which was enough to shut them up.

McCluer found his hat and put it on, placed a foot in the stirrup of his saddle, and swung aboard—or started to. The girth which I'd loosened the night before turned, the entire saddle slid down the side of the horse, and McCluer spilled into the street with a foot still stuck in the stirrup.

This time, even McCluer's fearsome reputation couldn't stop those around him from bursting out laughing. By now, there were so many gathered around him that even he couldn't have shot them all.

I decided I'd seen enough, from my vantage point on the roof of the bank building where I'd been lying flat since leaving Star tied down near the city's acres and acres of stockyards. They made up such a sprawling and busy place at all hours that I figured nobody was going to notice an extra horse.

I climbed over the railing at the back of the building, shinnied down the same drainpipe which had provided me access, and walked as fast as I could to the yards. Sure enough, Star was right where I'd left him, nibbling on a fence post, and my gear was where I'd concealed it the previous night when I'd started out of town but changed my mind.

I sat down and thought it over. I'd come to a dead end in trying to find Jack. I simply had no idea where to try next, and the West was too big for me to just hope to run across him and Callie again. But McCluer must have sources almost as good as Ned Buntline's, because he, like the writer, had tracked me here. It occurred to me that McCluer might have a better idea than I did as to where to go next.

His most likely inclination would be to try and track me, I supposed, but good luck on that. If I'd ridden out of town ahead of him as I'd originally planned, he might have managed it. But the best tracker in Kansas City wasn't going to pick out Star's trail through the mass of cattle and horse hooves around the stockyards.

I had hit McCluer where it was bound to hurt him the most, and I don't mean with fists. It didn't bother me one whit that, although I was still a youngster, I was already bigger and stronger than he and had used that advantage—not when I knew he would have killed me or Jack, if he could, as casually as swatting a fly. To me, he was a cowardly murderer who killed from ambush, and I felt no pity for him. From what I'd heard, he didn't even care if people knew about his killings, so long as there was no evidence which would hold up in a court of law. That reputation was what made him a fearsome figure.

What I had done, and done quite deliberately, was to make him a laughingstock—at least momentarily.

And it had all worked out just as I'd hoped. Enough people in Kansas City had now seen McCluer trussed up, staggering about drunkenly, and even falling flat on his back from his horse, for the story to spread. Westerners in every saloon in the territory would hear about it, sooner or later. The awe in which they held him had to change at least a little after that—or, at least, I hoped so.

Humor could be as deadly to someone like McCluer as a gun, maybe more so. All the reading I'd done back home had showed me how satire could humble even a giant, in the hands of, say, someone like Mark Twain whose "Celebrated Jumping Frog of Calaveras County" was the last story I remembered reading before I left Virginia.

I saddled Star once more, attached my saddlebags, and guided him along the road in the direction I'd started last night, the direction I figured McCluer would be taking in hopes of catching up with me and settling the score for his humiliation. I hoped it wouldn't occur to him that I might be following him instead.

I was counting on that as my edge, because I wasn't kidding myself: being close to McCluer after what I'd done to him. I had a tiger by the tale, and didn't dare let go.

I drifted off the road at the first clump of trees large enough to conceal me from other passing riders, and waited. Sure enough, it wasn't more than fifteen minutes before I saw McCluer's horse moving along at a rapid clip as I peered through the branches—too rapid for him to keep up the pace for long. I let him get well ahead before I remounted Star and followed in his wake.

In the days that followed, I would become very familiar with every nail and indentation of each shoe on that horse of his.

His right rear shoe, I quickly determined, was set slightly off angle from the others, and maybe was working loose. The right front had a worn spot along one side. I didn't know a lot about tracking, but I was learning.

My survival depended on him not realizing that I was behind him. If he should guess that, I was dead. He would be waiting somewhere up ahead with that Sharps of his, and I would never know what hit me.

All the while I was riding, I pondered things I'd learned during my long talk with Ned Buntline, or Colonel Judson. I wasn't sure whether to believe the twenty thousand dollar figure he'd cited as his annual income from writing but, even allowing for exaggeration, he was obviously making a good living. As I say, I'd read plenty of dime novels by him and others, *Rough Riders of Durango* being one I'd breezed through while doing odd jobs around Kansas City. I would one day steal that title for a movie.

The thing was, I believed I could write blood and thunder as well as what I'd been reading. Besides, I'd actually seen Hickok and Earp and many of the other legends of the West up close and personal, maybe more so than Judson himself. I could weave fact and fiction into stories as well as he could, I thought.

As westerners go, I wasn't much of an outdoorsman yet. But I had done enough hunting and trapping small game in the mountains of Shenandoah County to be able to avoid starving. I encountered enough water holes for drinking and washing. Strange as it seems, McCluer seemed to be even more of a greenhorn outdoors than I was. When he would camp out overnight, it was easy for me to make a cold camp nearby—near enough to smell his coffee and wish I dared light a fire of my own—and to keep a distant eye on him. He never cleaned up a campsite when he moved on. Sometimes, I would do it myself, after he'd abandoned it. Eventually, I got so I could practically track him by his campsites, and didn't have to stay quite so close and worry about him hearing me if I shot some game. I even dared have my own campfires, too far off for him to see or smell.

I had no idea where he was headed. By now, he must have given up any idea of catching up with me, so he must have some destination in mind.

Sometimes he'd stop off in a little trailside village, or a place the size of Beatrice on the Big Blue River where they had lodging accommodations. Of course, I didn't dare use a hotel or stable in the same town while he was there. But, by now, I was getting used to fishing and washing up in the occasional stream, catching what I could cook on the trail, and that had the advantage of not diminishing my remaining little bankroll. Star, of course, got by on grass and water, and whatever else he decided to chew on, until I would pick up some grain for him in one of those towns after McCluer passed through.

Besides the grain and occasional food, the main thing I spent money on was paper and pencil. I began sending letters and writing samples whenever I ran across a Railway Mail Service location to some of those eastern publishers I'd heard Colonel Judson mention, giving them a return address of the next municipality of any size I figured we'd pass through as we moved across Nebraska. I quickly learned that there was indeed lots of space that needed filling in those publications, and I began writing my first stories while trailing along behind McCluer. Whenever I would complete one, I'd package it and mail it to one of the magazines.

For someone who stalked others, he never seemed to think he might be followed himself. The days became weeks, and finally months. I got used to being sunburned and rained on. At least it was closer to summer than winter.

When the rain came really hard, I would either find a town or residence for refuge, or Star and I would just get wet. But I had picked up some waterproof wrappings to keep my various writings dry.

It became apparent early on, in the various communities where I followed McCluer, that my ploy in Kansas City had done just what I'd hoped and more. People who talked about McCluer passing through seemed less fretful of him and more amused at what they heard had happened to him. Some of the fearful aura which had previously surrounded him was gone.

We passed a number of sodbusters' homes, and sometimes I'd trade my help in plowing a field or clearing some trees in return for a roof over my head. Once in a while, I'd find that McCluer had stayed at the same house, although he never paid for the hospitality with money or work. He still relied on his reputation, what was left of it, when he stopped at an isolated home and demanded a bed or a meal. He left folks behind with a big dislike for him, both among the farmers and in the towns.

At one point, that growing dislike and the diminishing of his reputation forced me to get a lot closer to McCluer than I'd wanted.

It was one of those rare nights when I'd settled down within sight of McCluer's camp. I felt no need to do that at every opportunity anymore, but I did it occasionally. And one night I realized I wasn't the only one.

I heard the sounds of two horses pushing through the trees and bushes not far from where I'd been about to wrap myself in a blanket and go to sleep. I was some distance off the dirt trail McCluer had been following. I could think of no reason for other riders to be in the same wooded area as McCluer or myself, unless they were trailing after one of us.

I crept over to Star and held his nose, to make sure he didn't whinny at one of the passing horses. I'd been right, there were two of them. Once they'd passed by us far enough so I figured Star wouldn't call to them, I pulled on my moccasins—some of the more useful items I'd gotten from Warbonnet Gonzales after we'd gotten out of that Sioux village—along with Jack's black shirt, hat and trousers. I figured they'd blend in with the darkness. I stuck one of his pistols in my belt.

It was easy to keep up with the two riders on foot. They were picking their way through the trees cautiously and, in the dark, that was a slow job.

"That's got to be him up ahead," I heard one of them whisper. "You can see the glow of his fire."

"Yeah. The great man-killer, Cord McCluer," the other said, and gave an unexpected giggle. They both sounded about as young as I was, and perhaps slightly tipsy as well. "He can't get away with talking to us the way he did back in the cafe. He probably don't know we heard how some guy treed him back in Kansas City. He ain't so tough."

"And when we gun him," the first voice said, "it'll be us people talk about, not him. Better tie the horses here, Steve. We'll sneak up the rest of the way on foot."

"Yeah." I could hear leather creak as they got down, but we must have still been too far off from McCluer's fire for him to hear it. Carefully, I moved closer as the two would-be gunmen crept ahead.

I came onto their horses, and gave the saddles a once-over as best I could in the dark. I'd hoped one of them might be packing a rifle in a scabbard. I didn't want McCluer killed, not now, not until I'd learned whatever was to be learned from dogging him. With a long gun, I could've stationed myself on high ground above McCluer's camp and placed my shots close enough to the pair of intruders to chase them off, and McCluer would never see me. But there was no rifle on either horse.

I fished out a black bandana which had been an occasional part of Jack's showy clothing, and tied it behind my head, highwayman-style. With the handkerchief covering the lower part of my face and my hat pulled down, and if I could alter my voice, I didn't think McCluer would know me. I hoped not.

I moved through the trees slowly and quietly, easing around the bigger ones so as not to rustle the growth near them. As it was, I was almost too late.

"Howdy, Mr. McCluer," said a voice I recognized as belonging to the youth called Steve. "Remember us?"

I stopped at the edge of the campsite, still within the trees. The speaker had his pistol out and pointed at McCluer, who was armed with nothing but a half-empty whiskey bottle. His shotgun lay to one side of his saddle, where his Sharps was also sheathed, but both were well out of reach. If he'd replaced any of the pistols I'd taken from him, I couldn't see them.

I was surprised that anyone who made his living the way McCluer did would not have taken more precautions. I guess he saw himself as always the stalker, never the one being stalked. Or maybe my treatment of him had caused him to fall apart more than I realized. The whiskey pointed in that direction. Courage in a bottle, I thought.

Still, there was no give in the man. "Yeah, I remember you," he said. "A couple of louts who didn't like having to back down like whipped puppies for sassing their betters. What do you want now?"

"You ain't pointin' that sawed-off at us this time," Steve's companion said, holding his own pistol down by his side. "How's it feel to be on the other side of a gun, Mr. McCluer?"

"You going to shoot, or talk me to death?" McCluer said, glaring.

In reply, Steve cocked the hammer on his pistol and took careful aim at the unmoving figure sitting on the ground. But I was taking an even more careful, at the pistol in his hand.

I squeezed the trigger, and the weapon went flying with a clang as he spun around and yelped in pain, shaking the hand as though it had been stung by a nest of bees. "Drop it," I told his companion, before he could locate me.

The other youth hesitated, then let his pistol fall to the ground. I stepped out from behind the tree, and their eyes widened, even McCluer's. I guess I did make a pretty outlandish figure, all in black and wearing a mask as I stood in the flickering firelight. I picked up the dropped pistol with my left hand, and kept both weapons on them.

McCluer started to move to where his shotgun lay. "Leave it alone," I said, pitching my voice as low as I could and swinging the borrowed gun in his direction.

He settled back and stared at me. "Who the hell are you?" he said. His words sounded just a little slurred.

Remembering the title of that last dime novel I'd read, I made up a name on the spot, a name I would use one day over at Columbia. "Call me the Durango Kid," I said. "All right, the two of you—start drifting. Get back to your horses and vamoose, before I turn McCluer loose on you."

They didn't need a second invitation. I stepped back into the trees as they rushed past me, tripping over themselves and various bushes in their haste. Once I heard the sound of their horses pounding away, I faded further into the trees myself.

"Hey! Who are you? Why'd you help me?"

I didn't answer, I just kept moving into the woods. McCluer didn't seem inclined to stir from where he sat. In fact, instead of reaching for either of his weapons, he reached for his bottle and took a healthy swallow. Once I could no longer see him, I moved faster back to where I'd left Star. I didn't think McCluer would feel like trying to follow me, but it wasn't a chance I was willing to take. I packed up my gear and saddled up to put some distance between us. Steve and his friend might not have been afraid of him, but I was.

It didn't take long to get my stuff together, get mounted and ease my way clear of the woods. I still moved carefully, and it turned out to be a good thing, as I almost crossed trails with Steve and his friend down the path. But I heard them before they heard me. I pulled up, dismounted and put my hand over Star's nose again to make sure he didn't respond to their horses.

I could hear them talking for just a minute and then they were gone. The last thing I heard one of them say was, "Who the hell was that masked man?"

# TWELVE

*Roy Barcroft: "Yeah, if Sharkey had listened to me, he wouldn't be layin'*
*out stiff and cold tonight. I told that birdbrain that wasn't Leslie Rawlins."*
*Gene Stutenroth: "Don't speak ill of the dead. I feel very deeply about Sharkey.*
*Cut down in his prime."*
*Roy Barcroft: "Don't tell me you got a heart!"*
*Gene Stutenroth: "Of course. Besides, Sharkey was still useful to me."*
*Roy Barcroft: "You had me worried."*
Oklahoma Badlands *(1948)*

T*he snub-nose automatic felt cold where it was taped against the wrist of the man in the hospital elevator. The wide sleeves of the white coat resembling a doctor's would make it easy to pull it loose, when he was ready to use it. He hoped its silencer would make the shot quiet enough so he could leave before anyone realized what had happened.*

*Neither the pretty young woman nor the man in the suit, in the elevator with him, gave him a second look. Although they didn't talk to each other with him in there with them, it was obvious that they had eyes only for each other. Good. They wouldn't remember him if they were ever asked to describe him.*

*People had tried to describe him before. They usually ended up saying he was of medium height, average build, dark hair which could have been brown or black, pale eyes, no distinctive features they could recall. No, sorry, they weren't even sure they could pick him out of a police lineup.*

*Police in several states had suspected Clayton McCluer of being involved* in killings before. But none of them had been able to make it stick. He was too average-looking for anyone to identify him, and that was his protection—the ultimate camouflage.

The elevator stopped at his floor. The woman and man preceded him out the door. Now, if the information he'd been given was correct, Jonathan Six was in a room just around the corner from the nurses' station...

He started in that direction, his doctor's disguise diverting any inquiries as to where he was going, when he realized the couple in front of him were walking in the same direction. Then they turned and went into the room where he'd been headed.

Without breaking stride, McCluer continued right past the room and kept going. He didn't know who the two people were—his intended victim was not supposed to have any family or close friends—but it was obvious that he could not do his job today. His best bet was to get back to the elevator fast and leave, before someone looked closely enough to penetrate his disguise. It would not set well with Old Man Sutherland, but there was no choice.

There would be another day.

# THIRTEEN

*Randolph Scott: "Are we going to give in to that? Or are we gonna do what we came out here to do—build a railroad?"*
Canadian Pacific *(1949)*

I'm glad you decided to join us today, Detective Martin. Yes, I know I'm not getting where you want as fast as you'd like. Please believe me, if I don't tell you the entire story, you can't possibly understand what led up to the incident over at Gower Gulch.

Where did I stop yesterday, Miss Hamilton? Oh, yeah, the two young men who wanted to gun down Cord McCluer. And my inspiration of becoming a masked rider right out of a dime novel. Of course, that came in pretty handy when I was helping out with scripts over at Columbia, where they choose the titles for their westerns by drawing staff suggestions out of a jar in an office lottery. And when they wanted Charlie Starrett to settle into a permanent series character, the Durango Kid just seemed a dramatic name. Besides, it was another way for me to worry some of the people I'm going to be telling you about, my way of letting them know there's still someone out there who knows what's gone on in their pasts.

I don't know how much you know about my work in Hollywood. I've never been under contract to any single studio. I've moved around, mainly to keep the people I'm talking about from catching up with me—although, as you can see, they finally did. I've developed a kind of network among western writers and producers, who call on me to help out anonymously with a script, or make suggestions for some new series, or discuss the most authentic direction for a story to take. Only a few of the producers and directors even know me by sight, although I've made some good friends among the actors and stunt people over the years. I'm sure they all find me rather eccentric, insisting on meeting with them at odd hours, in empty offices, or out on location, for story conferences.

Maybe now they'll all understand why I've had to do it that way.

It's not as though I'm the only survivor from the old days who's worked in Hollywood. Heck, even Wyatt Earp did some technical advising out here in his final years. He conferred with John Ford who wanted to use some of the events in his life in *My Darling Clementine*, where Henry Fonda played Wyatt. Not that Ford used much of what old Wyatt told him. When Wyatt died, Bill Hart and Tom Mix were among his pall-bearers, you know.

Come to think of it, I guess every film about a town peace officer owes a debt to Wyatt's biographer, Stuart Lake. Although Wyatt's widow insisted until the day she died that Lake made up most of the stuff in his book, *Wyatt Earp, Frontier Marshal*. And it's true that Lake didn't publish it until 1931, two years after Wyatt passed on, so who knows what Wyatt really told him in those interviews? But I don't suppose Wyatt would have minded someone embellishing his life story, since he often embellished it himself.

But Wyatt's basic story in that book has been acted out by everybody from Hank Fonda to Randolph Scott, even using some of the same dialogue, and probably in a hundred other movies where Wyatt's name wasn't used. They were actually afraid to use his name the first time they did his story, when Walter Huston played him but called himself "Frame Johnson" to keep Josie Earp from filing a lawsuit. George O'Brien played him in *Frontier Marshal* in 1934, then Randy Scott re-made it in 1939, and then O'Brien turned around and did it once again in *Marshal of Mesa City*. Singing cowboy Eddie Dean even did a version of it in *Check Your Guns*. I think they all did that scene in Lake's book where Wyatt was supposed to have arrested Ben Thompson in Ellsworth, after Thompson's brother shot the sheriff. It never actually happened, but it's a western cliché now.

And Wyatt sure isn't the only one to take advantage of his notoriety. Did you ever see the silent picture back in 1914 that "Buffalo Bill" Cody made about the frontier Indian wars? Charles King—no relation to the Charlie King who's played as many bad guys as Roy Barcroft by now—did the screenplay. That earlier King may even have published the first western novel, *The Colonel's Daughter*, back in 1882, unless you count James Fenimore Cooper's stories as early westerns, even though they took place in the east, or maybe the dime novels by people like Buntline and, later, people like me.

Come to think of it, Cody appeared in at least ten movies I can think off offhand before he died, back in 1917.

Then there was Al Jennings, the reformed Oklahoma outlaw. He made a bank robbery movie in 1908 along with Bill Tilghman, the lawman who captured him. Talk about art imitating life. Tilghman did some movie advising for Bill Hart, too. Hart used to call him "Uncle Billy," which Tilghman didn't particularly care for.

So yeah, there were ex-outlaws a-plenty making the rounds. Remember Cole Younger, and Frank James? They toured together in Wild West shows right up until 1915, the year both of them died. Fonda not only played Earp, he played Frank James in a couple of movies, too, although Frank was never as easy-going as Hank made him seem. For that matter, Cole wasn't quite as nice as Dennis Morgan or Wayne Morris made him look in movies, either.

Then there was Emmett Dalton, the last survivor of the Dalton gang of bank robbery fame. Emmett went into real estate out here in California after he got out of prison, and turned into a law-and-order advocate right up until he passed in 1935. He even co-authored *When the Daltons Rode*, the book that Randy Scott, Brian Donlevy, Broderick Crawford, Andy Devine and some others did as a movie just a few years ago.

So, Detective Martin, you shouldn't be surprised to find there are others besides me from those times still kicking around in Hollywood.

All right, yes, I'm sorry, you're right—I am rambling. Let me get back to when I was still shadowing Cord McCluer through Nebraska.

He seemed to be making for the Wyoming Territory, but he didn't stop to shoot anybody on his way out there. I wondered, as I had with Jack, just how he was keeping himself solvent. He always seemed to have money for supplies and the occasional town lodgings and meals.

The railroad had gone through the southern part of Wyoming by then, creating boom towns at stops like Cheyenne and Laramie. Midway through 1868, the Fourteenth Amendment was ratified granting citizenship to blacks, naturalized citizens, and practically everybody but the Indians who were here before anybody else. Wild Bill's old buddy, Lieutenant Colonel Custer, had gained a modicum of fame by leading an attack on a Cheyenne encampment on the upper Washita River that killed more than a hundred Indians. It wasn't until much later that some of us found out most of those Indians had been women, children and old men. But that was Custer, sure enough.

I'd actually gotten some of my stories in print by then in the penny dreadfuls, and gotten a little bit of money for them. That was the meager start of what has supported me in all the years since, spinning yarns out of stuff I'd seen or just heard about, painting story pictures of a west that never was quite what the myths and the movies made it.

If it hadn't been for the bits of writing I managed to do during those long hours of travel, I'd probably have dropped off McCluer's trail after the first six months, out of plain boredom. The man didn't do anything but drift, and drink. I didn't know how much drinking he'd done before our little encounter in Kansas City, but I don't think he could possibly have been putting away as much liquor as he was doing now, and still have made those long-distance kills I'd heard so much about.

Maybe I really had gotten to him, hit a nerve and shaken him up. Maybe he couldn't handle being a hired gun anymore, having been humiliated as he'd been.

I was quite wrong about that, of course.

He and I had gradually drifted into what was left of Utah, after parts of it had gone to Wyoming, Colorado and Nevada. It hadn't been necessary for me to stick very close to McCluer. Word about him would get around so it would be easy for me to pick him up, after dropping off and getting my latest manuscript into the mail.

Utah was still a territory. It would be almost twenty-seven more years before it got admitted to the Union, mainly because the Mormons there enjoyed having more than one wife.

Six years earlier, the Central Pacific Railroad had started laying rail east from Sacramento, and the Union Pacific west from Omaha. They would soon be meeting at Promontory in Utah, and the country would have its first transcontinental railroad.

Promontory was crowded on the day Star and I rode into it, and it didn't take me long to find out that people had come from all over the country for a ceremonial driving in of the last rail spikes—gold and silver spikes, no less. I didn't think I stood a chance of spotting McCluer among that mass of humanity, unless it was by accident—and I realized he might spot me the same way. I decided to take precautions.

Since I had accumulated a bit of spare cash by now, I stabled Star and found a hotel room for myself—which wasn't all that easy, with all the people coming in for tomorrow's ceremony. I also paid for one of my rare hot-water baths, instead of soaping myself in cold creeks and streams. I hadn't seen a barber in months, so my hair had grown considerably—enough, I hoped, to provide me with a little disguise.

I cut off bits of it, and fashioned heavier eyebrows for myself, attaching them with spirit gum I'd learned about from a traveling stage actor I'd interviewed when I'd passed through Denver, the new territorial capital of Colorado. I was making a little extra as a feature correspondent for some eastern newspapers I'd hooked up with, doing occasional pieces like that.

Next, I outfitted myself with a suit, complete with vest and bowler hat, similar to the styles I was seeing on many of the other folks gathering in town. I hoped I'd appear different enough from my usual look so McCluer wouldn't know me even if he did happen to look my way.

I needn't have worried. It wasn't McCluer who saw and recognized me.

I'd returned to the stable where Star was happily cribbing at the wooden sides of his stall, and made sure he'd been cared for as promised. I was walking down a long line of stalls on my way out when another horse stretched out its neck over the rail and snapped at me.

I jumped back, and its teeth clicked where my shoulder had been.

The horse and I glared at each other. Its lip was curled as though in a snarl, exposing its yellowed teeth, and one of its front hooves pawed at the floor of its stall.

"I should'a warned you about him, mister," a grinning stable hand said. "He's a mean 'un. Got me a time or two when I was brushin' him for his owner." He held out his forearm, on which a purple bite-mark showed clearly.

"Who's his owner?" I asked, although I knew.

"Fellow name of Quinn," the stable hand said. "You may bump into him. I sent him to the same hotel as I suggested for you. Big fellow, heavy jaw, tough-looking…"

"Yeah," I said. "I believe I know him."

It took me until evening to spot Quinn and McCluer, on their way into a restaurant. I was ready for some dinner myself, but I didn't want to follow them too closely. I needed a way to get close to them that wouldn't put them on their guard.

It didn't take long to find one. Actually, it found me.

"Hey there, sonny," the wizened old codger with the chewed-looking hat and patches on his vest and pants called out to me, as I stood outside the door pondering my next move. "Hey, how's about buyin' us a drink? It's been a long dry spell."

I looked at him. I figured the panhandler might have been a down-on-his-luck miner, or maybe a saloon sweeper like I'd been. He had a short beard which jutted out aggressively, sort of like the one that Al St. John, the former Keystone Kop, developed for his "Fuzzy Q. Jones" character that he used in support of maybe half-a-dozen cowboy stars. It wasn't as long or neat as the one George Hayes grew for his "Windy" and "Gabby" portrayals, but he definitely fit the mold of the old-timers we put into those pictures as sidekicks.

Instead of just a drink, I invited him to have dinner. That didn't particularly excite him, until I added that he could order drinks to wash it down. He followed me in, smacking his lips loudly, and I led him to an empty table next to where I saw Quinn and McCluer sitting. They didn't even glance up as we passed by them, and I seated myself with my back toward them—but within earshot.

A woman in an apron who would one day remind me of Marjorie Main took their order, and then ours. She apparently knew my companion. "Zeke," she said, "you ain't gonna drink your dinner again, are you?"

"Jest enough to whet my appetite," Zeke said with a grin. When she went away, he added, under his breath, "Durned persnickity women." The perfect line for Gabby, I would realize one day.

My beef and potatoes were good, but I didn't appreciate them the way I should have. I was too busy trying to hear what Quinn and McCluer were saying behind me and, unfortunately, it wasn't much. I realized it had been foolish of me to think they'd reveal much about their activities in a place as public as this.

The most surprising thing I learned was that McCluer had a wife and some kids somewhere back east. Quinn asked with a sarcastic chuckle if he'd heard from his wife lately. It was apparently a sore point with McCluer, who grumbled something about that being one reason he didn't stay long in one place long. Quinn found that hilarious.

I found it hard to think of McCluer as ever having been married. I mean, when you watch the movies, do you ever think of Roy Barcroft or Charley King or Kenne Duncan as having a family off somewhere while they're rustling cattle or holding up stages?

Zeke's running commentary on life in general and Utah in particular didn't help me in trying to listen to what was being said at the next table. I didn't want to hush him up, though. His continuous gab made good cover for my eavesdropping. Quinn and McCluer, if they paid us any heed at all, could only assume we both lived around here and had known each other for years.

I'd about given up when I heard Quinn say something about the two of them getting together in his room, "to discuss that little matter about the trains tomorrow." That told me something was afoot, even if it provided no hint as to what. My goal after that was to get out of there before they did, and it cost me a third drink to get Zeke to abbreviate his meal.

On our way out, Zeke kept assuring me he'd enjoyed our conversation and we'd have to get together and do it again soon. We parted company and I hot-footed it back to the hotel. On the pretense of having forgotten my room number, I got a look at the register and saw which room Quinn had. My room was on the second floor, and his was on the top, one story up.

I unlocked my door, secured it behind me and walked over to my window. It would not be as easy a climb as when I'd gotten to the top of that Kansas City bank to observe McCluer's humiliation. I peeled off my hat and coat and then my light-colored shirt. It was time to put on Jack's black one again. The growing darkness outside should keep anyone in the street below from seeing me hanging onto the outside of the building, or so I hoped.

I had figured Quinn's room should be one level up and three windows to the left of mine. Luckily for me, all those windows had decorative wooden ledges outside. I hoped they were as solid and secure as they looked.

My tree-climbing skills, developed during my boyhood in the Virginia mountains, seemed intact. I blew out the lantern in my room, and crawled very carefully out my window and made my way to the ledge above mine. Again, my luck held: it was warm enough on this May night for the window to be cracked open enough for me to hear the voices coming from inside.

But they weren't the voices or Quinn or McCluer.

"...hard to believe it's been seven years already. Seven years since President Lincoln signed the Pacific Railroad Act and authorized the transcontinental rail," a man was saying. "Of course, Tom, our two companies were originally supposed to meet at the eastern boundary of California."

"The war kind of changed that," someone else said.

"Yes, the war took the iron we needed to make rails, and the able-bodied workers we needed were off fighting for the North or South. I'll tell you, there were times when I thought this event would never come."

"It'll come tomorrow," said the second man. "Theodore Judah was right, back in Connecticut when he said people someday would be able to ride from New York to California in a matter of days. 'Crazy Judah,' they called him. It's a shame he's not still around to have the last laugh."

"Yes, it is. He was the one who talked me into investing in his railroad idea. But private investments would never have gotten it done by themselves. It took government backing from the Congress to do it—assuming we do get it done tomorrow."

The other man laughed. "You're not having doubts at this late date, are you, Leland? Ben Holladay sure didn't. Don't forget, he built up his stage line for years by putting the little fellows out of business with cut-rate fares. Then the so-called stagecoach king turned around and sold all his holdings to Wells Fargo. Don't you think he realized what the coming of the railroad would mean to transportation?"

"I've ridden in some of Holladay's coaches," Leland said. "Passengers packed in like sardines, but often that was the only way to travel. Of course, you could go part of the way across the country by steamboat, if you didn't worry about hitting a reef or having a boiler blow. Or you could join a wagon train, and go maybe a few miles a day. But I don't think any but the most visionary men in Washington realize even now what this linkup will mean to the nation. For the first time, the United States will actually be united…"

This was all very interesting, but it wasn't what I'd clambered up all this way to hear about. Obviously, I'd miscalculated the location of Quinn's room. I should have gone upstairs and looked for myself to see how they were numbered, but I might have bumped into him or McCluer on their way back from dinner and they might get suspicious. Ducking my head, I shuffled along on hands and knees to the next window, only to find an empty room. I moved again, to the next, and nearly lost my balance as I heard Quinn's voice sounding as though he was right next to the window.

"…use some of their own nitro stuff," he was saying. "The Old Man wants this transcontinental thing to end up enough of a disaster so they won't try it again for years. I don't know if he's doing all this for some other country, or some renegade Confederates, or what, but it don't matter. His money's good."

"What makes him think the two companies won't just pick up the pieces and build it all back?" McCluer asked.

"I don't know. Maybe they will. Who cares? But with two wrecked engines and a bunch of bystanders blown to bits in that crowd tomorrow, Washington's sure not gonna keep investing in it. And Stanford and Durant ain't gonna be able to find any more private investors, not if we get people talkin' up the railroad as the devil's plaything and all that stuff. Anyway, that's how the Old Man's got it figured."

"So when do we get the explosive in place?"

"Tonight, soon as the boys swipe it out of the Central Pacific supply cache west of town. The Chinese workers have been riskin' their necks clearing obstacles with it so other workers could lay track. We'll swipe some before dawn and get it set up, so I'm gonna catch me a few winks while I can…"

I started scrambling back down to the second level, and then to my room's open window. As soon as I swung inside, I grabbed up my carpetbag, dumped its contents on the bed and belted on Jack's pistols. Then I pulled on his black hat, and went downstairs and toward the stable as quickly as I could without breaking into a run and drawing attention.

My guess, and I was sure it was right, was that the Old Man was none other than Colonel Sutherland. I didn't know why he wanted to wreck this transcontinental rail link, other than his hatred for the nation that defeated his beloved South, but I knew I had to find some way to stop him.

# FOURTEEN

*William Elliott: "I swear, sometimes I think I'll turn you out to pasture and*
*just let you run. What in the world are you talkin' about?"*
*Andy Clyde: "I'm talkin' about that smoke yonder, which is*
*our StationSeventy-Six, afire."*
*William Elliott: "Why didn't you tell me before?"*
*Andy Clyde: "I hate to fight on an empty stomach."*
The Plainsman and the Lady (1946)

I'd been worried that Star wouldn't be in shape for a long run, since we'd been dawdling along at an easy pace on McCluer's trail for so many months. But he seemed not only willing but eager as I guided him parallel to the tracks into the night. That was good, because I needed all the time I could get at the railroad's supply cache.

The stable boy had no idea where the supply depot was. Neither did the first three rail workers I stopped along the muddy street to ask. It was a wiry-looking Chinese laborer in work clothes who finally pointed me in the right direction, west along the tracks for three or four miles.

The Chinese have never gotten proper credit for their part in building that railroad. Thousands of them poured into California during the gold rush, and the Central Pacific hired about fifty of them when its regular workers were threatening to go on strike. The Chinese did such fine work that railroad officials went back to the Chinatowns of California for more of them, and eventually even sent recruiters all the way to China itself. The CP construction crews ended up about ninety percent Chinese. So far, though, I've never managed to get any of that into a movie script.

I spotted the depot by moonlight when Star topped a small rise, and I pulled him to a halt. He'd been running, resting up at a walk and then running again long enough by now that he was ready to stop for a bit. The building stood in the open in the grassy meadow, away from the few rocky outcroppings on either side. A buckboard with a two-horse team stood parked alongside the small structure. Lamp light from inside spilled out through a small window, facing in my direction. There was no way to sneak up on the place, even in the dark. If Quinn's men were already there, they could hardly miss seeing me approach.

Maybe they'd be less alarmed if I simply walked in, instead of approaching on horseback. Then again, they might just open fire anyway.

I guided Star into the rocks and picketed him there. He immediately started eating what grass was nearby. Then I made my way back down to the rail bed on foot and began walking along it, openly, as though I had not a care in the world.

"Hold it!" A man stepped from the moon-cast shadow of the roof's overhang, his hat pulled low over his eyes and a rifle in his hands, pointed in my direction. I stopped. "Just keep comin', mister," he said. I thought about telling him to make up his mind.

"It's all right," I said, preparing to bluff. "Quinn sent me."

"What?"

"Yeah, he and McCluer will be along soon. He just wanted me to make sure we were getting the right kind of explosive."

"Ben sent you?" The rifle wavered slightly. Then the man lowered it. "Who are you? I don't remember seeing you with..."

That was as far as he got. I laid the barrel of Jack's heavy pistol against his head as hard as I could, and he dropped like a chopped tree. I stuck the pistol back in its holster, picked up the rifle and searched the unconscious man to make sure he wasn't carrying any more armament. He seemed to be breathing. I was glad I hadn't killed him, but even more glad that he hadn't fired off that rifle when I clobbered him.

I dragged him back into the darkness against the wall of the shack-like depot, and checked again to make sure he was out cold. Then I made my way carefully around to where the buckboard was standing, ducking beneath a small window and parking the lookout's rifle against the wall. I took off my hat and peered through a corner of the window.

The light was coming from a lantern which hung from a rafter inside. Two men were wrestling some cases toward the door. More cases of the same type lined the far wall, and the figure of a third man lay near them. At first I thought maybe they'd killed him. Then he moved slightly, and I could see he was tied and gagged.

The men had maneuvered one of the nitro containers through the door. Between them, they managed to ease it onto the buckboard, to the accompaniment of grunts and curses. I saw another container already aboard.

"That's probably enough," one of the men said. "But I guess we better take one more, just to be sure. Quinn'll be here in time to tell us where to put them."

"How's he gonna blow them after they're placed, anyway?" the other man asked. "I mean, he can't exactly walk up to them in broad daylight between two engines and shake 'em."

"I dunno, that's his problem. I figure he'll have us put 'em on top of one of the cars, where McCluer can get a shot at 'em with that Sharps of his. As good as he's supposed to be, it should only take one shot to set 'em off. Hey, Jake," he called out, raising his voice. "C'mere and give us a hand with these things."

Jake, I figured, was the lookout I'd managed to cold-cock. He wasn't going to answer them, so I did.

"Jake can't hear you," I said, stepping out where they could see me and holding cocked pistols in both hands. "Just put that stuff down real easy, and raise your hands. Don't forget, even if I miss one of you, those bottles next to you are easy targets."

Both men stared at me. "You, you're crazy," one of them sputtered. "If you blow up one of those, you'll be blasted to kingdom come along with us."

"I'm willing to risk it if you are," I told him.

"He's crazy! Do like he says," the man told his companion. They eased the container onto the ground and raised their hands. The man doing most of the talking wore a single pistol, holstered butt-forward on his left side. The other appeared to be unarmed. I had him remove his companion's pistol using a thumb and one finger, and toss it lightly in my direction.

They may have figured I didn't know Quinn and McCluer would be showing up out here and, if they could just keep me occupied until then, the odds would be in their favor. If that was what they were thinking, they had a point. If I started to tie up one of them, the other would have a chance to jump me—and that third man wasn't going to stay unconscious forever.

I holstered one pistol and picked up the guard's rifle. "Walk over here," I ordered. "That's good. Now move to your left. You see Jake lying there? All right, pick him up. One of you take his legs, the other his shoulders. Move!"

They jumped to do as I'd instructed.

"That's fine. Now, I want you to start walking west along the track. I'm going to be watching you, with this rifle. If one of you drops ol' Jake, or if you make a break to one side or the other, I'll shoot you on the spot. You understand?"

They looked at one another. "But he's heavy!" the less talkative of the pair protested, shifting his grip on Jake's shoulders. "He might slip…"

I raised the rifle. "He'd better not. You drop him, I drop you."

"Maybe you'll miss," suggested the first man.

"Have you ever heard of Double-Six missing as easy a target as you'll be?"

That stopped them. I could see their startled gazes shifting from my clothing to my gun belt to my face and back again. "I thought you was dead," the man said.

"Well, I'm back." I hefted the rifle. "I'd advise you to get a good solid grip on Jake. Now, start walking. And don't look back! You might turn into a pillar of salt."

With pained expressions, they began shuffling along the track. I slipped into the shadow under the overhang once more, watching their slow progress past the buckboard and down the long track. They had to have felt exposed in the moonlight, and you could almost see them resisting the urge to glance back at me. If they really believed I was Jack, they would also believe I could hit them if I fired.

I gave them a minute and then called out, "No slowing down, boys. This rifle's still pointed at your spines. Just keep on going."

They shifted the still-unconscious Jake to get better grips on him, and kept moving. I lowered the rifle and moved inside. I went to where the man on the floor was tied, and undid the knots as quickly as I could, then ran back outside. As I'd hoped, the pair had kept going without checking to see if I was still there. Behind me, I could hear the man I'd freed murmuring to himself once he pulled off his gag and started untying his feet.

"Dirty spalpeens," he growled in a rumbling voice. He got to his feet and made his way unsteadily to where I stood by the door. "Drove right up to the door, they did, and threw guns on me before I knew what they were about. Sure an' you did a fine job of headin' 'em in, laddie. I heard it all. Was I you," he said, gazing at where they were still making their way in the distance, "I wouldn't be above goin' ahead and droppin' 'em where they stand."

"Let's move this nitro back inside," I said. "We can check on their progress between trips."

"Aye, laddie, let's be about doin' that very thing. And my thanks for gettin' me out of that scrape," he added, offering me his huge paw of a hand. "Me name's Paddy Welch and, if there's ever a thing I can do for you, just name it."

"I'm Johnny Six," I said, my hand engulfed in his. "No thanks necessary. I overheard two of the men they're working for back in Promontory, talking over their plans for all this."

"Yeah. About that," Paddy said, as he carefully hefted the first nitro container. "What exactly are they planning? They didn't bother to take me into their confidence."

I carried another behind him. "They were going to plant some of these on one of the trains tomorrow and blow it up with a rifle shot during the ceremony," I explained.

"Why would they be doin' that?" he asked, sliding his load into place and making way for mine. "Just for the nastiness of it?"

I parked my burden, checked again on the dwindling figures walking the rail line, and wondered how to answer that. I wasn't sure myself what lay behind this attempt at sabotage. I admitted as much to Paddy.

"Well, whatever it is, they'd best not be thinking of trying it again," he said, picking up the rifle where I'd placed it. "I'm going to sit on this spot until my relief gets here and, if somebody else shows up, I'll be about emptying their saddles."

"I wouldn't wait outside, Paddy. They mentioned having a sharpshooter to blow up the explosive tomorrow. I know who they have in mind, and he's good. Somebody like that could pick you off from a distance, as long as he could see you."

"Saints preserve us," Paddy said, scrambling back inside. "But this building is poor protection, laddie. A heavy rifle could shoot right through the wall, until he managed to hit some of that stuff and blow meself clear back to Ireland!"

"Yeah," I said. "Unless we figure some way to beat them at their own game."

# FIFTEEN

Gary Cooper: *"There's no Sunday west of Junction City,*
*no law west of Hays City, and no God west of Carson City."*
The Plainsman *(1936)*

It was still a good three hours before dawn when the silhouettes of two men on horseback, whom I took to be Quinn and McCluer, appeared on the rise and moved down toward the supply depot. I was sitting on the driver's seat of the buckboard, with four barrels loaded on it.

"That you, Jake?" Quinn called out as his horse made its way down the hill. I gave him a wave which I hoped he'd take as an affirmative. "Tell the boys to come on out," he said as they drew closer. "We gotta get back to Promontory before first light and get this stuff planted where it won't stand out but where Cord can get a clear shot at it."

McCluer was riding slightly in front when their horses hit the level bottom, and I hunched over some more, hoping he wouldn't recognize me. It was too much to hope for.

"Ben!" McCluer called out. "That's not Jake! That's…"

Paddy didn't let him get any farther. From a perch we'd picked out among the closest rocks, he fired the rifle I'd appropriated from the real Jake. The bullet scattered dirt in front of Quinn's horse, which already had its ears laid back in its perpetual state of pique. That was my cue. I yelled at the buckboard team and snapped their reins, and they rolled by McCluer and Quinn as Paddy fired a second shot from where he was hidden.

Either the shots, the buckboard rushing past or my shouts caused Quinn's and McCluer's horses to rear up and dance around, just as Paddy and I had hoped they would. It gave me a head start, and I wanted to get a good distance away from them before they hit the top of that rise again when they came after me.

"Hey, what's goin' on?" Quinn yelled, fighting to bring that half-savage horse of his under control.

"Someone's shooting at us from the rocks!" I heard McCluer respond, as Paddy let off a third shot. "I can't see where he is!"

"Never mind him. The stuff's on that wagon. That's all we're worried about. Come on, before he hits a bump and blows it all up," Quinn ordered, wheeling his horse after me.

"Ben, watch it," McCluer called after him. "That's not Jake. It's Six!"

I had made it to the rise by then, but I could hear the sound of hoof-beats pounding after me. Now, I had to depend on Paddy's marksmanship, which hadn't been all that great up to now.

His marksmanship turned out to be all right. But his timing wasn't.

Paddy and I had gingerly buried a several bottles of the nitro just at the summit of the rise, where he could get a clear shot at it from the vantage point we'd chosen. The idea had been for me to lead Quinn and McCluer in that direction and, when they reached it, Paddy would concentrate his fire on the barrel and explode it when they got to it.

I heard a fourth shot, and a fifth, and then an eruption of dirt and rocks from behind me that spooked the team, causing the two horses to pull against each other in their traces and almost overturn the wagon. It took me some time to get them straightened out again. Once they were lined up properly, I risked a glance over my shoulder.

Quinn was on the ground, but not for long. As I looked, he got to his feet and started chasing after his horse. McCluer was still mounted, and still pounding after me.

Paddy must have missed an earlier shot at the explosive, which might have taken both men out of action. Now, they had ridden far enough past it to escape the worst effects.

I drew a pistol, and fired back twice at McCluer. He veered off to one side but didn't slacken the speed of his horse. I whipped up the team again, but I doubted if they could outrun a man on horseback. And, farther back, I saw Quinn had caught up with his hammerhead of a horse and was climbing aboard. They were both after me now, and my brilliant idea for taking them out of the picture had failed miserably.

My only chance was to make a run for it. I was sure I wouldn't make it back to Promontory before they caught up with me, but I didn't know what else to do.

I could hear pistol shots behind me, and risked another look back at the two men. Quinn was doing the firing, but having no better luck at hitting me than I'd had with McCluer. McCluer had ridden still farther off to one side, as though trying to get around me and maybe cut me off. I leaned forward, hoping I'd offer a little less of a target, and kept yelling at the horses in front of me.

The next time I glanced back, I could see just one horseman. I couldn't spot McCluer anywhere, which seemed wrong because he'd been gaining on me pretty fast. Then I had to concentrate on my driving, to keep the horses running straight and avoid any rocks or obstacles that might wreck the buckboard.

Where was McCluer? Probably I should have guessed the answer, having heard how he worked, but I hadn't realized how far ahead of me he'd gotten. It was far enough for him to have taken up a position off to one side and wait for me with that Sharps of his.

I realized what he'd done only after something struck me, and knocked me not only off the driver's seat but clear off the wagon. I hit the ground with a thud that knocked whatever wind I had out of me, rolled several times and then lay there, unable to move.

"I got him!" McCluer yelled back at Quinn. "That makes us even for Kansas City, by damn! I knew I'd get him in my sights one day!"

"Never mind all that," said Quinn, riding right on past where I lay. "We gotta catch that wagon, or we'll lose the nitro. They'll be laying for us back at the depot, if we try to swipe any more."

Both of them rode on in the wake of the driverless buckboard, as a wave of darkness swept over me. But even as consciousness faded, I felt a flicker of elation at what their reactions would be when they opened the containers in that wagon and found them filled with dirt.

# SIXTEEN

*Clayton Moore: "Won't they let a man be honest?"*
*John Compton: "Not if the man is Jesse James."*
Jesse James Rides Again *(1947)*

I'd always had my doubts of making it into Heaven, but it seemed like maybe I had. At least I didn't think they had angels in Hell.

She caught me looking at her and grinned. That made me wonder about her divinity; it was a very down-to-earth grin. There was also a small but un-angel-like sprinkling of freckles on her cheeks.

"Well, well," she said. "You're finally awake."

I started to sit up but changed my mind when pain surged through my left side at the effort. Moving my head as little as I could, I found I was lying in a bed inside a small but homey-looking room with curtains at the windows, pictures on the walls, and flowers in a vase on a corner table. It was the first time I'd been in a room even close to this since I'd left Virginia.

I turned back for a closer look at her. She was a little thing, with lively dancing eyes and a very un-angelic figure from a tiny waist to enticing curves above and below. She wore what looked like a man's shirt, although it would never have looked that way on any man I knew, plus a long riding skirt.

If I had to describe her, I guess I'd say she was a combination of Jane Frazee and Adele Mara, two of the gals who helped improve the scenery in some of the movies over at Republic.

"Where am I?" I managed to croak. As soon as the words were out of my mouth, I realized how trite it sounded, but I really wanted to know.

"You're in my mother's boarding house," she told me, almost in a whisper. "The doctor said you needed all the rest you could get. Mr. Stanford is paying the bills. You must've made quite an impression on him."

Her answer raised so many more questions in my mind that I didn't know where to start. I didn't know anyone named Stanford. I noticed bright daylight streaming through the curtained window. "How...how long...?"

"You've been here for three days," she said, and her smile widened. "I'm glad you're finally wide awake. Ma and I have had quite a time getting you to swallow water and soup and such."

The mere mention of food made me realize how hungry I was, even hungrier than some of those days I'd spent following McCluer across several states. And that reminded me of something else. "My horse," I said. "He must have been tied out there for three days..."

"A railroad man brought your horse in. He's fine." I thought maybe I detected a tone of approval in her voice that I'd thought of Star. "We've got him stabled here with some of the livery horses, and he's been keeping them pretty well stirred up. It seems he's been kicking and nipping at any who come too close."

I felt compelled to defend Star. "He's a little on the small side. He thinks a good offense is the best way to keep from being picked on."

She laughed, and I found the sound absurdly pleasant. "Well, it's working. They're leaving him strictly alone."

The door opened behind her, and an older version of my angel came in, a little more gray and matronly but with the same uninhibited grin. She might remind you of Sarah Padden, the lady who always plays somebody's mother or the woman ranch owner or whatever in her westerns. "Our guest is awake, Ma," her daughter informed her.

"So I see. We were getting worried about you, young man. Do you think you could eat something a little more substantial than soup, now that you're able to do your own chewing?"

The next few minutes involved some logistics in getting some pillows behind me without causing me too many grimaces. I found my left arm was in a sling beneath the sheet, although it was my chest that hurt. I could feel the wadding under a bandage apparently wrapped around me. Still, I could wield a fork and spoon with my right hand, and proceeded to do that. The ladies had to cut my meat for me, but I consumed a lot of it plus some beans and corn they put on a tray across my lap, washing them down with some dark, rich coffee.

Tasty as it was and hungry as I was, I couldn't quite finish it all. My stomach told me in no uncertain terms that it wasn't ready to keep down a meal like this, so I stopped while I was ahead.

"It was so good that I forgot my manners," I told the two ladies. "My name is Johnny Six."

"I'm Liddy Wells. Folks mostly call me 'Ma,'" the older lady said. "But my daughter, Ginny, is the only one who can do it legal."

"Ginny? Short for Virginia?" I asked the daughter. She nodded, being occupied with the removal of my dishes and silverware. "I'm from Virginia," I added helpfully.

"You're a long way from home, then, aren't you, Mr. Six?" Ginny said over her shoulder, as she carried the remains of my meal through the door.

I must've faded out again. The next thing I remember, I opened my eyes and the two women had been replaced by a large bearded man who stood by the side of my bed. He was perhaps forty-five years of age, with strong features and dark hair, and wore a long black coat and tie.

"Hello," I said. "Are you the doctor?"

His features relaxed into a smile. "Nope. My name's Stanford, and I'm one of the men whose railroad you kept from being blown up three days ago. The ladies have told me your name, Mr. Six."

It took me a minute to figure out why his voice sounded familiar. Then it came to me. He was one of the men I'd overheard when I was hanging outside that hotel window, trying to locate the room occupied by Quinn and McCluer.

"Are you Leland? Or Tom?" I asked, remembering the names I'd heard them use.

"Perhaps you're thinking of Tom Durant. He's president of the Union Pacific. Anyway, yes, I'm Leland Stanford. Head of the Central Pacific. Both he and I owe you a great deal, Mr. Six."

I shook my head. "I didn't do much except get myself shot."

"Paddy Welch, our employee at the supply depot, told me what you did. He said how you chased off the gang that had made him a prisoner. He'd overheard them talking about what they planned to do with the nitroglycerin they were trying to steal. Dangerous stuff—we once had a crate of it blow up in a Wells Fargo office in San Francisco. After that, we decided to make our own instead of shipping it in. Paddy also told us how you made a decoy of yourself, and drew the others away."

Put that way, it all sounded a lot more heroic than it was. I'd planned for Paddy to take down McCluer and Quinn by exploding those bottles we'd planted. I'd never planned on getting shot myself.

"You deserve public credit for what you did, young man," Stanford went on. "Not only did you save a lot of lives among those attending the ceremony, you also averted an incident which could have ruined our venture just now when it's just getting started. By rights, you should get a medal." I started to protest but he added, "May I tell you why none of that can happen?"

"Uh…well, sure."

"I'm quite serious about you meriting all that," he said. "If people back east or west of here began reading about a disaster when U.P.'s Engine 19 and our Jupiter engine touched cow-catchers, it might have taken years for them to regain confidence in the safety of rail travel or shipping. I'm not even sure either of our railroad enterprises could have withstood the financial losses that such a catastrophe would have meant. We were both stretched to our limits from laying track to where it finally connected up."

The last thing I wanted was to be put on display as a hero. That kind of publicity would make it all too easy for Quinn's men to find me again. As things were, McCluer probably believed he'd finished me off. He would have, too, I thought, if I hadn't messed with the sights of his Sharps back in Kansas City. I'd figured it might save somebody's life down the road, but I hadn't known it would be mine.

"Frankly, Mr. Stanford, that suits me fine. I don't want any public credit. In fact, I'd be just as happy if nobody even knew I survived."

He gave me a long, shrewd look.

"A little law trouble, Mr. Six?" he asked. "Is there a past you're trying to put behind you?"

"No to the first question, and yes to the second," I said.

He looked at me and frowned. I wasn't sure how much I wanted to tell him. But it seemed to be a matter of letting him believe the worst or telling him everything.

"Mr. Stanford, the same people who were out to ruin you, for whatever reasons, have been after me for some time now. If they think they finished me, I'll be better able to stay on their trail and get to the bottom of whatever it's all about."

I gave him an abbreviated version of my treatment by the Sutherlands, my trip west to find my brother, and how I wasn't sure whether he was still alive.

The bearded man had pulled up a chair, and sat there listening patiently and without interrupting. When I finished, he leaned back.

"That's rather a fantastic story," he said. "Like something from one of those magazines with drawings of Buffalo Bill or Kit Carson on the covers."

I chuckled, and immediately regretted it as pain ran up my chest and shoulder. "Funny you should say that," I told him. "I've been supporting myself by writing stuff for some of those magazines."

"Well, our interests certainly coincide insofar as keeping quiet about your part in all this," he said. "It would be helpful to us, my friends and me in the railroad business, if nothing ever became known about what almost happened. If the public realized how close we came to such a cataclysm, it might serve the purpose of the enemy almost as well as if they'd realized their plans."

"Why is that?"

"Well, it could only make people connect danger with railroads," he said. "Bad press reports, bad reputations, bad all the way around. But you've made things very easy for me, in that connection."

"I have?"

"I'd envisioned myself trying to talk you out of taking public rewards for preventing what almost happened, and figured I'd have to come up with some other way for us to express our appreciation to you. I'm not even sure what that other way would have been. Money?" he suggested.

"I guess a fellow could always use money. But, with what's sitting in a bank in Virginia and what I'm getting now from these little magazine pieces, I seem to have all my needs covered." I looked around the room again. "Except maybe for whatever this place and the doctor is costing."

"Don't even think about that. It's on me," he said, standing up. He hesitated, then spoke again. "So these people still think you are your brother? They don't realize there are two of you?"

"Well, there's a little more to the story."

"I would be fascinated to hear the rest of it."

So I spent the next hour telling him, pretty much the way I'm telling you two right now. And with me in roughly the same condition, come to think of it—flat on my back from a bullet.

Leland Stanford shook his head when I'd finished.

"Incredible," he said. "But I cannot deny what almost happened at the ceremony. There is nothing made up about that." He grew thoughtful. "So you think the Sutherlands hired this Ben Quinn and the others to kill your brother.

I don't understand how they would be connected to this sabotage business."

"I overheard Quinn refer to someone he called 'the Old Man' as the person giving him his orders. I can't prove it, but I'm betting it's the Colonel Sutherland I've told you about."

"I'd be more tempted to identify their unknown boss as Ben Holladay, except he's already sold his Overland Stage monopoly. He wouldn't profit from discrediting rail travel at this point. Is there anything else you can tell me about the motives of this Sutherland?"

"Yeah," I said. "Did they bring in my saddlebags when they got my horse?"

He got up and moved to a chest of drawers in one corner of the room, and opened the top drawer. "They're right here, along with your weapons and clothing."

"There's a .44 pistol in one of the bags. Reach under that, and you'll find an envelope."

It was the envelope I'd taken off McCluer in Kansas City. I'd read it quite a few times in front of small campfires during those long nights when I was following him. I practically had the thing memorized:

*McCluer:*
*No further payments in reference to Six without confirmation*
*of assignment having been completed. Quinn has instructions*
*from S for your next task, which may be the biggest since we*
*started working with Q and later B to eliminate the top problem*
*four years ago. Y and J venture in Russellville successful*
*last March. May try another with them in December.*
*The Colonel*

Stanford tugged at his beard as he studied the letter. He read through it several times, then shook his head.

"This is like reading someone's private grocery list," he said. "You can't tell what he's ordering if you don't know what the abbreviations stand for. The 'Q' could refer to this man Quinn—but, then, why does he use Quinn's name in the previous sentence?"

Good question. "I thought maybe if I could find out where Russellville was, and learn what happened there in March…"

"Good idea," Stanford said. "Offhand, I can think of three Russellvilles. In Alabama, Kentucky and Arkansas. There could be others." I must have looked surprised, because he smiled. "You have to develop a memory for place names when you're mapping railroad routes," he explained. "May I keep this letter? Maybe next time I see you, I'll have found out something about it."

I didn't want to let the letter go. I knew it wasn't evidence that would stand up against the Colonel in any court of law, but it was all I had. Still, I had gotten nowhere trying to puzzle it out by myself. Maybe Stanford would have better luck. He certainly had more resources to work with.

So I agreed.

I slept through most of the rest of the day, and so was wide awake when Ginny brought my supper that evening. Again, she helped me handle the silverware. Between bites, I asked her questions about Leland Stanford. He seemed trustworthy, but I wanted to be reassured.

Ginny knew a lot about him. He'd practiced law in Wisconsin, moved to California nearly twenty years ago and started a general store. Shortly after the start of the Civil War, he became governor of California and helped keep it loyal to the Union.

So he and I had been on opposite sides of that conflict. But he certainly seemed a solid enough gentleman for me to rely on his word. In retrospect, it was one of my better judgment calls.

He came back to see me the next day, and he was holding a hand full of telegrams.

"I think I may have the answer," he said, pulling up a chair.

"Governor, if you've figured out in one day what's stumped me all these months…"

"I haven't solved it, Johnny. But I did find out something about Russellville." He handed me one of the telegrams, but didn't wait for me to read it. "On March 20, in Russellville, Kentucky, a man asked a bank cashier to change a fifty-dollar bill. Then the man pulled a gun. The cashier was shot and wounded, but managed to make it outside and alert some townspeople that the bank was being robbed. The gunman and the men with him shot their way out of town."

He handed me a second telegram.

"The bankers hired a Louisville detective to try and track down the gang. They traced one of the bandits, a man who'd fought in a guerilla band in the war, named George Shepherd. Shepherd was arrested following a gunfight at his home. The rest of the gang is still running loose."

"The note could have been referring to holding up a bank," I said. "But how can we know for sure?"

"There's more," he said, peeling off yet a third telegram. "You may have heard of the Pinkerton National Detective Agency?" I nodded. "They've been around for quite a while. They even foiled an assassination attempt on President Lincoln shortly before he took office. Too bad they weren't around last time. Anyway, I know some of the Pinkerton folks, and I managed to find out who some of their suspects are."

He pointed at a name in the telegram.

"Remember Shepherd, the man they caught? He'd been associating lately with a couple of brothers visiting from Missouri—Frank and Jesse James. It turns out those two have been linked to several other bank robberies in recent years, back in their home state."

"Frank and Jesse James," I repeated. "Do we know anything else about them?"

"We know they rode with William Clarke Quantrill and 'Bloody Bill' Anderson in the war. So had a man named Cole Younger, a cousin of theirs who joined up with them in Kentucky shortly before that Russellville robbery."

"Well, they were in the right place, but..."

"The robbery had some things in common with some of the guerilla raids they'd have been involved in. For example, these robbers believed in firepower. They each carried extra guns, so they wouldn't have to waste time reloading. That kind of thing fits both Younger and the James boys."

I still didn't get it.

"Cole Younger and the James boys," he repeated. "'Y' and 'J,' perhaps?"

# SEVENTEEN

Max Terhune: "There they are, Johnny,
and they're afteryour hide."
Johnny Mack Brown: "You'd better stay out of this."
Max Terhune: "I should say not."
Law of the West *(1949)*

"Why the long face, Rick?" Nancy asked as she and Rick Martin walked through the wide hospital doors.

Rick sighed, but he was glad not to always be "Detective Martin" at work. "The boss is pulling the plug, Nancy," he said. "It's been nearly two weeks, and we still haven't gotten the first clue out of him as to what that shindig at Gower Gulch was all about."

Nancy's face fell. "Oh, Rick, how are we going to tell him?"

"Tell who? You mean Jonathan Six?"

"He'll be so disappointed. Sometimes I find myself thinking that his telling these installments of his life story are all that's keeping him going."

Rick stopped and looked down at her. "I thought you'd be happy about it. You're the one losing time and money from your regular steno work."

"Yes, but..." Nancy returned his look. "Rick, I like him. Apart from the job, I mean. And I've got to admit," she added with a rueful smile, "he's really got me curious about how all this ties together."

"Well, sure, me too. I've felt from the start there's more to that fracas than the captain wants to admit, himself, because he's afraid we'll get into bad publicity or complicated court proceedings involving all those actors." He found himself grinning. "Hey, maybe I ought to be jealous of Mr. Six."

"Maybe you should." But she was grinning back, and even touched his arm reassuringly. "Well, is there any point in holding another session with him today?"

"Well..." Rick let it hang there for a few seconds.

"Well? What? Out with it, Detective Martin."

"Well—Nancy, what we could do, if you were willing, we could both put in for a week's vacation time. We could..." He was stopped again by her stare.

"You want me to use up my vacation time as well as lose the work? And suppose he isn't finished even after a week? Suppose...Rick, you look funny. What's the matter?"

"I was thinking," he said. "I mean, coming in here just during the afternoons would leave us the rest of the day. There would be time before we talk to him, and after..."

"Rick, what are you babbling about?"

"Well—I mean, if we were taking vacation time anyway, I thought we could... we could..."

"We could what?"

"Get married!" There, he'd said it. It surprised him almost as much as it probably surprised Nancy. "If we told our bosses we were getting married, we'd get the time off right away, no questions. The weekend's coming up. We could drive to Vegas. There'd be no waiting period..."

"Whoa!" She raised her hands to her cheeks, which were flushed. "Hold your horses, Detective Martin!" Her eyes were wide. "You're asking me to marry you just so we can keep taking down Mr. Six's information, not even have time to invite my mother and sister to the wedding, just like that? Why, you haven't even proposed, you idiot. Aren't you're taking a lot for granted?"

"Nancy," he said, reaching down and taking her by the shoulders, as people passing in the hallway regarded them curiously and then looked quickly away again, "I know I'm doing this badly..."

"'Badly' is not the word!"

"But you must know by now how I feel about you, how I've felt about you for months. Don't you?" he pleaded.

She had been trying to pull away, but stopped. "How would I know?" she said softly. And then, a bit louder: "Just how is it you feel about me, Detective Martin?"

His throat felt dry, but he managed to get it out without croaking. "I love you, Nancy. That's how I feel."

Her gaze softened. "Why, you big sap, why didn't you say that in the first place?"

"Well, I just…"

"You know what it sounded like? Like you wanted us to get married just so you could get work on your pet cop case!"

"I've wanted to marry you for a long time," he said seriously. "I didn't know how to say it. I chickened out whenever I tried. I was afraid you'd say no." He took a deep breath. "Nancy—are you saying no?"

"No," she said. His face fell. "I mean, no, I'm not saying no. I'm saying yes."

"Yes?" His face lit up. "Yes? You mean it?"

"Of course I mean it," she said, laughing. "But I've got to tell you, Rick, this is not the kind of honeymoon I thought I'd have when you finally got around to popping the question."

# EIGHTEEN

*Whip Wilson: "So you stole a horse, too?"*
*Andy Clyde: "Yeah, and we better steal two more. Here they come!"*
*Whip Wilson: "Here we go!"*
Haunted Trails *(1949)*

Well, congratulations! I couldn't be happier for you both. Of course, I've got to tell you, it's been pretty plain you two were sweet on each other. I just couldn't imagine, Detective Martin, what was taking you so long. She might have gotten away!

I see you nodding, Nancy. Shoot, you two shouldn't be spending the afternoon you got engaged with the likes of me. You should be out somewhere celebrating…

Well, all right, then. But I assume that you'll make up for lost time when you leave. Surely you're going to at least take Nancy to dinner at some nice romantic nightclub, right? I'll miss seeing the two of you tomorrow. I've gotten used to your visits every day. But I'll console myself with the thought that, when I see you next time, you'll be mister and missus.

So let's get through this part fast.

Okay, for some reason, I seemed to have made a hit with the ex-governor. Stanford offered me a job, sort of what might be described today as being his personal private eye. He wasn't altogether satisfied with his contacts in Allan Pinkerton's agency, the one with the picture of an open eye as its trademark and the motto, "We never sleep," on its business cards. Folks began referring to Pinkerton himself as "The Eye." In fact, that's where the term "private eye" came from.

I would still pose as a writer of dime novels. Well, it wouldn't be a pose. But Stanford thought it would be a good cover. As for getting around, he made me a permanent pass to go anywhere the CP had laid track. I could take Star along, assuming he didn't chew his way out of a rail car, or just rent a horse wherever I ran out of rails, and bill it in my expenses.

It had been seven years since Stanford served as governor, but he was still a good deal-maker. He sold me on this one in one sitting.

It didn't do me any good to protest that I had no experience at detecting. My friend Paddy apparently exaggerated my role in what happened at the supply depot, because Stanford had more faith in me than I did.

We worked it out that, as soon as I got back on my feet, I'd head for Clay County, Missouri, and try to get a line on Cole Younger or the James boys. Jesse was the one people heard about the most. He was more flamboyant than his older brother, Frank. The thing was, while they were both suspected of being involved in any number of bank robberies, nobody had proof. Their mother, their family, their sympathizers all alibied them.

Their very first robbery, if it was them, had probably been the Clay County Savings Bank in Liberty, Missouri, three years earlier around Valentine's Day. In the next few months, there were bank robberies in Lexington and Richmond, and then the Russellville robbery in another state altogether.

Now, I know how the movies have portrayed Dingus—that's what people called Jesse, I found out later—as a man forced into outlawry by Yankee carpetbaggers and all that. He's been played sympathetically by everybody from Tyrone Power to Roy Rogers and Don Barry. Maybe not quite as sympathetically in a picture last year by Reed Hadley, but that one was more about Bob Ford. Even Clayton Moore, before he started doing that Lone Ranger thing on TV last fall, played him in a couple of serials, as someone who'd been framed, or misunderstood, but was really a good fellow beneath it all. Heck, our most decorated war hero, Audie Murphy, just finished playing him in a picture with a bunch of up-and-coming actors over at Universal-International. Of course, Audie played Billy the Kid over there, too, but at least that one wasn't quite as whitewashed a version as that little series with Bob Steele and then Buster Crabbe that made him a B-western hero.

Well, that's not the way it was, not with Billy and not with Jesse. Try asking the college student who got gunned down when the James gang was riding out of Liberty. Or the mayor of Richmond, or the jailer and his son there, all killed in another of their robberies. But Jesse and his family had the best public relations you ever saw, with his mother at the head of it. She would have put our Hollywood image-makers to shame.

I mean, it was always the railroad robber barons stealing land for their rights-of-way, or the big-money banking interests who drove Jesse to robbery, they would say. And he would give away his loot to those who had been decimated by those money interests, a Robin Hood. I never verified an instance of him giving away anything to the poor farmers or impoverished Southerners he was supposedly helping, but, you know, never let the truth stand in the way of a good story.

Anyway, I found myself riding a train to Clay County. At that time, nobody had managed to tie any of those boys to a single robbery. Stanford wanted me to scout around for evidence that might implicate them in one holdup or another, so I was studying up on them as much as I could during the trip.

I hadn't taken Star along this time. Instead, I'd arranged to pay Ginny and her mother to keep him boarded with the livery horses while I was gone. I guess you two, of all people, can understand why I wanted an excuse to see Ginny again.

Stanford and I had talked about getting arrest warrants for Quinn and McCluer, even getting out wanted posters on them. But, for that, I would have to come out in the open to testify, being the only one who could identify them. We decided it was more advantageous for me to stay dead for now.

So the last man I expected to see in Clay County was Ben Quinn.

Luckily, I saw him before he could spot me. And I was wearing a suit, not the kind of outfit he'd expect to see me in, which gave me some camouflage. I'd invested in a variety of clothes before I left Utah, now that I actually had money to spend on such things. Stanford had started issuing me paychecks before I was even out of bed. I guess it was his way of saying thanks for what had happened the night before the Golden Spike ceremony—the spike they immediately pulled back out and replaced with an iron one.

McCluer's bullet had been high and to one side, but it had still clipped me pretty good. It would be some time yet before I would be fully functional. Any sudden movement, especially involving my left arm, reminded me of just how close I'd come to joining McCluer's list of victims.

That was one reason why I'd chosen to dress more eastern style. Nobody would expect a lot of physical prowess from a visiting magazine writer, I hoped. And in my case, at least for now, they'd be right.

Just carrying my suitcase into the hotel at Liberty was enough of a strain to leave me hurting a little. I wasn't looking forward to renting a horse and riding to Kearny, where the Samuel farm was located. Jesse's mother had outlived her first husband, divorced the second and was now married to a Ruben Samuel. I picked up a few more tidbits just chatting with folks around town. I had already found that people enjoyed telling things to a writer, particularly if I hinted that I might attach their names to characters in some story.

I had about decided on the bold approach—renting a buckboard and team rather than a saddle horse, riding to the Samuel place and telling Frank and Jesse I was a newspaper reporter, interested in writing their side of the story in response to the gossip associating them with outlawry. If Jesse was as talkative as I'd been lead to believe, he might let something slip if I got him on a roll.

I still think that might have worked. Or it might have gotten me killed. But everything changed when I spotted Ben Quinn riding that hammerhead horse of his into town.

I kept walking without breaking stride in the direction I'd been going, which was toward a little restaurant. I made no sudden movement, like turning my head or breaking into a run. But I was no longer hungry, and no longer thinking of renting a buckboard. I'd need to rent a horse to trail Quinn.

Luckily, Quinn was hungrier than I was. While he was having his meal, I was back in my hotel changing into trail clothing, then heading for a stable to see what kind of transportation I could rent. By the time Quinn got back to where he'd tied his horse, I was aboard a big black Tennessee walker named Shaker, who had energy to spare.

It looked as though Stanford had guessed right. There was a tie between the attempt to put the transcontinental rail link out of business, and the James and Younger gangs. Why else would Quinn turn up here?

Now I was glad of what trailing skills I'd developed following McCluer all those months. But Quinn wasn't traveling that far—just to Kearny, and the Samuel farm. Surprise, surprise.

At least, following him saved me from maybe drawing suspicion by asking directions.

If the James brothers had been involved in as many robberies as folks suspected, it stood to reason that they'd have lookouts posted around their farm. So I gave it a wide berth, going around it and into the town of Kearny proper where I found a place to buy that meal I'd missed in Liberty. The beef jerky and other trail food in my saddlebags wasn't that appetizing.

All I had to do was listen to the talk around town to confirm that the farm indeed belonged to Ruben Samuel and his wife, Zerelda, the former Mrs. James. I even picked up the tidbit that Jesse had recently gotten himself baptized at the local Baptist church.

I would soon find out that the baptism didn't take.

# NINETEEN

*Roy Barcroft: "Very good, stranger. Very good. See you around?"*
*Allan "Rocky" Lane: "Probably will…"*
*Fred Graham: "See what I mean? That stranger, he don't fool around."*
The Bold Frontiersman (1948)

It was a cold day in December when we all rode into Gallatin, Missouri—the James boys, followed at a good distance by me. I was getting pretty used to trailing people at a distance by now.

Most folks remember that particular month as when the Wyoming Territory became the first jurisdiction in the country to give women the vote. Utah would be next, three months later. But I remember it because it was the day I shot it out, kind of, with the James gang.

The little community of Gallatin was the seat of Daviess County, not far from St. Joseph on the Grand River, and it didn't take long for me to figure out its main point of interest for the pair I was shadowing—The Daviess County Savings Bank.

Shaker shook his head impatiently as I slowed him down. I'd been noticing that habit all the time I'd been riding him. Maybe that's how he got his name.

I had wondered whether I might be wasting my time, riding along in the wake of the notorious brothers when they left Kearny. It was easy to see that they were carrying provisions for more than a day's ride, but there had been no sign of Cole Younger or any of the others supposedly associated with the James boys in their forays. Even Ben Quinn had dropped out of sight a few days after I'd spotted him, and I'd been very careful about watching out for him.

Once I saw what building interested the boys, I figured they must have decided they didn't need a gang to knock it over. They were going to handle it all by themselves.

Also, it was December, the month cited in McCluer's note from the Colonel. *May try another with them in December*, it had said, referring back to what Stanford thought must have meant the Russellville robbery. Well, the month was right and, sure enough, here they were lounging outside another bank.

What connection could Colonel Sutherland have with a couple of backwoods bank robbers, though? True, he was the one who had hired Quinn and the others to kill Jackson, and I'd seen Quinn in Clay County. But it made no sense for Sutherland to be involved in crimes like this. He already had more money than God, and why would these bank robbers share with him, anyhow? What could he be doing for them?

I had Jackson's pistols belted under my coat, but I couldn't just start shooting at them before they did anything to justify being shot at. Looking back, it was too bad I didn't. I might have saved a life.

In studying up on the James boys, I'd learned about their association with Quantrill's guerillas where they'd learned a lot of what became their trade. In 1864, Frank had left Quantrill's outfit to ride with another band under the aptly-named "Bloody Bill" Anderson. That was when Jesse, only seventeen at the time, joined his big brother. They had both taken part in Anderson's raid on Centralia, Missouri, which they followed by stopping a train and taking about $3,000 from its express car. Next, they shot down some twenty-five Union soldiers who'd been passengers on the train. Later that same day, they ambushed a unit of troops sent out after them. Supposedly, Jesse himself had shot and killed the commander. They'd had a busy day.

After I arrived in Clay County, I'd contrived to be around Kearny whenever Frank or Jesse rode in from the farm, and I actually overheard Frank describe the Centralia raid to a group of admirers. Frank must have had something of a classic education; he compared the raid not only to the Alamo but the Greek battle of Thermopylae, where a band of Spartans fought odds as overwhelming as those Texans had against Santa Ana. Only this time, in Frank's telling of the tale, the smaller group had won and the vanquished perished in a bloodbath.

No wonder the guerilla bands were denied the amnesty which regular Confederate soldiers got after the war. But Frank was paroled in routine fashion when he gave himself up to authorities. Jesse tried to give himself up, too, riding into Lexington, Missouri, holding up a white flag. Some over-eager federal troops shot at him anyway and wounded him badly.

If the saga of Jesse James had ended there, you could sympathize with him. The federal commander in Lexington allowed him to be taken to his home, figuring he should at least be allowed to expire under his own roof after being shot under those circumstances. But Jesse recovered, and western folklore was changed for all time.

Supposedly, he was still nursing those wounds when the Liberty bank was robbed. It made for a fine alibi, and was one of the reasons why authorities never tied him to that crime.

Frank and Jesse had been drilled in riding and shooting along with the other recruits in Quantrill's and Anderson's bands, just like in that Audie Murphy picture, *Kansas Raiders*. They learned the value of advance intelligence, of knowing the layout of a town before they raided it. They applied what they'd learned to raiding banks. In Liberty, they'd even known the names of the tellers.

I wondered how much time they would spend checking the layout of the bank in Daviess County. Or—a thought struck me—could Ben Quinn have already done that for them? Maybe that's what his trip to Kearny had been about.

I rode Shaker on past where the brothers had stopped outside the bank. I was close to them, so close I could actually see Jesse's eyelids twitching. It was a mannerism I'd noticed whenever I'd seen him around Kearny. He was dismounting from his mare, and handing the reins to Frank.

I heeled Shaker around the first corner I reached, quickly found a place to tie him, and crept back. Frank still sat there in his saddle, holding Jesse's horse. I paused, wondering whether to try and slip past him into the bank, when the first shot rang out.

Frank heard it, too, and immediately jerked a pistol from under his coat. I eased back into a doorway before he could decide to use it on me, and reached with my right hand for the butt-forward pistol in my left holster.

"What's goin' on?" an old-timer with a mustache like actor Hank Bell's asked me. I grabbed him and pulled him back into the doorway with me, just as a bullet split the planking where he'd been standing. Frank was a good shot.

"Bank robbery!" I told him, although he'd probably figured that out by now. "Spread the word." I reached around and threw a couple of shots in Frank's direction, giving the old-timer a chance to scramble away.

At that moment, Jesse came bursting out of the bank with a bunch of greenbacks in one hand and a pistol in the other. I wasn't the only one firing at them by then, but none of us were scoring any hits. Frank dropped the reins of Jesse's mare to where Jesse could grab them, wheeled his own horse away from us and galloped off.

Jesse started to swing into his saddle. I took the opportunity while neither of them were shooting to aim carefully and put three quick shots into the dirt near the mare's feet.

She bolted as I'd hoped she would, just as Jesse got one foot into a stirrup. She went running down the street away from my position, dragging Jesse along bumping behind her until his foot finally came loose. We had him, I thought. This time, there was no way his friends and family could alibi him. And maybe we could make him tell us about any connection he had with the Colonel.

But then Frank was riding back up the street, spurring his horse to where Jesse was staggering to his feet. You've seen it in bunches of movies, but this was the only time I saw it happen: Jesse jumped onto the back of the horse behind Frank, and they went roaring right by me on their way out of town, riding double. I took careful aim at their dwindling figures, thinking I might have a chance of hitting one of them.

My hammer clicked on an empty chamber. By the time I'd switched guns, they were out of sight.

I followed the crowd which had materialized into the bank. One man lay on the wooden floor behind the cashier's cage, with another man bending over him. Several people asked how badly the man on the floor was hurt. "About as bad as he could be," the kneeling man replied. "He's dead."

"What happened?" I asked the survivor.

"I heard a customer ask him to change a hundred-dollar bill," the man said. "He started to make change and, just out of the blue, the customer said something about him looking like the Yankee officer whose men killed Bloody Bill Anderson. Before I knew what was happening, the customer snatched his bill back and started shooting, like someone crazy. Then he ran around to the cash drawer and scooped up a bunch of bills before he ran out."

"Do you remember anything about how he looked?" I asked.

"Young fellow, clean-shaven. Blinked a lot."

Jesse, all right. Well, of course, who else? But it still might not be enough to get him arrested back in Kearny, and brought into court for the man to identify. Then I got another idea. I went outside, and started talking to people who had gathered there.

"They left one of their horses behind," I said as loudly as I could. "Has anyone seen a loose mare on the street without a rider?"

"Yeah," a man in a heavy coat. "She's standing right over there." He pointed, and I recognized the horse I'd managed to spook.

"Don't let her wander off. Maybe we can find out who she belongs to," I said.

In the end, it was just as simple as that. Jesse's family would continue to insist that their darling boy was innocent—in fact, after future robberies, his mother would bring in written articles to various newspapers proclaiming the boys' non-involvement in the crimes—but once authorities identified that horse as belonging to Jesse, even their closest sympathizers began to realize her alibis for them were nonsense.

It was the next best thing to capturing him. But in the years ahead, as the numbers of bank and train robberies and the lists of casualties mounted up, I found myself wishing that I'd tried aiming at Jesse instead of around his horse's feet that day.

# TWENTY

*Buck Jones: "I'm a special investigator from the Cattleman's Association.*
*They wanted probably to impersonate me."*
*Tim McCoy: "That sounds like a smart idea.*
*I never like to pass 'em up when they're smart."*
Riders of the West *(1942)*

I could have telegraphed a report to Mister Stanford, but it was winter, I had no more leads to follow, I had free train transportation, and I'd never seen California. So I found myself, at the start of the decade of the 1870s, climbing aboard a Kansas Pacific train when I was astonished to hear someone call out my name. My real one.

"Johnny! Hey, Johnny Six!"

A man with long hair and a long coat was getting up out of his seat on the train car as I turned toward his voice. He was wearing a long coat, vest and hat. "Mr. Hickok!"

It was indeed Wild Bill. He shook my hand and guided me back to the seat beside him. "It's good to see you again, boy. I was just thinking about you before I left Hays City. Just ahead of the Seventh Cavalry, in fact."

I sat down, glad to see a friendly face—especially that of someone who had been such a good firearms tutor. And, truth to tell, I felt better about the possibility of running into Quinn or McCluer, with Jim Hickok sitting beside me. I still remembered spotting Quinn so unexpectedly before.

"The Seventh Cavalry?" I repeated when we sat down. "Isn't that the one commanded by your friend, Colonel Custer?"

Hickok chuckled, smoothing his mustache with a finger. "George and Elizabeth may still be my friends. But his brother, Tom, sure isn't."

"Tom?"

"He's a captain with the Seventh, and commands some pretty tough boys. I was sheriff of Ellis County, until I got un-elected last year. The troopers preferred a wide-open town, and I'd been hired to keep the peace, so you might say we were at cross-purposes."

"So the brother give you some trouble?"

"Well, he tried. When he got drunk, he liked to ride through town and shoot at lights and windows. Ride his horse into saloons. Finally, I had to drag him off his animal and arrest him for disturbing the peace."

"I guess he didn't take that well."

"Not very," Hickok said. "He and three troopers caught me coming into Paddy Welch's saloon during a commotion when the whole town was celebrating New Year's Eve. Before I knew what was going on, they grabbed me and lifted my guns. Next thing I knew, one of the troopers was drawing a bead on me."

I wondered if this could be the same Paddy Welch I'd met working for the railroad. "What happened?" I asked. "This isn't going to be another story where you got killed, is it?"

Hickok threw back his head and laughed. "What happened was Paddy tossed me a gun. I had to shoot the three soldiers."

"Oh oh," I said.

"You might say that. Tom went running back to Fort Hays. His brother wasn't there, but little Phil Sheridan was more than happy to issue an order to bring me in, dead or alive. At least that's what one of the scouts from the fort told me. He said I'd better leave town unless I wanted to take on the whole Seventh Cavalry. My term as sheriff wasn't officially up until midnight, but I decided to turn in my badge early."

"Sounds prudent."

"Since then, I've been traveling up and down the rail line, stopping off for card games and a little yarning here and there. It's funny how a few dime novels make people fall over themselves to buy you drinks and lose money to you at poker. But who am I to quibble?"

"How come you said you'd been thinking about me, back at Hays?"

"Oh, yeah. An acquaintance of yours is performing at one of the dance halls there—the singer you spent all that time looking for back in Kansas City, remember? After you had that run-in with the Silver Dollar Kid…"

"Callie is in Hays?" I interrupted.

"Well, she was when I left," Hickok said. "I don't know about now. As you recall, she moves around."

I waited impatiently for the train to reach its next stop before I could get off, and then I had to wait for the next eastbound back toward Hays. I passed the time as I usually did during periods of enforced leisure, writing. First, I wrote up as concise a report as I could to put in a telegram to Stanford, and I managed to churn out a couple more stories to mail east to paying magazines. It was a pretty long wait.

When I finally got turned around and reached the collection of shanties and false-fronted buildings that made up Hays City, I went straight for the dance hall Hickok had named. And, as I'd feared, Callie St. Clair had moved on.

I made inquiries, and finally found someone in whom she'd confided, up to a point. She'd told a fellow showgirl she was heading for Abilene, not immediately but round about. She knew someone who was going into the saloon business there, she said, and had agreed to perform in his establishment. Where would she be until then? Her friend had no idea.

I didn't want to show up in Abilene before she did, and maybe scare her off. She had to be avoiding me, having left Kansas City so abruptly. So I used my rail privileges to pay Ginny and her mother a visit in Utah, and give Star a little exercise. He seemed fat and happy, and actually a little glad to see me. Not as much as Trigger or Champion or Lightning or Black Jack in the movies, to see their masters, but at least he didn't bite me.

Neither did Ginny. I'm sure you've guessed by now that I'd developed a considerable liking for her. The idea of settling down with her, assuming I could persuade her, was tempting. But I couldn't help worrying how she might react to my mixed racial makeup, which I knew I'd eventually break down and tell her about. Besides, I still needed to find out from Callie St. Clair if my brother was alive or dead and, if alive, where I might find him.

That didn't keep me from enjoying the days spent with Ginny. By the time I left again, a few months after reading the news that Texas had finally been re-admitted to the union, Ginny and I had become quite attached to one another.

"Why do you have to go?" she asked me, as we sat on the front porch swing of her mother's home.

"I told you, Ginny. This singer who's headed for Abilene is my only clue to Jackson."

Ginny's brow furrowed in a tiny frown. Finally, she asked, "Is she pretty?"

"Sure," I said, speaking before I thought. "But not as pretty as you," I said, when my thoughts caught up with my mouth.

As it turned out, if I had simply joined Hickok in his travels, we'd have both ended up in Abilene at about the same time. The Abilene city council had recently lost a marshal named Tom Smith, killed on the job. Abilene was a rail shipping center for crops from Kansas farmlands, and now was becoming an even bigger shipping point for Texas cattle herded there over the Chisholm Trail to be loaded onto rail cars and sent east.

As always, the Texas cowboys liked to let off steam when they arrived in Abilene, after a drive. Abilene needed a new marshal, fast. And Hickok was ready to take on a new job.

Hickok and his deputies—one of whom turned out to be a nephew of Kit Carson, the scout whose exploits had helped inspire Hickok to go west in the first place—enforced a no-gun ordinance to keep a lid on potential trouble.

But there were always cowboys who didn't want to give up their guns, even temporarily.

Neither did at least one of the city residents, as Wild Bill would find out.

# TWENTY-ONE

*Tim Holt: "Keep your shirt on."*
*Richard "Chito" Martin: "I always keep it on,*
*except on Saturday nights when I take a bath."*
*Tim Holt: "Well, this is only Thursday and*
*I don't want to attract too much attention."*
Under the Tonto Rim *(1947)*

Once I arrived in Abilene, and found a place to settle in and start looking around, it didn't take long to get a line on where Callie St. Clair was working. As I'd admitted to Ginny, Callie was one good-looking woman, and a number of men waxed enthusiastic when I made inquiries.

She was singing in a place called the Bull's Head Saloon, which sported a replica of its namesake out front. There was no doubt about it being a bull; the replica had been extremely well endowed, even though that part of its anatomy had now been erased. During my chats with men for whom I was a good listener, I learned that the city council had required the owners to remove that particular feature. They objected, and folks said Hickok stood by with a sawed-off shotgun while the offending feature was painted over. That's one thing we never saw Billy Elliott do in any of his Hickok portrayals.

The owners of the Bull's Head had been Ben Thompson, a native of England whose family arrived in the United States about a year after his birth, and Phil Coe, a Texan who, like most Texans, disliked the local restrictions. Thompson was the same gunfighter that Stuart Lake's book had Wyatt Earp arresting in Ellsworth, in a manner re-enacted in dozens of pictures, even though I doubt that it actually happened. But Thompson had recently sold his interest in the place to Coe and moved on.

From the talk I picked up, there may have been more to the bad blood between Coe and "Wild Bill" than Coe simply being a Texan. Some said it involved a rivalry over a woman. Others said it was because Coe's business depended on the cattle-herding Texans being able to cut loose and spend freely, and Hickok's job was to keep them in line. I never found out which speculation was right. Maybe both.

I ran into Hickok as soon as I arrived in Abilene. As marshal, he made it his business to check on new arrivals by train or stage or horseback. He made sure they turned in their firearms or, if he decided a newcomer might be a trouble maker, that the person got right back on the train.

"Hey, kid, how are you?" he said when he saw me. "I didn't know you'd be traveling this way." I guessed he hadn't realized I'd tracked Callie St. Clair here.

Hickok seemed more uptight than the last time I'd seen him, more wary and expectant of trouble. His hands were never far from the two pistols he had stuck in the sash around his waist. I noticed he would ease into saloons in such a way that his back was always to the wall, and wore a perpetual scowl which seemed to discourage anybody from crossing him. "A mad old bull" is how I overheard one man describe him.

Not long ago, I learned, a mob of twenty or thirty Texans rode into Abilene with the avowed intention of taming "Wild Bill." Hickok met them in the middle of the street outside the Last Chance Saloon with a Winchester in his hands. "Get lost, you sons of bitches," he said, or words to that effect. One look at him, and the whole group did just that. I was never happier at being one of the few people still on friendly terms with him.

But not with Callie. She was obviously not happy to see me.

I'd come in during one of her songs and, when she spotted me, she actually missed a note. I sat at a table with a drink I'd ordered as an excuse to be there, waiting until she finished her number, took her bows, and walked over to my table.

"Johnny," she said in a whisper, "you shouldn't be here."

I started to stand up, but she pulled back a chair and sat down. "Sorry," I said. "I don't mean to bother you. I just want to know about Jack…"

"Keep your voice down!" She looked around quickly but, although she was still getting admiring glances, nobody seemed interested in me. "How did you find me?"

I told her about encountering Hickok on the train, then picking up her trail from her friend in Ellsworth.

"That'll teach me to keep my mouth shut," she mused. "Look, we can't talk here. Do you know where the Novelty Theater is?" I didn't, but she gave me directions. "Meet me there in an hour. Come around to the back," she said.

I nodded, pushed my chair back, and walked out of the Bull's Head. The street seemed noisier than it had been when I went in. The end of the trail drive season was near, and the cowboys were in even a more boisterous mood than usual. I took it all in, filing the atmosphere away for some future magazine tale, passing the hour until I was to meet Callie. Finally, I would find out whether Jack was all right, and maybe where I could catch up with him. I could make sure he got his share from Dad's farm at last, and then—what? Go back home? Keep writing magazine stories? Ned Buntline had been right. You could make a living at it.

Finally, I figured it was time. I followed Callie's directions and made my way to the back of the Novelty. The numbers around me thinned out as I went and, by the time I got there, I was alone.

I stood there in the dark, away from the crowds, waiting for Callie to show up. Maybe in my eagerness, I hadn't calculated the time right. I had waited for maybe five minutes when I heard a sound behind me.

I didn't see whoever it was that hit me.

# TWENTY-TWO

*Robert Bice: "How many times does a fellow have to kill you?"*
*Allan "Rocky" Lane: "One good job would do it."*
Bandit King of Texas *(1949)*

"Ben, you can't kill him! You promised!"

The voice seemed to come from far away, but I recognized it as Callie's. I tried to turn toward the sound, but I couldn't. When I got my eyes open, I found I was tied hand and foot, lying face down on a hard wooden floor.

"Sure we can, Beautiful," another voice answered with a chuckle. I knew that voice, too—Ben Quinn. "But not until we hear the shot," he went on. "The one that'll mean the marshal won't be botherin' us no more."

"They probably wouldn't notice the sound of a shot in here, anyway," said a third voice, and that chilled me even more. McCluer! "With the performance out front and all the hell-raisers in the street, we could go ahead and finish him off right now."

"It don't hurt to be careful," Quinn said.

Callie spoke again. "You said you were only going to give him a beating—enough to discourage him from finding me again. That's all you need to do…"

"Now, Beautiful, let us worry about that. He won't be followin' you around no more. Go on, now, you get out of here. We got things to do."

I strained to look toward the voices, but I couldn't get turned far enough around. Callie didn't say anything but, after what seemed a long minute, I heard the rustle of her skirts moving away and then the closing of a door. And I was here alone with Quinn and McCluer. What a comfort.

I could hear footsteps coming toward where I lay, and then they were close enough that I could turn my head enough to see them. They looked down at me, their faces barely visible in the light from a table lamp which was turned way down.

"Hey," Quinn said jovially. "Our boy's awake."

McCluer stared at me. "How many times do we have to kill you, anyway?" he said.

"Once would be enough, if you did it right," I croaked, trying to ignore the pain in the back of my head.

Quinn liked that. He actually laughed. Roy Barcroft says he patterned his movie bad guy performances on those of Harry Woods, but he could have used Quinn as a model. Barcroft has been in so many westerns that you could just about define them as a series of pictures where different heroes shoot him or beat him up. Between pictures, he'll sometimes left his whiskers grow, put on old clothes and lose himself in some disreputable part of outer Hollywood, getting ideas for character traits from the bums around him. But whenever I see him on the screen, I think he could be channeling Ben Quinn.

"You fooled me back in Nebraska, kid," he said genially. "I really thought you were your brother, when you came down those stairs. It'll be like killin' the same guy twice."

"Why kill me?" I asked. "You know I'm not Jack. Colonel Sutherland isn't paying you enough to kill both of us, is he?"

I didn't believe I was going to get out of that room alive. I was casting around desperately for some way to shake them up. And McCluer did raise his eyebrows when I mentioned the colonel's name.

He chuckled again. "What makes you think it was your brother we was supposed to kill?"

Now I was the one confused. "I heard them," I said. "I heard the colonel tell his son, 'That Six boy has got to die.'"

"I don't doubt that. But what makes you think he was talkin' about Double-Six?"

"Why…" I started to say something about Jackson's roll in the hay with the colonel's daughter, but then the import of Quinn's question sunk in.

"That's right, kid. The colonel wasn't talkin' about your brother dyin'. He meant you."

I stared up at him. My mind tried to reshuffle itself. Why would the Sutherlands want me out of the way? I barely heard McCluer say, "Ben, you're talking too much."

"So what? He ain't gonna tell nobody."

"But," I said, "then why did you shoot Jackson?"

"Had to," Quinn said. "He wouldn't have sat still for us gunnin' you whenever you showed up. We had to get him out of the way first. Besides, if you were lookin' for him like we thought, you'd show up where he'd been last."

My head was spinning, and it wasn't just from the after-effects of the blow.

"They don't have any reason to want me dead," I protested.

"Yeah, well, they think they do, kid. Said you knew too much about something the colonel had been involved in. His boy paid us enough to cover however long it took to track you down. Us, and the Silver Dollar Kid, rest his black little soul."

"How'd you find me?"

"You were trailin' around after Callie. We just kept track of her."

"But it's Jack that the colonel hated," I said, almost to myself, trying to work it all out. "Jack and the colonel's daughter…"

"Kid, don't you get it? Double-Six had been one of us, ever since we rode with Quantrill and Anderson in the war. Maybe the colonel didn't much like him, but Double-Six was too good a gun to worry about over some skirt-chasing with his daughter. Putting him out of the way was my idea, not the colonel's."

"Jackson was no outlaw!" I protested. "He was a deputy one time, I remember reading. A stagecoach guard…"

"Yeah, sure. Don't believe everything you read, kid." Quinn gave his raspy chuckle again. It was getting on my nerves. "If we hadn't had to get rid of you, he'd be ridin' with us yet. Or maybe with the James boys, or the Youngers, knockin' over banks or findin' other ways to hurt the Yankee economy. Blowin' up that transcontinental rail link would have been our biggest deal, 'cept you queered that." He shook his head. "Would've been the biggest thing since Quantrill tried to find a plan to kill the president…"

"Ben!" McCluer warned again.

Quinn waved a hand dismissively. "It don't matter, I tell you. Haven't you heard that shot yet?"

McCluer shook his head. "What shot?" I asked.

"You ain't much, kid, but you do have connections. Hickok's taken a liking to you. Like Double-Six, he might get perturbed about your demise, so he'd be best out of the way, too. As it happens, we got someone who's real willin' to do the job. He ain't even askin' for no money. Hickok imposed that no-gun ordinance so, when Coe fires off a shot, the marshal will come runnin', and…" Quinn pointed his finger. "Bang! Every Texan in the crowd will swear it was self-defense."

Since Quinn was being so free with his information, I decided to ask the question that had been bothering me all this time. "Is my brother alive?"

"Beats me, kid," Quinn said. "I was sure I'd finished him. And then we thought you was him. Since it was you and not him, I'm guessin' I did …Hey, there it is!"

We all heard the shot. "That'll be Coe, throwin' one into the air. Now, Hickok will come runnin'…"

We listened. Then came two more shots, right together. Quinn, who'd been reaching inside his shirt for what I assumed was a concealed pistol, probably for me, hesitated. Then another pair of shots sounded.

"Two guns," Quinn murmured. "Hickok shoots with two guns…"

"It doesn't matter now," McCluer said. "Whatever happened, they'll be too busy out there to worry about another shot before we're gone. Finish him."

"Yeah," Quinn said, pulling the small pistol I recognized as a two-shoot derringer all the way out and cocking it. "Yeah, I guess you're right…"

"Hold it, Quinn!"

It took a second for me to realize I'd heard the door burst open just before I heard that voice. But it was a voice I knew.

There he was, dressed in black from hat to boots, a red bandana hanging loosely about his throat, the Double-Six monogram on his shirt, the gunbelt I'd been keeping all this time belted around his waist, the twin guns in his hands.

It was Jackson.

# TWENTY-THREE

*Al "Fuzzy" St. John: "This is getting' confusing. First time I saw you,*
*I thought you were Lash. Then I saw Lash and I thought he was you.*
*I just left Lash, and I thought he was him. Now I see you and*
*I don't know who's who. Are you you? Or who's who?"*
*Lash LaRue: "Yes."*
Outlaw Country *(1949)*

Jackson was alive! And right here. I watched as Quinn and McCluer stared wide-eyed at him, then me, and back at him, but they couldn't have been more shocked than I was.

Quinn was still holding the hideout pistol pointed toward where I lay. Jackson was holding a single-action revolver on Quinn, and I could see that it was cocked. McCluer doubtlessly had his ever-present shotgun hanging under his coat, but not where he could get at it quickly. The trio looked like three frozen statues, each waiting for someone else to move first.

"You shoot, I shoot, Double-Six," Quinn said, finally breaking the silence.

"You'll be just as dead," my brother said. "And don't you move, Cord," he added, as McCluer shifted his position.

But that was all the edge Quinn needed. He snapped his little gun toward Jackson and fired, quick as a striking snake. The weapon only made a popping sound, but I could see Jackson stagger. Then Jackson was firing and Quinn was driven backwards by the impact of bullets. I heard a shattering of glass behind me, and twisted around in time to see McCluer clambering over a window sill.

Quinn got off a second shot as he fell to the floor. It shattered the lamp.

Silence. At least, the broken lamp hadn't started a fire, but it left me in darkness. Outside, I could hear the distant sounds of a crowd, more clearly than before with the glass being gone, but they didn't seem to be moving in our direction. My guess was they were focused on whatever had happened out on the street.

I began scrambling around on the floor, afraid of drawing someone's fire but more worried about doing nothing. My bound hands finally got hold of a piece of glass, perhaps from the lantern or the broken window. I cut myself several times before I made any progress on the ropes. The circulation in my fingers had almost been cut off, and they felt like sausages, but I finally managed to manipulate the glass shard around enough to saw through one strand and then work myself free.

I felt around in my pockets until I came up with some matches. After several attempts, I managed to light what was left of the lamp, still on the table and intact except for the glass globe.

Quinn was staring right at me, or so it seemed, from where he lay on the floor. He wasn't seeing me, though. He'd been hit several times, judging by the blood-spattered marks on his shirt. Then I heard a groan behind me.

"Jackson!" I picked up the remains of the lamp in both hands, and carried them over to where he lay.

"Hey, kid," he said weakly. "We got to quit meeting this way." He tried to laugh, but it quickly turned into a cough.

"Jackson, hang on. I'll go find a doctor…"

"Not…not this time, Johnny. Ben…he did a better job of it…"

"No!"

It wasn't fair. I'd been living with the fear that Jackson might have been dead. Now I'd found him. And he was dying.

He swallowed before he managed to speak again. "You kept the outfit and guns all this time," he said. "I got them out of your hotel room, when Callie told me what was going on." He tried to laugh again. "The clerk handed me your key without a second look…"

"Jackson, don't talk, just hang on. I'll be back as quick as I can…"

He held onto my arm with surprising strength, given his condition. "Got to talk," he said. "Things you got to know…"

And he did talk, for several minutes, his voice getting weaker with each sentence. Finally, I could barely hear him at all.

"You've got to stop them, Johnny," he concluded. "I've been on the wrong side, most of my time out here. But maybe you can help me make it up…"

And then he was gone, this time for good.

# TWENTY-FOUR

*Dave O'Brien: "I tell you, Tex, my way is the right way."*
*Tex Ritter: "So far, there hasn't been any right way."*
Three in the Saddle *(1945)*

"For once," Rick said to his wife of five days, "I can understand why he wanted to stop his story at a certain place."

Nancy nodded, as he pulled their car into a slot in the hospital's parking lot. "Oh, Rick, it's so sad," she said. "Can you imagine? Your whole life being centered around something, and then you achieve it—and then it's gone. It must have been awful for him. And you could see how telling it affected him, even after all this time."

They got out. He locked the car, and his hand found hers as they walked up the steps to the entrance. "I guess the lesson is that life is precious, enjoy it while can."

"I guess."

Inside, Rick asked Nancy to wait for him a minute, while he went into the hospital's gift shop. Nancy drifted into the waiting room. There were five visitors seated there, three women and two men. She sat down and flipped idly through a month-old copy of Life Magazine until Rick rejoined her.

"Here," he said, as they waited for an elevator. He opened a tiny box, extracted a pin with a floral design, and carefully attached it to her blouse.

"Rick, it's lovely," she said. "But you don't have to keep buying me things. You'll spoil me."

"But it's our five-day anniversary. Only one we'll ever have." Then, more seriously, he went on: "You've given up a lot to help me on this thing, Nancy, more than any girl I know would consider giving up. You're more special than even I'd realized." Nancy actually blushed a little. "I hope someday I can find a way to make it all up to you. I can't even explain why I'm so bent on seeing his story through. I do think we're getting close to something I'll be able to take to the boss, to keep this case active. Heck, maybe it'll be whatever we get today."

The elevator door slid open. Rick pushed a button. As the car began to rise, Nancy felt something click in her memory.

"Rick, do you remember the man who was in the elevator with us one day last week? Dressed like an operating room physician?"

Rick frowned. "Yeah, vaguely, I think. I don't really remember what he looked like."

"I do," said Nancy. "Because I just saw him again, sitting in the visitors' lounge. Last week, he was a doctor. Today, he's a visitor." She and Rick stared at each other. "Makes you wonder, doesn't it?"

# TWENTY-FIVE

*Kenne Duncan: "Never did like actors. My wife ran away with one.*
*But I still don't like 'em."*
Hidden Valley Outlaws *(1944)*

For a long time after that, "Wild Bill" and I had something in common. We were both living with bitter memories.

When that first shot went off, Hickok came running out of the Alamo Saloon across the street from the theater building, just as Quinn and company had anticipated. He found the gambler, Phil Coe, holding a pistol he'd just fired into the air. What Coe must not have counted on was that Hickok emerged from the saloon with both his pistols in his hands.

Bill would tell me later that Coe snapped off a shot at him, the bullet plowing through his long coat and leaving a flesh wound. Hickok fired both his guns and Coe fell into the dust of Texas Street, not dead but fatally wounded.

Then, Bill said he heard someone running toward him from behind, and spun around in time to see another figure with a gun in his hand. Once more, he fired both guns.

But the running man had not been some Texan taking up Coe's battle. It was Mike Williams, a special policeman at the theater and a friend of Hickok's. Williams probably thought Bill needed him, surrounded as he was by hostile Texans. But Hickok assumed it was another assailant.

That instinct had saved his life before. This time, it ruined his life. We used a variation of the incident in one of Billy Elliott's movies about Hickok over at Columbia, *Across the Sierras,* having him accidentally shoot a friend. But we didn't use the rest of the story, which I heard later from people who were in Abilene that night.

They all said a change came over Hickok, as he stood up from seeing Williams' body. I wasn't there to see the expression on his face, but it must have been cold enough to frighten even the boldest of the surrounding Texans. They scattered. Bill proceeded to go through every saloon and dance hall in Abilene, closing them down. The cowboys outnumbered him everywhere he went that night but, after one look at him, they left without argument. There were a few who started to protest. He clubbed them to the floor.

For hours, people said, Hickok prowled the darkened Texas Street and the streets and alleys around it. Nobody got in his way.

Two things ended that night. No more cattle drives came to Abilene. And Hickok never served as a peace officer again.

The end of the cattle drives made things more peaceable, but it led to economic stagnation for Abilene. As for Bill, the town council dismissed him near the end of 1872, no longer requiring his protection from rampaging cowboys.

And as you know, something ended for me that night as well.

Callie and I were the only ones to attend Jackson's graveside service. With the excitement over the other shootings and Coe's protracted death as he lay in bed with his fatal wounds, nobody showed interest in another death. If they'd realized it was the once-notorious Double-Six, maybe some would have. But it was Jackson's given name, not his better-known moniker, that we put on the wooden grave marker, and nobody realized.

"It's your fault," Callie told me afterward, in an emotionless monotone. "If you hadn't kept chasing after us, Quinn would never have known he was here."

"Callie, Quinn didn't know," I told her. "Neither did I."

My words didn't seem to register. "I didn't know they planned to kill you," she said. "When I told them where we were meeting, I just thought, if they worked you over like Quinn promised, you'd be in no condition to come after us." She dabbed at her eyes with a tiny lace handkerchief. "When I found out what they really had in mind, I had to tell Jack. He would never have forgiven me."

And instead of me dying, he had. Jackson had been concealing his identity, I learned from Callie, ever since he'd recovered from Quinn's shot—or at least partially recovered. Callie said he had seemed sickly to her when they finally got back together, that he had a racking cough he couldn't shake, and that physically he seemed a shadow of himself. He knew Quinn and McCluer were in town, but had no trouble concealing himself from them—or from me, when he spotted me just before I'd approached Callie. That was how he knew where my hotel room was, when he went to take back his guns and outfit.

"Callie, what are you going to do now?" I asked.

She pondered that. "Pretty much what I'd been doing, I guess," she said. "Women entertainers are still liked out here. If you're a little bit pretty, it helps. I'll do all right." She turned to look at me. "I'm sorry for what I just said, Johnny. It wasn't your fault. If anybody's to blame…"

I saw where she was going and stopped her by putting my hands on her small shoulders. "When the chips were down, you went to Jackson," I said. She would have known the odds against him, in his condition, facing two professional killers.

"If you ever need anything," I went on, "you can reach me through Leland Stanford, in San Francisco. He's well enough known so mail with his name will reach him."

She nodded, then looked away again.

"There's something else," I said. "Jackson had what you might call an inheritance coming to him. I'm sure he'd want you to have it."

She looked up at me again, and even managed a tight smile. "Thanks, kid,"

she said, using Jackson's term for me. "I'll keep it in mind. I'm all right, for now."
Then she turned and walked away.

Much later, when I took a train out of town and was walking through a
passenger coach, I was surprised to find Hickok sitting by himself.

He invited me to join him, and told me he was headed for Kansas City. My
destination was California. I had a lot to report to Stanford, and I couldn't put
it all in a telegram.

Even San Francisco was a pretty wild place back then, but not where the
mansions stood on Nob Hill. Stanford ushered me into the library of his palatial
home, once I'd convinced his man at the door that the man would really want
to see me.

"Mr. Stanford, I think I've got that letter from the so-called Colonel figured
out," I told him after bringing him up to date. "Jackson told me a lot in the little
time before he was gone."

Stanford waited for me to go on.

"Before Quinn shot Jackson that first time and left him for dead, he'd been
part of their outfit. He didn't know who was giving them their orders—he
would never have guessed it to be Colonel Sutherland, I'm sure. But he did
know it was someone from the east. And that someone had nothing less in
mind than the destruction of the United States."

"Now wait a minute, Johnny…"

"I'm not exaggerating, sir. These people are still fighting the Civil War. They
think anything they can do to bring chaos to the country will help them re-do
its government to their liking."

The stout figure across from me pulled at his beard. "I believe I see where
you're going with this," he said, leaning back in his chair. "But let me hear your
conclusions."

I took a deep breath. "When Ben Quinn was talking to me, he said the
colonel's son had paid them to track me down and kill me. I think Sean is the
'S' who signed those written instructions in that letter about the so-called big
assignment."

"The biggest since we started working with Q and later B to eliminate the top problem four years ago," Stanford recited. He'd obviously studied that letter. "Four years before that letter would have been 1865."

"The year President Lincoln was killed," I said.

We considered the implications in silence for several minutes. Stanford still looked doubtful.

"Quinn said Quantrill had once planned to do it," I reminded him. "And we know the Sutherlands have connections with men who rode with Quantrill— the same ones who are still robbing banks."

"At least we think we know who the major bank robbers are," Stanford said. "The editor of the Kansas City Times is still printing denials from the James family, but the Pinkertons have identified Frank and Jesse as having held up banks in Iowa and stolen a cashbox at the Kansas City Fair."

"They get around," I said.

"Yes. A ten-year-old girl was trampled to death when they made their getaway from the fair. But their pet newspaper still refers to them as Missouri's version of the Knights of the Round Table. It's generated enough sympathy so the Pinkertons are getting no help from the citizenry. Of course, I suppose it doesn't help that Pinkerton's agency worked for the North during the war."

He stroked his beard some more, and looked at me from across the small table between us. "So you're thinking that, if the Q referred to Quantrill, the B could be John Wilkes Booth." He nodded to himself. "It does seem obvious that Booth was part of a larger group. We know now they'd planned to get the vice president and the secretary of state as well. Secretary of State Seward and three others at Seward's home were wounded by another would-be assassin. And we know that a man assigned to kill Vice President Johnson simply lost his nerve."

"Booth broke a leg when he jumped from the presidential box at the Ford Theatre," I recalled. "Mr. Stanford, when I was a kid back in Shenandoah County, I stumbled into Colonel Sutherland talking to a man whose leg had been injured. This was within days of the president's death."

"You think it might have been Booth?"

"I never thought about it. I guess Colonel Sutherland gave me credit for being smarter than I was. Or maybe he was afraid that, with a little prompting, I might remember more details. I overheard him tell Sean that they had more at stake than family honor. I thought he was talking about going after Jackson. Now we know he meant me."

"Because you might've linked him to Booth, before they got him," Stanford said in his thoughtful way. "But, Johnny, it's all conjecture. There's nothing in the letter that would prove any of this. We can't even prove that Sutherland wrote the letter."

"McCluer could prove it, if we could ever get him to talk."

"McCluer seems to have dropped out of sight. At least, nobody's been able to locate him."

"It would be nice if one of Jackson's bullets hit him," I said.

"I've had some research done on your Mr. McCluer," Stanford informed me. "Did you know he has a wife and three children living in New York City? He abandoned them when he came west, but who knows? Perhaps he would seek sanctuary with them now. At the least, his wife might be able to provide information about him."

"Maybe one of your detectives could check on them."

"I think you'd do it better. You've encountered the man several times. You know more about him than they do."

"You want me to go to New York when I'm clear on the other side of the country?" I asked.

He gave a bass laugh. "A long train trip would give you time to pursue your story writing."

As a matter of fact, I thought I had a good cover for making a trip to New York. And Bill Hickok was the key.

Hickok had been invited by none other than "Buffalo Bill" Cody to join him in a touring stage show called "Scouts of the Plains." The idea was that the

two Bills would play themselves. Hickok knew about the dime novel stuff that I had done, and invited me to join him and maybe provide some advice on story lines, things with which he was totally unfamiliar. I hadn't taken him seriously then, but, luckily, I hadn't given him a definite no.

Hickok told me that he once tried a Wild West show himself. Shortly after leaving Ellsworth one step ahead of Custer's cavalry, he accumulated enough poker winnings to hire three cowboys, four Comanches, and to somehow cram six unruly buffalo into train cars to transport them to the Canadian side of Niagara Falls, where the tourist season was in full swing. Somewhere along the way, they picked up a monkey and a bear for their entourage. Hickok had planned to put on an outdoor show called "The Daring Buffalo Chase of the Plains," and several thousand people showed up at the arena where the first performance was to be given.

It didn't go exactly as planned.

The buffalo, after being cooped up for their ride across the country, weren't much interested in being chased. Hickok and his folks herded them into the center of the arena, and they just stood there.

Finally, Hickok fired a shot into the air to encourage them. It worked, too well.

The animals charged out of the arena and ended up stampeding through a nearby residential section, where they terrorized folks who had no idea what they were or where they'd come from. About that time, the bear managed to get out of his cage. He promptly started gobbling up the offerings of a nearby sausage vendor, and seemed about to start gnawing on the vendor himself before a bunch of spectators managed to chase him away. The monkey got loose, too, and climbed up on top of a wagon where he began throwing things at the crowd.

When it was all over, Hickok said he had lost his shirt. He decided that card tables were a much more reliable source of income. But Kansas City had started to crack down on gambling, to the point where Hickok was broke when

he received Cody's invitation. Reluctant as he was to involve himself in another show, he finally agreed to give it a try.

I sent him a telegram saying I'd thought it over and would like to join him, after all. It was a long trip, but I filled the hours as Stanford had suggested, composing more magazine stories—and letters to Ginny.

My arrival in New York City was a lot more quiet than Bill's had been. No sooner had he arrived at Cody's hotel than he got into a fight with the driver of the hansom which had brought him there.

"He tried to overcharge me," Bill told me later. I could just picture Mr. Cody being informed that the gentleman he was expecting had just flattened a hansom driver right in front of the hotel. "Ah, yes, that would be Bill," he reportedly said.

The script being used by the show had been perpetrated by my old acquaintance, Ned Buntline, who didn't remember me. I didn't tell him that it was he who had inspired me to follow in his footsteps.

Mr. Buntline not only provided the script, but played several of the roles he'd written, not all that well. To me, his script read as though he'd pounded it out in a few hours while under the influence. And I learned later that this was pretty much the case.

The storyline was a mishmash of Indians chasing whites and being chased by the heroic scouts. Buntline even threw in an occasional temperance lecture, during a scene where the Indians were about to burn him at the stake. Most nights, the audience would applaud, not at his speech but at his character's impending demise.

I read a review of a performance by a couple writers named Henry Blackman Sell and Victor Weybright, in which they wrote that yet another character played by Buntline died again in the next act, "to the delight of the spectators, who felt he couldn't die too often. For weeks afterward it was said that the dazed playgoers would shout, 'The Indians are upon us!' and explode in maniacal laughter."

The script rewrite which added Hickok to the brotherhood of scouts eliminated Buntline's roles, but it wasn't much of an improvement—not when it stuck Bill with such lines as "Fear not, fair maid! By heavens, you are safe at last with Wild Bill, who is ever ready to risk his life and die, if need be, in defense of weak and defenseless womanhood!" I mean, even Coop or Bill Elliott couldn't have done that with straight faces.

Well, for that matter, neither could Bill himself, no actor to begin with. Cody was a ham at heart, and seemed to relish such outrageous dialog but, to Hickok, it was all foolishness. Often he couldn't (or wouldn't) remember his lines at all, which left Cody and "Texas Jack" Omohundro, the other "scout," having to ad-lib until Bill got back on track.

He got through it only with lavish amounts of liquor. One evening, during a scene where the three scouts were sitting around a campfire passing a whiskey bottle among them, Hickok stopped the show when he tasted it and found it to be nothing but tea. He refused to continue until he had the real stuff, and the audience seemed to be in total agreement. They loved it. The play resumed once the stage manager provided a bottle of the real stuff.

Bill was always unpredictable. Sometimes he would burn a "dead" Indian with a blank cartridge around the actor's legs, making him jump. More than once, when he was rescuing the "fair maid" played by a pretty lady named Giuseppina Morlacchi, perhaps the only "Indian maiden" to have an Italian accent, she had to be rescued again from his all-too-amorous embraces.

But audiences ate it up. They had come to see the mythological frontier figures of him and Cody, not the play. I thought Hickok's antics improved the show, myself. It actually helped give me ideas about what kind of entertainment western fans liked, which I capitalized on much later.

While all this was going on, I was slipping away during the day trying to track down McCluer's wife.

She and her children had moved from the address the Pinkertons had given Stanford, but eventually, with the passing of a little cash, their former landlord came up with their new location.

The New York slums were worse in the 1870s than they are now. Molly McClure proved to be a rawboned woman with gray-streaked reddish hair, and a suspicious glint in her eyes. Marjorie Main could play her. "If you're selling something," she told me after responding to my knock, "we don't want it."

I was wearing a suit and tie, since western garb would have been out of place. But I guess the time I had spent in the west showed through, somehow. I didn't think I could fool this woman, so I told her straight out that I was looking for her husband.

She laughed bitterly. "I've been looking for him for six years, mister. Ever since he left us and started shooting people, or so they say. Now I'm not sure I want to find him. How come you want him?"

"I just need to talk to him, Mrs. McCluer." I was considering another offer of money, if she actually had any information. It was then that someone behind her pushed her aside and I found myself staring into McCluer's cold dead-looking eyes.

"We ain't talkin' with no Pinkertons," the newcomer snarled, and came through the door at me. I'd yanked the pistol I had under my coat before I realized that this was not McCluer, but a younger version of him. He'd come charging toward me with his fists cocked, but stopped at the sight of my weapon.

"Clay!" his mother screamed. She grabbed him by the shoulders and pulled him back inside. "Don't shoot him, mister. He don't mean nothin'. He's just got his father's mean streak…"

"It's all right, Mrs. McCluer," I assured her. "I'm not going to shoot anybody."

The boy was probably not much older than I'd been when I started out to find Jackson. But he was going to be a dead ringer for his father when he matured, I could see that. His eyes fixated on the pistol I was still holding.

"You're that Six man," he yelled. "Ma, that's Pa's spare gun, the one that got stolen from him in Kansas City."

He was absolutely right. It was the same shiny factory-converted .44 revolver I'd taken out of McCluer's saddlebags where I'd found Colonel Sutherland's letter. I'd hung onto it for use as a spare, when it wasn't practical to strap on Jackson's artillery. Now I slid it back under my coat.

"You want to be more careful about who you go after, Clay," I told him. "Some folks might shoot first and talk later."

My only answer was a steady stream of curses, words I was surprised he even knew at his age. His mother managed to pull him the rest of the way inside. "I don't think we got anything to talk about," she said, slamming the door in my face.

But they had already told me a lot.

The fact that the boy recognized his father's weapon, and knew how and where he'd lost it, meant that McCluer had been in touch in recent years. And if he had been here before, he might come back.

# TWENTY-SIX

*James Stewart: "Clever fighters, those Sioux. It seems*
*they knew all about your Springfields being single-shot."*
*J. C. Flippen: "You mean they had repeaters?"*
*James Stewart: "Yep. They sent in the first wave light, so it'd draw the fire. Then*
*they sent in a heavy second wave before the Custer men had a chance to reload."*
Winchester '73 *(1950)*

During July of the same year Hickok and I came together at Buffalo Bill's Wild West show, the James gang held up its first train. The outlaws derailed it on the Rock Island Line in Iowa, killing the engineer and several passengers. I think Stanford had seen this coming—first banks, then trains. We'd been exchanging telegrams and, after several weeks of my watching, he decided the McCluer family in New York was a dead end.

I wasn't so sure. But he was paying me, and I had to agree that the family now knew me by sight.

With the train robbery, Stanford wanted me to get back on the trail of Jesse James and company. Before I left New York, I made the acquaintance of a man who lived near McCluer's family and, in return for periodic bits of cash mailed to him, agreed to keep me posted if someone answering McCluer's description showed up.

Stanford didn't seriously expect me to compete with the Pinkertons in tracking down Jesse James. But he and I were the only people who knew about the connection between these outlaws and Colonel Sutherland's seditious leanings. Stanford wanted me to try and counter the James gang's propaganda machine, the one thing for which I might be better qualified. I would try and place freelance articles on their outlawry in eastern newspapers and magazines, and paint a less glamorous picture than the ones they painted themselves.

Hickok had abandoned Cody's stage show by now, disgusted with its pretense and, I think, with himself. "Don't they look foolish?" he whispered to me one night while we watched some of the show from backstage. "Kid, I'm not going to do it anymore."

He didn't say where he might go from New York, except for some vague remarks about hitting the gambling circuit again. His notoriety was still such that people would happily lose to him just so they could say they had played cards with him.

As for me, I took a train west and visited for a time with Ginny and her mother in Utah. "Johnny!" Ginny called out when she saw me walking up to their little house. She ran to me before I'd reached the porch and threw her arms around me.

I was delighted.

Even Star seemed to remember me when I groomed him that evening. I found a room not far from their boarding house; Ginny's and my relationship had progressed to the point where it would hardly be proper for me to rent space under the same roof with her.

And I settled down to start picking up accounts of the James and Younger gangs. I sent off some of those pieces depicting them as less than angelic, and some of those found homes. But it was sedentary work, and the only exercise I got was going on horseback rides with Ginny.

I had not been away from the west all that long, but there had been changes. In the summer of 1874, Bill's old military friend began making news. Custer and around a thousand soldiers set up a "military outpost" in what was supposed to be Sioux territory in the Dakota badlands. The reason was obvious: gold had been found on those Indian lands, and the Custer expedition followed.

Soon, what had been a few trespassing miners turned into a gold rush. By the following year, the gold seekers had brought enough pressure on the government to get Army protection for the Sioux withdrawn. By the end of that year, the government had done a complete turnaround and ordered the Indians out of the Black Hills of the Dakota and Wyoming territories.

While all that was going on, the Red River Indian wars were winding down. Over a period of months during 1874, hundreds of Comanche and Kiowa warriors surrendered themselves at Fort Sill, in Texas. The invention of the Winchester '73, named for the year in which it was produced, gave soldiers more range and impact than they'd had with the older 1866 rapid-fire, and it was becoming obvious how the battles that had been going on between whites and Indians all these years would end.

You might have thought that the diminished Indian threat would have increased migrations westward but, also in 1874, the worst grasshopper plague in history devastated croplands from Canada to Texas. Nobody had ever seen anything like it. It became so bad that the insects would actually block railroad tracks at times, and darken the sun by sheer numbers. Instead of moving west, thousands moved back east.

Yet another development marked that year, when Joseph Glidden invented and patented something called barbed wire, which was much less expensive than wooden fencing for dividing up the prairie. It provided a way to cut up the vast previously-open cattle ranges.

As much as I was enjoying my time in Utah, it was getting me no closer to the James boys. By now, they had held up yet another train at Gads Hill, Missouri. The leader gave a report of the robbery, apparently written in advance of the act itself, to a conductor to be passed on to newspapers. Jesse was apparently acting as his own press agent now, but I thought maybe I detected Sean Sutherland's fine hand in this. I even wondered if it was deliberate, to counter the stuff I was getting placed in publications.

Of course, the outlaws' account didn't give the real descriptions of the five masked robbers. The story described them as "all large men, none of them under six feet tall...all mounted on fine, blooded horses."

Jesse and his boys came up with other antics to curry favor with the public. After robbing the train's safe, they turned to the passengers and loudly proclaimed that they would examine each man's hands before deciding whether to take his money. Working men with calluses would be left alone, and money would be taken, as they put it, only from "the capitalists, professors and others that get money easy."

Stanford had written to me about a Pinkerton man who tried what I'd managed to do once before, spy on the James farm from Kearny. The man planned to seek a job with Jesse's and Frank's mother, and use it to see when the boys came home again. His body turned up shortly afterward, shot through the head and the heart. I guess that was Stanford's way of telling me not to try that stunt again.

Other Pinkertons were hot after the Younger brothers around Monegaw Springs, Missouri. They caught up with the fugitives and one of the clan, John Younger, was killed in the shootout along with two of the lawmen.

The resulting publicity went in a less favorable direction this time, for the James and Younger gangs. The Missouri legislature actually put up $10,000 to pay for undercover agents to try and break them up. The Jameses and the Youngers must have started to feel the heat, because they vanished from Missouri.

Jesse did make it back for his wedding. He married a cousin, Zee Mimms, whom he'd been courting for something like nine years. Not to be outdone, a young woman named Annie Ralston bought a train ticket to "visit relatives" in Kansas City, and soon wrote back that she was now Mrs. Frank James.

Matrimony didn't slow the boys down. They joined some of their fellow ex-guerillas from Kentucky to Texas in more robberies. But people who had been applauding their exploits before now began to see them as a national disgrace.

Frank and Jesse did win back some of their public sympathy when a squad of Pinkertons, in the mistaken belief that the boys had returned home, surrounded the place and threw a metal object inside. Some idiot shoveled it in the fireplace. The result was an explosion. Mrs. Samuels, Jesse's and Frank's mother, was injured so severely that she lost an arm. A foster son, only nine years old, was killed.

The Pinkertons claimed the object had been a flare. The James partisans insisted it was a bomb. Whatever it was, it made martyrs out of the brothers even though they hadn't been there. You probably saw the whitewashed version of it in that Jesse James movie Tyrone Power made about twelve years ago. Pretty inaccurate. The only good thing that came out of that picture was its abuse of horses caused the American Humane Society to start monitoring films and put a stop to that stuff, and it boosted Randolph Scott, who'd already made a bunch of little Zane Grey adaptations, into some really good westerns like he's making now.

As for me, I found myself about written out as far as generating articles and stories showing the true colors of the James gang. My last two efforts hadn't even been accepted for publication; the accounts of the gang's activities, the attack on their mother's house and the depiction of the brothers as put-upon farmers all made for better copy.

And then my attention was totally diverted by a short letter from none other than Bill Hickok.

He'd finally gotten married, he wrote, to a woman he'd met five years ago when he was marshal of Abilene. She'd been the owner of a circus performing there, as well as one of its trick riders. She and Bill crossed paths again in Cheyenne, Wyoming, and were married on March 5, 1876, in the home of some friends she was visiting.

It was hard for me to picture Wild Bill settled down as a family man. But it seemed that he had.

Well, maybe not completely. His letter said he had joined the migration to the Black Hills, in the Dakota Territory. He invited me to join him there, painting a rosy picture of the money to be made—in his case, more at the gambling tables than in the gold fields.

I wasn't a gambler or a prospector, and was in no immediate need of money. In fact, I still hadn't touched the money I'd banked for Jackson. My writing income, plus the financial support from Stanford when I did stuff for him, took care of my needs which weren't really all that much. But I sent Stanford a letter saying I was taking a leave of absence. I already felt a little guilty about him paying me when I didn't think I'd accomplished much for him. I didn't wait for a reply, but took a train north through Wyoming to the end of the line, toward the Dakotas.

Star was getting a little old for such confined train trips, so I rented a stable horse at the end of the line and rode north. Hickok had written that he was located in a boom town called Deadwood. It was a long ride, but I kind of enjoyed the experience of camping out again, living off the land when towns were scarce and not sitting at a table scratching out magazine tales. It proved to be a quiet and uneventful trip—until the night I looked up into the faces of about a dozen Indians.

I had weapons within grabbing distance, but I had better sense than to grab any. Instead, I stood up and made motions of welcome. I raised my arms in what I hoped was non-threatening sign language, and found each of them held by a brave.

The next thing I knew, I was being hustled off into the darkness, while others in the band picked up my horse, camping equipment and other possessions.

I chafed at my own stupidity. I should have known what I was riding into, with the Indians being forced off their land so the gold-hunters could come in, extending the string of broken promises that always marked our relations with them. I'd heard about the Sioux, Arapaho and Cheyenne joining up to make probably the largest force of Indians in the history of North America. I guess I thought a lone rider could just sneak through all this. Well, now I knew better.

It was still dark when the fires of an Indian encampment came into view. It was huge, the fires stretching out as far as I could see, almost seeming to challenge the stars overhead in number. I'd had no idea there were this many Indians left in the entire country.

In no time at all, I was tied hand and foot and dumped unceremoniously into a teepee. They didn't even give me the dignity of a guard. As thoroughly trussed up as I was, they didn't need one.

I don't know how long I lay there, but I could see through a tent-like flap that dawn was approaching when the shadowy figure of a brave pushed the flap aside and came in. He walked slowly over to where I lay, and squatted down beside me. He started speaking words I couldn't understand. I shook my head to try and show incomprehension.

"I asked if you were scouting for Long Hair's soldiers," he said, surprising me as he switched so casually to English.

"No." My own voice sounded strange in my ears, after so long a silence. "I'm not a scout. Who is Long Hair?"

"Then you must be a gold seeker," he said.

"Not that, either. I was just traveling through. I was going to a place north and east of here."

He pondered that for a minute or so.

"You did not have any digging tools," he said finally. "You do have some fine weapons. We can use those. And they are not the sort of firearms a scout would carry. You may be speaking the truth."

He stood up and started to leave.

"Hey! Does that mean you'll let me go?" I called after him.

He paused. "That means we will give you a quick death—unlike the kind we will give the soldiers approaching us along the Greasy Grass. Their carcasses we will scatter to the winds."

And then he was gone, his parting words giving me no comfort whatever.

When I'd faced the possibility of death from Quinn, and later from the

Silver Dollar Kid, at least I was armed and had a chance. Not this time. I found myself regretting things like not having gotten Jackson's money to him before he was killed, of never seeing Ginny again—those two things, mainly. There's nothing like the prospect of death to find out what's important to you.

It was bright outside by the time two other Indians came in. The noise of whatever was going on had increased. One of the newcomers said something in his own language about first blood. He reached down and grabbed me by the hair. He pulled my head back and, with his other hand, drew a wicked-looking knife from his belt.

Then his companion said something I didn't understand. Whatever it was, it caused the first one to pause, although it seemed to come reluctantly. The second one pulled me roughly into the light and stared into my face.

I stared back, recognizing him first by the scar and then by his features. It was the same brave that Warbonnet had called Curly. He looked me over a bit longer, said something unintelligible to his companion, and they both slipped back out.

What the hell was going on?

Once more, I was alone with dark thoughts. I had no idea what might happen next, but it wasn't long in coming. As the noise of raised voices and shouts increased even more, Curly came back in by himself, this time holding his own knife. He made two quick slashes, and the thongs around my wrists and ankles were gone. He dropped an animal-skin bag down beside me, and said something in his own language about a debt being paid, or at least that's what I thought. Then he spoke more slowly, and I thought I got the substance of it as being that he would now go into battle owing nothing to any white-skin. He referred to himself by name in this little speech, but the name was no longer Curly. As close as I could make it out, he was now calling himself Crazy Horse.

Then he turned and was gone.

The first thing I did was dig into that bag. It contained a little of the food I'd been carrying when I was captured, some of my campfire cooking implements and, most important, Jackson's gun belt and pistols.

I didn't go out until the sounds of the war cries started to fade, and I heard the sounds of feet walking rapidly away, and the clopping of a few horses. Despite what you see in movies, it was only the Comanches back in Texas who fought from horseback. The other tribes were mostly ground troops. I guessed they were heading off for their encounter with Long Hair, whoever he was.

Still, I hesitated to go out, where I'd be visible to anyone who might have stayed behind. Instead, I slithered under a flap in the back, and crawled slowly and carefully away, using every tree and bush I could find. It seemed like hours before the huge encampment dropped out of sight behind me, and only then did I dare to stand up.

Based on where I figured the sun had come up, I moved in a northwesterly direction. In the distance, I thought I heard the sounds of gunfire, lots of it. The distant noise lasted maybe half an hour. Then, there was silence—a silence I didn't care for at all. Still, I kept moving, keeping to cover, but I didn't see a single living thing until I spotted buzzards circling in the distance. Then I saw movement, and jerked to a stop. A black and white pony was chewing on some grass. I guessed he had lost his rider in whatever battle had just taken place, and gotten separated from the other horses. Considering what a herd instinct horses have, it must have taken something extraordinary to frighten this one into taking off by himself. He wasn't wearing cavalry trappings, so I presumed he'd belonged to one of the Indians.

The pony's head came up when he spotted me. He laid his ears back, and tensed as though ready to bolt. I rummaged in the bag I'd been dragging along with me, and came up with a couple of carrots from among the garden vegetables I'd been carrying since my last stop at a store.

The pony mellowed when I offered him a carrot. While he munched, I spoke softly to him, got my hand on his rope bridle, and swung into the saddle. Yes, I know, the movies don't have Indians using saddles, but they used them whenever they could steal one. This saddle didn't amount to much, but it was a lot better than riding bareback.

I continued northeast, pretty much letting the horse run or fast-walk whenever he was inclined to do so. I didn't want any argument with him, and he seemed to become pretty used to me as the journey stretched into days and weeks.

And I found myself awed by the realization that Jackson had reached out from the grave, to save my life yet again.

# TWENTY-SEVEN

*Raymond Hatton: "Why, doggone, John,*
*you never whistle that tune unless there's trouble brewin'."*
*Johnny Mack Brown: "It's brewing, all right. Take a deep seat and hold on."*
Back Trail *(1948)*

Long before I finally rode into Deadwood, I learned at stops along the way what had been the source of all that gunfire—the demise of Lieutenant Colonel George Armstrong Custer, known to the Indians as Long Hair, along with more than two hundred of his men, along a bank of the Little Bighorn, which the Indians called Greasy Grass.

"None of us is safe now," declared a Montana farmer who had invited me in for a sit-down meal in return for my doing a few chores. "The Indians never got together before like they have now. If they take a notion to come this way, we wouldn't have any more chance than Custer did. I don't know, son, I don't know…it could be the end of white men livin' in this part of the country. Maybe the west is meant to belong to the red man."

He shook his head. His eyes lingered on the rugged black and white pony I'd left tied outside.

"I swear, if that don't look like an Indian cayuse you're ridin'. What do you call him?"

"Name's Curly," I said around a mouthful of mashed potatoes. Actually, I hadn't even thought of what to call him until then, but that was his name from then on. The way he'd acted up on me a time or two before we got used to each other, I might as easily have called him by Curly's new name. But I doubted that would endear me to people who lived in the country I was moving through now.

Deadwood was almost as crowded as that big Indian encampment had been, and just as noisy. The wooden store building, hotels and many saloons lining both sides of the narrow, crowded street looked like they'd been slapped together about as fast as movie props over at little PRC Studios. Horses, mules, oxen and men jostled one another as they moved along that muddy, rutted thoroughfare and I saw at least two fistfights break out as I edged my way past them on horseback. Curly had gotten along fine on the grass and water whenever we'd stopped to camp along our trek, but he was clearly uneasy around so much civilization. I hoped he'd stay tied when I got off, jumpy as he was.

You might think it would be hard to find one man among so many, but not when that man was Wild Bill Hickok. The first person I asked pointed me right toward Nuttall & Mann's Number Ten Saloon and, sure enough, no sooner had I started toward it than I saw Bill coming out through its batwing doors.

I almost didn't recognize him at first. He was wearing some kind of darkened glasses. Today we'd call them sunglasses, and he'd fit right in with the Hollywood crowd. But in Deadwood in the summer of 1876, they looked weird.

"Bill! Hey, Bill."

His right hand disappeared under the coat he wore, but then he recognized me. "Kid! You made it."

For the next hour, we sat at a table getting a bite to eat and catching up with one another. Hickok had arrived in Deadwood four months ago, with some companions called Colorado Charlie and Calamity Jane. And he hadn't been the only one with a colorful reputation to try his luck here in the gold camps of the Black Hills.

"Earp's been here," he said. "Doc Holliday, too, but I think he was calling himself something else. Bat Masterson showed up, took one look around, and said he was going back to Cheyenne." Hickok gave his familiar chuckle, but then turned serious. "Some folks here wanted to pin a badge on me again. Wanted me to clean up Deadwood."

"Are you going to do it?"

He shook his head. "I've picked up some kind of eye inflammation. It's not getting any better," he said in a low voice. "Bright light hurts 'em. I get along okay indoors, but outside's different, especially on a sunny day. No, I'm making my stake at the card tables, kid. The guys who are doing all the digging and panning for gold ain't very good poker players. So I guess I won't be providing you much for your stories, will I?" he said with a trace of his old humor.

I can remember that conversation like it was yesterday. Bill and Charlie Utter and some of his other friends were living in a tent, just outside the main part of Deadwood. He invited me to join them. He said he'd missed me, that I reminded him of "old times" when he and the other shooters would gather around Tom Speers' Bench in Kansas City, and of some of the escapades he'd gone through before Abilene, where it all went wrong. "Even if my eyes were as good as ever," he said, "I'd never pin on a badge again."

Now I wish I had joined him and his friends. Maybe things would have turned out differently. But I wanted to get acquainted with Deadwood, learn what I could to bring verisimilitude to my writing, stuff like that. I told Bill I'd look him up tomorrow.

Bill drifted back to his poker, and I went out to find a stable for Curly. He didn't like stalls, it turned out. He tried to kick down the first one that the stable hand and I eased him into.

"What kind of wild pony you got there, mister?" the hand demanded.

I ended up persuading him to let me picket Curly in the little corral back of the stable. By the time I'd given him a rubdown and fed and watered him, the sky over Deadwood was getting as dark as the trees on the hills around it.

I bought myself a leisurely evening meal, soaking up the atmosphere and people-watching the same as I'd done in any number of towns. I'd become pretty good at it. Probably that was how I managed to spot the two men who were watching me.

They were both young guys, younger even than I was by then. The two leaned against the bar, seemingly in earnest discussion except for when they would take quick, furtive looks my way. They weren't good at subtlety. One of them had a slightly askew eye and a bent nose, but he was no one I'd seen before. The other, even across the smoke-filled room, looked eerily familiar to me but I couldn't figure out why.

When a man from the kitchen brought me the apple pie I'd ordered for dessert, I asked him about the pair. He said he didn't know but, when I slipped him a silver dollar and promised another if he could find out, he turned into the most enthusiastic sleuth you could imagine.

He was back before I finished the pie.

"The bartender knew one of 'em, the cockeyed gent—name of Jack McCall. Don't do much 'cept play cards, and usually loses. The youngster with him calls hisself Alias. Funny name, but it's the only one he'll give. He told one of 'em a pal of his named Billy Bonney pinned the name on him last year, back in Arizona."

The two young men had left the bar by now. I still wondered why the kid who called himself Alias seemed so familiar. "Who's this guy, Bonney?" I asked.

"Dunno, but Alias says this Bonney killed three Apaches for their guns and horses. An ambush, the way he told it. Don't know why he'd brag about that. But I guess it don't matter none, these days. Only good Indian's a dead Indian, right?"

"I doubt if the Indians see it that way."

He gave me a look that said I was even more stupid than he'd thought. His attitude once more made me a little ashamed of whatever white blood I had in me. But I could understand how he felt. Even here in the Dakotas, people were on edge all the time that this new confederation of Indians might move this way.

I was more careful than usual when I made my way through Deadwood's central street that night, checking to make sure neither of the two who'd seemed interested in me were anywhere around. I'd learned to trust my instincts in such matters, and my instincts told me they boded no good.

The stable hand had no objection to my bedding down in the stable that night, and I made myself a place in the loft so anybody who tried to find me would have problems. I slept with one of Jackson's pistols close to hand.

In my dreams, I was still looking for Jackson and, every time I'd spot him somewhere, he'd smile at me and fade away. Then I would see the late Ben Quinn, and the Silver Dollar Kid, and Cord McCluer, all coming after me on horseback. I could see McCluer's cold dead eyes, no matter how far away he seemed at any given time.

I snapped out of my dream and sat straight up. It was not quite sunrise, I could see through the slats in the barn, but it wasn't the dawning light that had wakened me. I realized where I had seen the kid who was calling himself Alias.

The foreboding I'd experienced last night came back in spades, as I pulled on my shirt and boots, ran a hand through my hair, and saddled Curly. I followed the directions Hickok had given me yesterday, riding out of town to where he and his friends had set up housekeeping. Hickok had not yet gotten up when I finally figured out which of the many tents was his. Another man at the tent told me Bill didn't usually arise until about noon. I scrounged a pan of water from him, enough to wash up and shave. I still didn't have to do that too often, but it had been a while.

Hickok had mentioned me to his tent-mates. Colorado Charlie Utter knew who I was before I had a chance to introduce myself, and seemed to take it for granted that I would be moving my bedroll in with them. I debated waking Bill to tell him what I'd remembered about Alias, but I couldn't see where the kid could be any potential problem for Bill. Just me, maybe.

He'd probably recognized me right away. I hadn't changed as much as he had, nor had I changed my appearance in any way, as I would when I thought there was a chance of running into McCluer or any of his playmates. It hadn't been all that long since the kid and I first saw each other, in that hovel where he'd lived back in New York.

I realized now he was Cord McCluer's boy, the one who'd recognized his father's spare pistol—which I supposed was now in the hands of some Sioux brave—and had been ready to come at me in spite of it. Maybe he was doing exactly that, right now. But how could he have managed to track me through all the country I'd traveled through coming to Deadwood? Even with McCluer for a father, the kid would be a tenderfoot—although it seemed, if his bragging meant anything, that he'd already managed a few kills with his friend, Bonney.

It sure hadn't taken him long to fall in with his father's kind of people.

What worried me most was the possibility that his father, too, might be lurking somewhere in Deadwood. Maybe he and his boy had gotten together. I hadn't strapped on Jackson's pistols; I was afraid that my sporting them might be taken as an invitation for some Deadwood tough to try and take them away from me. If I'd still had McCluer's less ostentatious pistol, I'd have stuck that in my belt. But at least neither he nor his kid could gun me and claim self-defense. Not that any such consideration ever stopped the elder McCluer, but those kills hadn't been in public.

I didn't spot either young McCluer or his friend from the night before as I roved through the town during what remained of the morning. I bought myself a leisurely late breakfast or early lunch, then resumed my exploration of Deadwood. I had found that anything I could soak up during forays through frontier towns would be valuable, just as Roy Barcroft finds new character traits and material for his grungy roles when he loses all identification and visits with unsavory characters along Poverty Row.

It was past mid-afternoon when I found myself approaching the Number Ten saloon where I'd met Hickok yesterday. I figured he'd probably be back there by now, dealing his cards, raking in winnings, and maybe telling that story again about how he'd been killed by all those Indians. I eased through the boisterous and noisy throng which, by now, filled the street as it had yesterday.

I heard what sounded like a shot. With all the clamor going on around me, I didn't think anything of it. In Deadwood, you could hear shooting at any hour.

Someone backed out through the saloon's swinging doors and brushed against me, knocking me off balance as he rushed by. I barely recognized him. It was the cross-eyed and broken-nosed Jack McCall.

I watched as he plowed through the crowd, leaving a few angry curses in his wake. I shrugged, and went on inside.

It took a few seconds for my eyes to adjust to the darker interior. And then I saw Bill, lying on the floor by a table, his legs drawn up as though he'd simply slid off his chair.

"Bill!"

An older man seated at the same table, with his back to the wall, gripped a bleeding arm. "Wild Bill shot me!" he was saying. Others stood around, staring down at where Bill lay.

"It wasn't Bill, Cap'n Massey," one of the others at the table told him. "Bill didn't draw. It must have been the bullet that hit him."

They figured out later that the one shot fired by McCall had passed through the back of Bill's head and struck the river boat captain. It all happened so fast that the captain, shocked to find himself wounded, hadn't realized where the shot came from.

I dropped down beside Bill, but it was obvious there was nothing I could do for him now. His fingers were still bent, as though holding invisible cards. There were several of them, aces and eights, scattered on the floor by him.

"Wild Bill Hickok is dead!" someone yelled from behind me. And then others took up the cry.

Even without thinking about it, I reached under Bill's coat and found a revolver he hadn't had a chance to use. I went back out the door, holding the gun down by my side.

Although it takes longer to tell it, less than half a minute had passed since

McCall bumped me while fleeing the scene. I looked in the direction where I'd seen him go, and there he was, starting to climb onto a horse. I raised the pistol, but there were too many people between us. He swung into the saddle and kicked the sides of the horse, which started galloping down the street. I hadn't a prayer of catching up to him on foot.

All at once, McCall tumbled from the horse, and I realized the entire saddle had come off with him. The horse ran on, as McCall staggered to his feet.

We learned later that the cinch on the saddle broke, but right then I thought only of the chance I'd been given to catch him.

Nobody else seemed interested in anything beyond Hickok's death. I guess they were all stunned. Wild Bill Hickok had always seemed larger than life, the stuff of legend to which even I had contributed bits and pieces. To think of him gone seemed unbelievable. If McCall had simply walked off through the crowd of people running up and down the street, he might have gotten away unnoticed.

He began to move again now but, by this time, I was right behind him holding Bill's pistol. He started to run, rounding the corner of a building. I went after him. I thought about trying to put a bullet into his leg, but he didn't seem armed now and I hesitated to shoot. I did wonder what had become of his gun.

When he turned around to see who was making the running footsteps behind him, I slammed him across the face with the barrel of Bill's revolver. With a cry, he fell back against the wall of the nearest building, holding his hands over his face. Deliberately, with my left hand, I hit him in the stomach. He doubled up, then slid down to a sitting position against the weathered wooden wall.

I stood over him and pointed the pistol. He looked up, and his eyes widened. "Double-Six," he said in a whisper.

The ramifications of that didn't sink in right away. "You shot Hickok."

He shook his head. "I ain't got nothin' to say…"

I snapped the pistol to within an inch of his crooked nose and thumbed back the hammer. It gave an ominous metallic click. "Why?"

"Don't shoot. My God, don't shoot. It was Alias. He paid me, told me I'd be a big man, even gave me a gun…"

He clamped his mouth shut as others came pounding up to where we were. I recognized one of them as the young bartender from the saloon. Before I could ask McCall anything further, three of the men seized him and dragged him away.

I was left standing there, holding a pistol on nobody. I put it away, and walked back to the saloon along with the bartender and several others.

"Bill hadn't wanted to sit with his back to the door," the bartender was saying. "The other three players kind of joked about it. Said nobody was going to shoot him in the back." He shook his head. "And that's just what happened."

When we re-entered the saloon, an undertaker was examining Bill's body. I waited around until they carried him all the way to his tent outside town. That was where he would be laid out for burial.

"Look at this," the young bartender said, picking up a pistol from the floor. "McCall's gun. He tried to take a shot at me with it, when I came over the bar after him. It must've misfired. He threw it at me before he backed out the door."

That explained why McCall had been unarmed when I caught up with him. And McCall had blurted out that the McCluer kid had provided him that gun, before he shut up.

"It misfired, you say?" I asked the bartender.

He nodded. I hung around a little longer, when they started examining the bullets. They found all but the first one, the one which came up under the hammer when the gun was cocked, had been defective and probably wouldn't have fired.

McCall had only one working bullet in that gun, and that was the one he had put in the back of Wild Bill's head.

Had the McCluer boy planned it that way? Had he meant for McCall to be left with a useless weapon after the first shot, and perhaps gunned down so he couldn't say who had put him up to it?

But why should the McCluer kid want Hickok dead? I didn't know, but I decided to stay in Deadwood long enough to find out.

# TWENTY-EIGHT

*Roy Rogers: "Ever hear what William Shakespeare said?*
*'All's well that ends well.'"*
*John Wayne: "Shakespeare, huh? He must have come from Texas.*
*We've been saying that for years."*
The Dark Command (1940)

They held Bill Hickok's funeral the day after he was killed. The grave marker was just a stump—I know it's been changed since then—with a few words carved on it:

"A brave man, a victim of an assassination, J. B. Hickok, age 39 years; murdered by Jack McCall, Aug. 2, 1876."

Townsmen convened a miners' court right after the funeral, and chose a jury to decide whether the carved words were true, whether McCall was legally a murderer. Twelve jurors, drawn from thirty-seven names written on slips of paper and placed in a hat, heard the bartender and two of the men in the card game testify that McCall walked up behind Hickok, said something like "Take that!" and fired, then ran for it. Three other men testified to McCall's "good character" and managed somehow to do it with straight faces.

Then McCall himself took the stand. He claimed Hickok had threatened to kill him. He also claimed to have been the brother of a man Hickok killed back in Hays City, and said he'd sworn to his mother on her death bed that he would avenge his brother.

Yep, it sounded like something right out of a dime novel. And, of course, it would be, eventually.

It was true that Hickok had killed a man in Hays City, a fellow called Jack Strawhan. Less successfully than McCall, Strawhan had tried to shoot Bill from behind in a saloon. I never found any relationship between Strawhan and McCall, other than both being back-shooters. But McCall's story suggested to me that someone who knew a few details about Bill's history might have coached McCall a bit.

Ninety minutes after retiring, the jury came back and found McCall not guilty.

I was standing in the back of the Bella Union, where the trial was being held, trying not to show my shock. I didn't want to make Bill's mistake and let anyone get behind me, especially not knowing where the McCluer boy, otherwise known as Alias, might be.

But it wasn't long before I spotted him, strolling out with a smirk after the verdict was announced. I followed him. I'd gotten good over the years at following people. Behind me, I overheard the prosecutor shouting that he just learned that two hundred ounces of gold dust had been slipped into the jury room during the proceedings. No one seemed to care. The onlookers were in too much of a celebratory mood to worry about a little detail like that. But I noticed that Alias' smile widened a bit when he overheard the prosecutor make that claim.

I wasn't a Pinkerton man but, as I say, I had become adept at shadowing without being noticed. In Deadwood, with so many people milling around, it was easy—much more so than it had been tracking Alias' father. With all the prospectors, gamblers and townspeople gabbing either about the trial or their latest worry that the Sioux who had wiped out Custer might move this way, there was too much activity for Alias to notice me.

It was several days before Alias finally rode out of Deadwood.

When I saw that he was buying trail supplies and packing up, I secured

Curly from the corral outside the livery stable, paid for his keep, and had him saddled and ready to go when Alias pulled out. Alias still looked to me like a kid who should be in school somewhere, except for the cold glint in his eyes. Just as I'd tracked his father across several states a decade earlier, I trailed after him for quite a while, staying anywhere from an hour to a day behind him. Another thing I'd cultivated over the years was patience.

The journey took us east, eventually into Minnesota, over several months. When he would drift into a town somewhere, I would take the opportunity to post a letter to Ginny or Stafford. Time in the saddle seemed to last forever, but it did pay off. Alias finally hooked up with his father.

It was in a town called Mankato, southwest of Minnesota. As had become my custom, I picked up changes of clothing at stores in towns we'd passed through. I'd learned a bit about applying makeup during my stint with Buffalo Bill's Wild West Show. In Mankato, I'd powdered some white into my hair and eyebrows, walked with a slight stoop, and wore a long coat to cover Jackson's gun belt which I'd thought it prudent to wear.

I'd concocted other disguises in other towns tracking Alias, but started to wonder if it wasn't a waste of effort. He never seemed to have any inkling that he was being watched. This time, it probably saved my life. Cord McCluer would have been more watchful than his son.

I recognized McCluer's gaunt figure the minute I saw him, seated in a restaurant into which I'd followed his son. I did my thing at taking my own midday meal at a table close to theirs, sitting with my back to them—and don't think I didn't have cold chills over the possibility that Cord McCluer might recognize me.

It was too noisy to hear everything they said, but I managed to pick up a few words. I heard Hickok's name mentioned, and something about having made sure he wouldn't help nail "the boys," whoever they were. I heard a mention of the First National Bank of Mankato. And most importantly, I heard Cord McCluer say the colonel's son was on hand to coordinate the upcoming bank jobs.

As soon as they left, I paid my bill and slouched outside in their wake. I saw them stop to talk to a group of four horsemen, but couldn't recognize any of the mounted men, and I wasn't about to move closer. I eased my frame into a chair under the restaurant awning, pulled my hat down as though napping in the noonday sun, and watched them from under its brim.

And then I had a rare stroke of luck.

A man in work clothes came walking past the little group, and came to an abrupt halt. He peered up at one of the horsemen. "Hallo, Jesse," the man said. "What are you doing up here?"

One of the men stiffened visibly in the saddle. "Hell, man," the horseman said, "I don't know you." With that, he turned his horse down the street and walked it away. He gave a slight jerk of his head to the other mounted men, and they moved their horses in the same direction, away from the man who had spoken. McCluer and his son came walking back my way, and I sat perfectly still until they passed.

Then I got up, stretched, and ambled along after the man who had greeted the horseman. Once we had gotten some distance away, I started a conversation with him, and worked it around to the man he'd seemed to recognize.

"Well, I really thought it was Jesse James," he said, shaking his head. "I seen him a few times when I lived down Missouri way."

That was what I'd thought he'd meant. But what would Jesse James be doing this far north? Well, what would Jesse James be doing wherever he happened to be? I decided my best bet was to keep an eye on that band of horsemen, even if it meant losing the McCluers for a while. But I'd have to be even more careful than I had been. If these were members of the James gang, they would be more watchful than McCluer's son. And I couldn't forget what had happened to the Pinkerton detective who'd gotten too close to the Jameses.

But none of the gang knew me by sight, as the McCluers did. And I knew them from my visit to the area around the Samuels farm in Missouri, where I'd watched their comings and goings.

By nightfall, the four horsemen I'd followed from Mankato had pulled up at an inn just outside of Northfield, where several more men joined them. I figured it would have been suicide to follow them inside the place. But I recognized Cole and Bob Younger among the newcomers. And Frank James.

Early the next morning, I was still in Northfield. There was a First National Bank here, too. Could the gang have switched targets, since Jesse had been recognized in Mankato?

I'd long since washed the powder out of my hair and looked more or less like myself. I'd made sure, first, that McCluer hadn't joined up with this bunch. In walking through the town, I noticed that its citizenry didn't routinely go about armed as many did in frontier towns. My own gunbelt would have looked out of place, so instead I stuck Hickok's pistol in my belt hidden beneath my coat.

I made a quick armament inventory. The only available weapons I saw were in the town's hardware stores. There didn't seem to be a gun shop.

"Help you?" A man in a white shirt and black vest smiled at me in one of the hardware places, where I was looking at a shotgun on display on a store rack.

"Just looking," I said. "Do you carry ammunition for your rifles and shotguns?"

"Sure do. You know, you're the second man who's asked me about that."

I felt a stab of alarm. "Really. Who was the other man?"

"Never saw him before. He was a stranger here, like you. Big man, though. Hair was starting to thin, big bushy mustache. Had another fellow with him. Another stranger, I think. Came in yesterday, checking out our line of guns."

Now I was more convinced than ever about Northfield being a target. The Jameses and Youngers had learned during their time as guerillas about reconnoitering a town before a raid. That was exactly what the two men had been doing.

I turned to the clerk. "Listen, I've heard there's a band of bank robbers in this part of Minnesota. You might want to think about keeping some of your guns loaded, in case those two were some of their advance men."

He stared at me. "You serious?"

I nodded, and left.

It was later that morning when they came, three of them riding leisurely across a small iron bridge toward the town square. All three wore linen dusters, but I recognized two of them when they dismounted—Bob Younger and Jesse James.

There are times when people somehow know they're being watched intently, and I figured that sense was well developed in these men. I was careful not to look directly at them, just glimpse them out of the corner of my eye and direct my concentration elsewhere while leaning against the outside of the store. I tried not to even think about them. Did you ever try to not think about something? You can't.

The men walked around the square. Checking out the bank, no doubt, and the buildings nearest to it. Apparently satisfied, all three ambled into a restaurant. I drifted that way myself, and came through the door in time to hear them order ham and eggs.

I knew what was coming. I could feel it. They would have the rest of their group waiting for a signal, or maybe they'd set a time already.

The three took their time eating. That gave me a chance to pick the spot where I wanted to be when things started happening. I chose the top of one of the buildings around the square, once I saw it could be reached from an interior stairway leading to its roof. But first I went back to the hardware store and found the clerk.

"I don't want to buy a rifle," I said, "but could I rent one?"

He looked at me as though waiting for the punch line. "Sounds like you really think those bank robbers are coming," he said.

"They're here already," I told him. "Three of them are sitting over there in Jeft's Restaurant having a meal."

He started to laugh again, but caught himself. "You're not kidding," he said. "Who are you, anyway? Why should I believe you?"

I'd been expecting that question and I was ready for it. I reached into my coat where I had two folded wanted posters, one on the James brothers and one on the Youngers. "Got a pencil?" I asked. He gave me one, and I circled the picture of Jesse James on one poster and Bob Younger on the other.

"If you're real careful about it," I said, "you can go see those two over in the restaurant right now."

His eyes widened, but it was the picture of Cole Younger at which he pointed. "That's one of them who was in here yesterday!" he breathed.

Without another word, he reached up on the rack behind him and lifted down a Remington repeater. He set out a box of shells from under the counter, and pushed them both toward me. Then he went out the door, almost at a run.

I loaded the rifle and walked out after him, more slowly. I made my way to the store I'd checked out earlier, near the bank. Inside, a clerk and two customers stared at me as I walked toward the rooftop stairway in the rear with the rifle. I jerked my thumb over my shoulder in the direction of the hardware store.

"The clerk over there just spotted some wanted bank robbers here in town," I told them. "He's loaning out guns, if you want to get one."

I didn't wait to see whether they believed me. I had barely gotten up to the roof when I heard the gallop of horses and the first shots below. I crept to the edge and peered down at the street.

Three more horsemen had come over the bridge, whooping and firing their guns. Two more came from the opposite end of the street, doing much the same thing. I was watching for the three men I knew had been already here, and saw them running into the bank.

Later, we would learn that one of the cashiers tried to bluff Jesse, telling him the safe had a time lock on it and couldn't be opened. Jesse struck him with a revolver, leaving him stunned on the floor. When the bandits were on their way out of the bank, Jesse turned back long enough to shoot and kill him. Yeah, Jesse was a real Robin Hood.

Another teller burst out of the bank door. He staggered and clutched his shoulder, but managed to make it around a corner and into an alley.

While all this was happening, I brought my borrowed rifle to the roof's edge. I aimed at one of the horsemen below who was firing indiscriminately at people running on the street. I squeezed the trigger but, if I hit him, it didn't slow him down any.

By now, though, I wasn't the only one shooting. Others had obviously armed themselves and were giving the outlaws a reception like they'd never had.

One of the riders tumbled from his saddle as a shotgun blast left him bloodied but alive. He got to his feet, grabbed his horse and climbed back on, but was promptly knocked off by another shot. This time, he didn't get up.

I spotted an unarmed townsman gawking at the horses jumping all around him, seeming not to comprehend what was going on. I yelled down at him to get away, get under cover. I don't know if he heard me, but it was too late, anyway. One of the horsemen dropped him with a single shot. Two or three more bullets struck the edge of the roof close to me. I'd just given away my position.

I eased back, counted slowly to ten, and peeked down from a different part of the roof, hoping none of the shooters down there was waiting for me to pop up. Three outlaws from the bank were making for their horses. One of the other horsemen outside threw up his hands and tumbled from his saddle. A hat flew off the head of another, as they all prepared to flee.

A horse being ridden by one of the robbers took a hit and tumbled over. The rider must have been hit, too. At least he was limping when he got up and moved farther into the street, where another rider swung back and picked him up.

Long afterward, when the townspeople put all the pieces together, we would find that it had been Bob Younger who lost his horse, and his brother, Cole, having already taken a hit himself, who came back for him.

I tried a shot at another rider and saw dust fly from a spot on his leg. But he stayed on his horse as the gang raced out of town.

It was over.

Nobody paid me much attention when I climbed down from the roof and went out through the store. I walked to the hardware building, empty at the moment, and left the Remington on the counter.

Outside, I heard excited comments from various folks and learned about the cashier being killed as the inside men left the bank. I saw the bodies of two of the would-be robbers lying in the street.

I didn't realize it then, but Northfield was the beginning of the end for the James gang. Within a few days, a posse caught up with all three Younger brothers along with a fourth robber. All four had been shot up pretty badly, and the fourth man died of his wounds.

The Youngers all recovered. All three went to prison. Bob Younger would die of tuberculosis in 1889 in the Stillwater Penitentiary. James Younger would be paroled in 1901; a year later, he would pick up a gun and commit suicide. Cole got out in 1903. He actually became a respected citizen, living until 1916, one year longer than Frank James. Frank died in his old bedroom on the Samuels farm. Cole and Frank did work together one last time, in 1903, but not robbing banks. They were appearing together in a wild west show.

Dennis Morgan played Cole sympathetically in *Bad Men of Missouri* nine years ago. Maybe you saw it. Wayne Morris, who'd played Bob Younger in that one, played Cole just last year in *The Younger Brothers*. The scripts made it seem like the big bad railroad drove them into banditry, the same way it was portrayed when Tyrone Power played the title role in *Jesse James* back in 1939, and Henry Fonda repeated his role of Frank in *Return of Frank James* a year later. Heck, even Don Barry and Roy Rogers have played Jesse as a decent guy. Dale Robertson made him seem positively cuddly last year in *Fighting Man of the Plains*, where he even saved Randolph Scott from the bad guys at the end.

And Clayton Moore, the actor behind the mask in that new Lone Ranger TV show, made it seem like Jesse was framed for almost everything he ever did in two movie serials over at Republic. I doubt that any of those killed during Jesse's robberies would see him in that light.

Frank and Jesse didn't get out of Northfield unscathed. Frank had a leg wound and was hit again, as was Jesse, when the two of them made a run on a single horse through a line of pickets shortly before the Youngers were captured. The Jameses dropped out of sight after that, for the next three years.

Then, with a new gang, they started robbing trains again. The railroads upped the rewards, until one of Jesse's gang gave in to temptation and shot him in the back at Jesse's home, where he was living under the name of Howard. You've probably heard the ballad:

"But the dirty little coward, who shot Mr. Howard, has laid poor Jesse in his grave…"

Sorry, I'm not much of a singer. After Jesse's death, Frank gave himself up, but the gang's public relations machine had built his legend sufficiently that he was let off in two trials, one in Mississippi and the other in Alabama. I guess the way Bob Ford killed Jesse contributed to the sympathy. Frank ended up working as a starter at a race track, except for his in-person time with Cole Younger.

And I ended up going back to California after Northfield, to bring Leland Stanford up to date. It would be six more years before Jesse's death, but his gang would never again approach the power it once had, and as Colonel Sutherland no doubt hoped it would. There were claims by government officials that fear of the James gang had actually slowed western migration and national development. Sutherland would love that. But it wouldn't do so any more. The gang that grew out of Civil War guerilla bands had finally been broken.

# INTERMISSION

*If Clay McCluer, Jr., had used a single gun as a hired killer and notched it for every hit he made, he would have whittled its handle down to nothing by now. And yet, here he was, actually sweating in fear of the frail old man seated behind the desk in front of him—a man he could have pushed aside with one hand, if he dared.*

*Such a thought would never occur to him. It would be like sticking his hand into a den of rattlesnakes.*

*"You're a disappointment to me, young Mr. McCluer," Old Man Sutherland said in his raspy voice. "Your grandfather would have had the job done weeks ago. Even your father might have managed it. And you call yourself a professional."*

*McCluer could feel the sweat trickling down his back, sticking his shirt to his skin. This old man was not someone you could disappoint.*

*"Mr. Sutherland," he said, "it's like I told you. I had everything set up, but he had visitors right then. It was a bad break, but I couldn't go back right away dressed as a doctor. I wouldn't be around long if I repeated myself..."*

*"Would you like to know who those visitors were, young Mr. McCluer? One of them was a Los Angeles police detective. The other was a police stenographer. Do I have to tell you what Mr. Six has been telling them, young Mr. McCluer?"*

*McCluer stood straighter. "No sir."*

*The Old Man nodded. "That's right, young Mr. McCluer. It's very likely about the organization I've built up over the years. The one my father started almost a century ago. You know more about it than most members, because your grandfather was one of the—ah, facilitators, shall we say. Blood is thicker than* water, young Mr. McCluer. That is obvious, the way you have followed in your grandfather's and your father's footsteps. That's why I'm disappointed in your not having finished the job I had arranged over at Sunset and Gower. At least it put him in the hospital, where it should have been easy for you to get at him."

McCluer agreed. But who could have guessed at all the allies that turned up to protect the target at Gower Gulch?

"If the authorities ever learn about me, young Mr. McCluer, you must realize they will learn about a lot of others, including you."

McCluer was tempted to say that, if the job had been done right at Gower, it wouldn't be necessary for him to clean it up now. But he didn't. He knew how much power the Old Man wielded. Although it now seemed that he might not command as much loyalty as old John Six did.

So he kept his mouth shut. He knew the man's tentacles reached throughout the country. While McCluer might hide from the authorities, he doubted he could hide long from the Old Man.

He swallowed. "I won't miss him next time, sir."

"See that you don't, young Mr. McCluer. See that you don't."

# TWENTY-NINE

*Audie Murphy: "Nobody takes my guns."*
The Kid from Texas (1950)

It's hard to believe so many things happened in just a single year: Wild Bill's death, the Custer massacre, the Younger Brothers all caught, and the beginning of the breakup of the James gang. But it all happened in 1876.

I didn't think there could be a year like that again—that is, until five years later. But we aren't through with 1876 yet.

Jack McCall didn't stay free long. He just couldn't keep his mouth shut about how he'd killed the greatest gunfighter of them all, and even re-enacted how he'd done it for any audience who would pay to watch. He made the mistake of doing that in Laramie, without knowing there was a deputy marshal among the spectators.

The marshal arrested him on the spot. It turned out that the miners' court in Deadwood had not been a legal tribunal, which took care of any argument about double jeopardy when he was tried again in Yankton. This time, the jury stayed out about five hours, until midnight, before finding him guilty.

McCall was hanged on March 1, 1877.

And I never got the chance to interview him, to try and get him to confirm publicly what he'd blurted out when I held Bill's six-gun on him—that the man called Alias had been part of the murder plot. I'd overheard enough in that conversation between McCluer and his son to know why: because Colonel Sutherland, or Sean, or maybe both, were afraid that the famous Wild Bill Hickok might somehow get on the trail of their outlaw army. Maybe they thought he'd even help me. There was no way they could have known that Bill had given up all that after Abilene.

A full confession from McCall might have uncovered the colonel's treason right then. Now I was left with just one lead: young McCluer, or Alias.

Leland Stanford still headed up the Central Pacific, and had enough pull with the Pinkertons for them to send him word if Alias resurfaced. During one of my visits with him in San Francisco, he got involved in a wager that would help create my future career, although neither of us knew it then.

He bet another man $25,000 that a galloping horse, at some point, would have all four hooves off the ground. To collect, though, he had to prove it.

Stanford hired an English photographer named Eadweard Muybridge—I'll spell that for you, Miss Nancy…to take care of that little problem. And darned if Muybridge didn't come up with a way to do it.

He set up a dozen cameras along a race track and attached trip-wires to them. Then he had someone gallop past them on horseback. As the horse tripped each wire, the camera snapped a picture. When Muybridge put all the photos together, sure enough, one showed the horse with all four feet off the ground.

Stanford won his bet, and Muybridge became intrigued enough with his idea of shooting pictures in sequence to look for a way to project them. He took his idea to—well, you know who, Thomas Edison, who created a "kinetoscope viewer," as they called it. The way that worked, you'd drop in a penny and peep into a viewer for a minute's worth of moving pictures. Those viewers became very popular. Rows of them lined penny arcades all over the country.

Then Edison developed a projector, so more than one person at a time could watch his little movies—everything from circus acrobats to vaudeville performers, not to mention western subjects like Indian dances, bronc riding, and even little Annie Oakley's trick shooting in a 1894 film.

But I'm getting ahead of myself. Something else happened, which was of more immediate importance to me than western history, or even what would become motion pictures. I proposed to Ginny Wells.

"Marry you?" she said, eyes twinkling mischievously. "Why should I marry you? I'm already cooking your meals, mending your clothes, taking care of Stardust and Curly when you're not off riding them somewhere across the country..."

"That's my point," I said with a straight face. "You're doing all that already, so why not—but never mind, if you're not interested..."

"I didn't say that!" She grabbed me by both ears and laid the biggest kiss on me I've had before or since.

For a few years after that, I was pretty much a homebody. We set up housekeeping in Utah, and the income from my magazine pieces supported us. I was writing stuff under various names by then, none of them my own. If they'd left us alone, I might still be doing it.

I never did get to see Curly—not my horse, but the Indian who changed his name to Crazy Horse—again. A soldier bayoneted him at Fort Robinson in Nebraska, after he supposedly pulled a knife after being told he was going to be locked up. That was in 1877, the same year that the Texas Rangers finally caught up with John Wesley Hardin and packed him off to prison.

Early the next year, an English rancher who'd established himself in New Mexico was shot and killed, supposedly for resisting arrest. People had the same kind of doubts about that as they'd had about Crazy Horse's knife. Besides ranching, John Henry Tunstall had been a partner in a store in Lincoln County, and had threatened the monopoly another group had been enjoying for a long time.

His death was the start of what they were calling the Lincoln County War.

I wasn't interested at the time, except, naturally, for its use as possible story material. The only thing I was interested in was that Ginny was carrying our child.

If only they had let us be!

Sorry, I didn't mean to choke up. The memory still gets me. She and I were eating supper in the little home we'd built not far from her mother's place. I was grousing about having to keep Star and Curly corralled or stabled separately to keep them from getting into a kicking contest. Funny, the things you remember. They'd both gotten a little spoiled, and each thought he should get the most attention from Ginny and me.

Then the shots rang out.

Five or six shots, the neighbors guessed later. All I really heard was the window glass breaking and something knocked me out of my chair and onto the floor.

We'd become so civilized in recent years that I didn't even keep firearms handy. I pulled myself up and crawled to the broken window, in time to see three men on horseback wheel around and ride out of our garden as other doors of nearby homes opened.

One of the riders turned and spotted me. He threw another shot my way. It missed. The flash from the gun showed me his face. To a lesser extent, it illuminated the faces of his companions. I didn't recognize either of them. But I recognized Alias.

"Ginny," I called, as I began to turn from the window, "it's all right now. They're pulling out..."

That was when I saw Ginny lying by the table, eyes shut, a red stain spreading across the front of her dress. I remember screaming her name, trying to stand up and go to her but my left leg collapsed under me. I had blood on myself, too.

As it turned out, I had bullets through my leg and shoulder, but had been too much in shock to feel them until I fell back onto the floor. The shoulder wound had been in and out, but they had to dig for the bullet in my thigh. That's why I still have a little limp today—same reason we gave for Bill Boyd's "Hopalong Cassidy" character in that first Hoppy movie.

I don't know if it was from pain or loss of blood, but I passed out several times between when I was hit and when a doctor removed the bullet. They told me I'd call Ginny's name every time I got semi-conscious, but I never heard what they tried to tell me about her. Not until later. Maybe I just didn't want to hear it.

It was Letty, Ginny's mother, who broke the news, once I was awake enough to comprehend it.

"She has a fighting chance, John. They got the bullet out of her, too. Doc Stark thinks it's a good sign that she's held on this long. He says things can only get better, the longer she's stable."

I breathed a sigh of relief. Ginny might not be out of the woods, but she was a fighter. But then I saw the tears in Letty's eyes.

"What else?" I asked weakly.

She put a hand on my uninjured shoulder. "The baby, John. She lost the baby."

It turned out to be worse than that. The damage from the bullet left Ginny so she could never have another child. I remember trying to get up, wanting to go to her right away, but Letty said she needed rest more than anything, and it turned out I couldn't walk yet, anyway.

When I finally could, I sat myself in a chair beside her bed and thanked the stars Letty was there to feed and wait on us until we could take care of ourselves again. Ginny's recovery took longer than mine, physically and emotionally. One minute, she'd be joking about something, and then she'd dissolve in tears. That always scared me, since that was so un-Ginny-like.

"I wanted to give you children," she sobbed. I said something about her being the most important thing to me, but that just made her angry.

I waited until she'd been on her feet for a couple of months before I told her I was going to do some wandering again.

"I need to do some fresh research for the writing," I explained. "I'm just re-doing the same old plots right now."

Ginny wasn't fooled. "You don't need to do research. You just make it all up, anyway. You're going looking for them, aren't you?"

"Who?"

"Don't treat me like I'm stupid, Johnny."

Reluctantly, I nodded. She was exactly right.

"I got a telegram last week from Mr. Stanford," I said. "It turns out that this Billy Bonney I heard Alias mention is making quite a name for himself down in New Mexico. If he and Alias were partners before, they might have gotten back together."

She turned away from me.

"I don't want you to go," she said in a small voice. "Not now. I'm afraid you won't come back."

"I'll come back." What I didn't tell her was, now that the colonel's people obviously knew where we lived, my best hope of keeping her safe was to keep myself away from her—at least until I put paid to the hired shooters. That should put a crimp in the colonel's plans.

I did explain all that to Letty. I didn't want her to think I was abandoning her daughter at a time like this. But her reaction was different from Ginny's.

"Good!" she said. "When you find them, put an extra bullet into each one for me."

# THIRTY

*Brian Donlevy: "Don't you get fed up sometimes?"*
*Robert Taylor: "Fed up with what?"*
*Brian Donlevy: "Oh, rollin' around like a tumbleweed, being hunted,*
*and never knowin' who's behind the next rock. I mean..."*
*Robert Taylor: "I know what you mean. I like it!"*
Billy the Kid (1941)

Star was no youngster anymore, but he was still a good, dependable horse. So I took him on this journey—first by rail car, then on trails like those he'd gotten used to over the years. Again, it was often a matter of camping out nights, staying in stables with him and the occasional hotel at other times, and always asking if anyone remembered three horsemen whom I would describe. By the time I crossed the border into New Mexico, I had even better descriptions of the two who had been with Alias, as well as some possible names—Clanton and Ringo.

It was a cold day in December, 1880, when Star and I rolled into Las Vegas, and into trouble right off. A train was parked at a small depot up ahead of us, and a mob of Mexicans and whites milled angrily around it, brandishing rifles and six-guns.

I tied Star to a hitching post, and loosened his cinch a bit, all the while watching the crowd. Everyone was concentrating on one of the train cars. I didn't have any trouble easing my way into the throng.

A bearded fellow bumped into me, and I asked him what was going on. "That Lincoln County sheriff's got some prisoners on that there train car," he told me. "We're gonna take one of 'em away and string him up to a telegraph pole."

"Who are you after?" I asked.

"Name's Dave Rudabaugh. He killed one of our jailers. But now that sheriff wants to take him to Santa Fe, on some other charges."

About that time, a tall man with a healthy mustache stepped out onto the platform of the car we were all surrounding. I found myself pushed forward as those around me surged in his direction. I tried unsuccessfully to back away from where I'd be uncomfortably close to any shooting that broke out.

"Go home, you men," the tall man call out, his voice carrying above the voices of the crowd. "I've got deputies inside with the prisoners. If you try and take them, some of you aren't going to be around tomorrow."

"Hang 'em all!" the bearded man next to me yelled. "The Kid, too." I wondered if he might be talking about Alias, who would be a pretty young outlaw. All this had just become more interesting.

Others took up the shouts. "Give 'em up, Garrett," another man yelled. "This train ain't leavin' 'til we get 'em. We done took the engineer off'n it."

The tall man held up a hand for silence and, such was his presence, he actually got it. "Besides being sheriff," he said, "I'm commissioned a deputy United States marshal. Rudabaugh's under arrest for mail robbery and that's a federal offense. The Kid's wanted for murder on Indian land, government land. That ranks any local charges. So, clear away, all of you."

Three or four men had circled behind Garrett and now surged onto the train car and grabbed him. One of them got hold of his pistol, jerking it from its holster and tossing it down into the crowd in front of him. The sheriff managed to shove all of them back away but, when he reached for his sidearm, it wasn't there. I could see the surprise on his face when he found his holster empty.

"Sheriff!" I called, and tossed up the spare pistol I'd had in my belt under my coat. It was the pistol I'd picked up from beside Hickok's body when I'd gone after McCall. With Bill dead, nobody had ever asked me for it and I didn't feel inclined to give it up, especially after the Deadwood populace had auctioned off Bill's other weapons to cover burial costs.

The tall man snatched it neatly out of the air, and swung it toward the closest members of the mob. He seemed pretty angry at having been disarmed.

"Now, damn it, back off," he said between clenched teeth. And, this time, they did.

Soon, the area around the train car was clear, and I drifted away myself, making my way back to Star. A few minutes later, the wheels of the engine up ahead began clanking against the track, and the rest of the cars began to move. I guess they'd found the engineer.

I decided not to hang around, lest someone in the mob realize I'd been the one who tossed that pistol to the sheriff. I untied Star and walked off, before it might occur to anyone to take his frustration out on me. I checked Star's cinch, and paused long enough before mounting up to get Jackson's twin guns out of my saddlebags and buckle them beneath my coat, just in case.

It was several days later when I arrived in Santa Fe, and found a stable for my horse and a hotel that supplied bathwater. I was signing the register when I felt a hand on my shoulder—the one still sore from that bullet wound—and turned around ready to fight or flee.

"Easy, friend, easy," the tall man with the badge said, smiling down at me. "I just wanted to thank you for the loan of that pistol. I recognized you when you came in just now. I'd like to buy you a drink, if you'll permit me."

He ended up buying me lunch. He introduced himself as Pat F. Garrett, recently-elected sheriff of Lincoln County, and proved an easy man to talk with. I decided he would do well in politics. I steered our conversation to the identity of the men he'd had as prisoners. It turned out that the one referred to as the Kid had not been the youthful McCluer, but McCluer's pal, Billy Bonney, apparently better known nowadays as Billy the Kid.

"We arrested Billy and three of his men when our posse surrounded them in an old house near Stinking Springs," he told me. "Killed a fifth man getting them out."

I told Garrett I was interested in finding another "kid" called Alias, whom I'd heard hung out with Billy. Garrett knew who I was talking about. He said Alias and Billy had been involved in the robbing and killing of some Indians. "But the one you call Alias hasn't been seen around here since then, far as I know," he said.

He put down the coffee cup from which he'd been sipping, reached under his coat and pulled out a pistol I recognized.

"I appreciate the loan of this," he said with a chuckle. "They kind of caught me with my pants down. I'm sure you want it back. Fine workmanship, one of the best guns I've ever handled."

"It ought to be." I told him who'd owned it, and how it wound up with me. "Why don't you keep it? I'm sure Mr. Hickok would have liked it being used on the side of the law again."

"Hickok's gun." Garrett handled it with new deference. That was when he insisted on at least paying for my meal, and indicated he'd do me about any other favor I might want. All I wanted was to find Alias and his two partners in crime, but I didn't tell Garrett that. He might not have favored my wanting to do to them what the mob had wanted to do to his prisoners.

Having gotten indications from those who recognized his description that Alias had been on his way to this part of the country, I decided to hang around at least for Billy Bonney's trial. Alias just might turn up in the audience, as he had in McCall's miners' court hearing.

It turned out to be several trials. In the first one, the Kid was acquitted in the death of a man named Buckshot Roberts, who had shot it out with some of the late Mr. Tunstall's ranch hands on Mescalero Apache land three years earlier. Billy had been with the bunch, but they couldn't prove he'd been the one to kill Roberts.

Billy wasn't so lucky with his second trial. That time, he was charged with killing a former Lincoln County sheriff, William Brady. Brady and two other men had been ambushed in downtown Lincoln on April Fool's Day two years earlier. The shootings had been part of the Lincoln County War, in which Brady was allied with the merchants competing with the Tunstall group.

The violence that followed Brady's death got so bad that President Hayes appointed Lew Wallace, a Civil War general, as territorial governor and declared Lincoln County to be in a state of insurrection. Wallace finally managed to end the war by issuing pardons to all those who agreed to put away their guns. But Billy never did that, even after a personal meeting with the governor.

I watched Billy closely during those trials, figuring I might be writing about him. He wasn't a bad-looking youngster, despite his buck teeth. But I can't say he resembled Johnny Mack Brown, Roy Rogers, Jack Beutel or Robert Taylor, all of whom would play him in movies at one time or other. In size, he was closer to Bob Steele. Or maybe to Audie Murphy, the young war hero who played him this year—and then turned around and played a young Jesse James next.

Bobby Steele had teamed up with Al St. John, better known as "Fuzzy Q. Jones," over at PRC for a Billy the Kid series. Talk about a white-washed version of Billy. Then Buster Crabbe took over the role. Buster is a strapping Olympic athlete, certainly nothing like skinny little Billy. But some PTA groups began protesting movies making a hero out of an outlaw, and I have to say I agreed. Anyway, Buster quit being Billy the Kid, and became Billy Carson still with Fuzzy as sidekick, and the series sailed right on.

The real Billy was convicted of being involved in Brady's murder, and the judge sentenced him to be hanged "until you are dead, dead, dead." Billy responded, "And you can go to Hell, Hell, Hell."

But he didn't stay around long enough to be hanged. Someone slipped him a gun. He killed two guards and escaped, leaving Garrett with the job of tracking him down all over again.

I'd wanted to question Billy about Alias, but that wasn't a favor Garrett could arrange. And then Billy was gone. I didn't figure I had a chance of finding him. I was no man-hunter and, besides, I was a stranger in a territory where the Kid had friends. If I kept an eye on Garrett, though, I thought I might get a lead on Billy's whereabouts, and then maybe Alias. Pretty thin, but it was all I had.

Garrett was an impressive six-foot-four, and actually better looking than his early movie counterparts like Wallace Beery, or Wade Boteler, or Thomas Mitchell. Monte Hale, who just played an early version of him over at Republic, came closer but Monte is actually too clean-cut.

People complained that Garrett didn't seem all that anxious to find Billy. But I'd gotten to know Garrett a little bit in the weeks I'd been hanging around, and he confided to me that he wanted to compile information on the quiet side before he acted. Once he figured out where the Kid was hiding, he'd move.

Later on, he took a couple of men on what he told folks was a business trip to Arizona. But they really rode to Roswell, and then Fort Sumner, checking out tips on the Kid's whereabouts. It was in Sumner that Garrett and the Kid came face to face.

They met in a dark room at Pete Maxwell's ranch, where the Kid had taken refuge. The Kid made the mistake walking into the room with Garrett there. Garrett recognized his voice, and fired.

You know, Garrett became one of the first actual figures of the historic west to tell his own version of events. He wrote an account of his hunt for the Kid—or, some say, newspaperman Ash Upson wrote it while clerking for him. The book came out in April, 1882, almost a year after the fatal confrontation.

There had already been eight quickie dime novels about Billy, since his death. Their shootout had nothing to do with a fast draw or anything like that. Garrett simply shot first, maybe even with the Hickok gun. He made no bones about it.

When someone accused Garrett of writing the book to make money, Garrett replied, "What the Hades else do you suppose my object would be?" I liked that.

He also made the point that, if Billy had realized the situation first, it might have been Garrett who'd ended up on the floor. Unfortunately, Billy's death at the age of twenty-one ended any hopes of my using him to track down Alias.

But by then, Leland Stanford had come up with a lead for me.

# THIRTY-ONE

*Roy Barcroft: "The president must die! When that coach*
*comes into town, he dies! Do you hear me? He dies!"*
Code of the Silver Sage (1950)

S tanford's informants had located the other two names I'd come up with—
Clanton and Ringo. It turned out there was a whole family of Clantons,
ranching, if you could call it that, in Cochise County, Arizona, and one of their
associates was a gunman called Johnny Ringo. I had no way to be sure they
were the men who, along with Alias, had injured Ginny and killed our child.
But it seemed very possible.

That wasn't the only news I got during that busy year of 1881.

The other news was that James Garfield, who'd been inaugurated as
president on March 4, had been wounded by a would-be assassin on July 2.
The gunman was described as an anarchist, but I couldn't help wondering if the
treasonous hand of the Sutherlands was involved.

Garfield did die two months afterward. Chester Arthur became our new
president.

Billy the Kid had met his demise on July 14 of that year. About a month
later, Star and I ambled into Tombstone, the seat of Cochise County. The place
had been born out of a silver strike, made by a man named Ed Schieffelin. A
well-known scout named Al Sieber once told Schieffelin that the only thing he'd

find, prospecting in Apache territory, was his tombstone. Schieffelin chose that name for the place.

Lots of its residents did end up under tombstones, including its last marshal, Fred White. White had been trying to disarm a cowboy called "Curly Bill" Brocius who had been in the process of shooting up the town's main street. In the struggle, Brocius' pistol went off—by accident, Brocius would claim—and fatally wounded the lawman. The town appointed a man named Virgil Earp to succeed him.

Tombstone had hundreds of stories, and I was able to write some of them for well-paying magazines. The town had four newspapers, the Expositor, the Evening Gossip, the Nugget and the Epitaph. Those last two represented the two competing factions and political groups.

The Epitaph was run by Tombstone's first mayor, John Clum. He'd started it just over a year earlier. I showed him enough of my publishing credits to get a temporary reporting job with him.

Clum had led quite a life. He'd been an Indian agent at the San Carlos Apache reservation, and was one of the few white men at that time who treated the Indians fairly. He had organized a tribal police force and used it to capture Geronimo without a shot being fired. Clum lasted three years before resigning in disgust, dogged by an Indian Bureau and military people who disagreed with his methods. His successor freed Geronimo, which resulted in fifteen more years of war with the Apaches until General Nelson Miles caught him again.

The rival paper's editor was Harry Woods—no, not the actor who plays bad guys in westerns, but the name is an interesting coincidence. Roy Barcroft, an even badder movie guy, once told me he modeled his acting style on Woods. Interesting coincidence, since Woods' paper, the Nugget, tended to support the lawless element in Tombstone.

I learned a lot of history from Clum, during the hours I helped him set type late at night, and not only about Geronimo. In his view, the Clantons' ranch was a cover for cattle rustling, most of the cattle coming from across the line in

Mexico and blatantly sold in Tombstone. Old Man Clanton, the patriarch of the clan, had been killed by Mexicans during one of those rustling forays, at about the same that Pat Garrett caught up with Billy the Kid in New Mexico.

Like I said, a busy year.

Clum doubted that the old man's sons—Phin, Ike and Billy—had what it took to keep the ranch going. Their hired hands, he said, were not cowboys but gunmen, like Brocius and Ringo. He thought Ringo might have been related to the Younger brothers of Missouri, which interested me. It might be another link with Colonel Sutherland's little renegade band.

"Does any one of the Clantons in particular hang out with Ringo?" I asked. Clum thought Ike was probably closest to him. When I asked about a young gunman called Alias, Clum couldn't help me. But he did say he wouldn't be surprised to find many of the Clanton hands living under assumed names.

Clum also believed that the county sheriff, Johnny Behan, was in sympathy with the Clanton cowboys if not actually in their pay. Clum may have been influenced by the fact that his rival editor, Harry Woods, was Behan's under-sheriff.

Virgil Earp had initiated a no-gun policy within the corporate limits of Tombstone and made it stick, so I never took Jackson's firearms out of my saddlebags. I wrote Ginny that I might be here a month or so, and that she could write me in care of the newspaper.

Marshal Earp had a couple of his brothers with him, Wyatt and Morgan. The three of them looked a lot alike, so much so that one would occasionally be mistaken for another. I noticed that neither of them checked their guns when they came to Tombstone. When I mentioned that observation to Clum, he said they often served as deputies for Virgil, as well as guards on Wells Fargo and stagecoach runs.

All three brothers held financial interests in the Oriental Saloon, and even a brothel or two—all of which were considered legitimate businesses in frontier towns—and so handled large sums of money that needed firearms protection.

It's a good thing I wasn't armed when I first ran into a friend of theirs, John Henry Holliday, a dentist better known as a gambler and gunfighter. "Doc" Holliday suffered from consumption, and I don't suppose his dental patients cared for his coughing. From all I heard, he knew his days were limited, and that gave him an advantage with both poker and pistols: he really didn't care whether he won or lost.

If I'd been carrying a gun when I first saw him, I might well have grabbed for it, and I wouldn't be here now to tell you about it. You see, from a distance, Holliday resembled Cord McCluer. They were both skinny and unhealthy-looking. Closer up, I could tell that Doc was younger. I would later learn that he had a redeeming feature which McCluer lacked: he was loyal to his friends, and apparently considered Wyatt and Morgan to be among them. Kind of a strange alliance, a cold-blooded killer and a couple who described themselves as law-and-order folks.

Once more, I had worked on changing my appearance—styling my hair differently, even growing a mustache of sorts—since I didn't want to be recognized by Alias or the two gunmen who had been with him in Utah, if I found them.

I had been in Tombstone for less than two weeks when I spotted all three.

They came riding into town with a group of cowboys who seemed interested only in drinks and a good time. They could well have been in and out of Tombstone on previous occasions since I'd arrived and we just hadn't crossed paths. I'd been staying close to Clum's office while getting the lay of the land. On this particular evening, Clum and I were having dinner in the Oriental when the cowboys came in.

Trying not to make a big thing of it, I asked Clum about the two I recognized as they were standing at the bar. "The one with the goatee and little bit of curl in the front is Ike Clanton," Clum said. "I told you about him and his brothers. The one with the big mustache and long face is Johnny Ringo. He's a little crazy."

Young McCluer, or Alias, was with them. Clum didn't know him by name, only that he seemed to be one of Curly Bill's pals of late. The changes I'd made in my looks and the non-cowboy clothing I wore kept him from recognizing me—I hoped.

The Earps and Holliday were in the Oriental, too, and seemed to me to be watching the newcomers warily. Well, not Doc Holliday. I could hear him verbally insulting some of the cowboys who had seated themselves at his poker table, smiling all the while as if he meant no offense. And they all knew better than to take offense.

The sheriff scurried around from one group to another. "No trouble, boys," Sheriff Behan kept repeating. "Don't let Holliday bait you," he advised the ones playing poker with Holliday.

Ike Clanton spoke up from the bar. "You sure you wouldn't like us to take on Wyatt for you, Sheriff?" he asked. His speech was already slurred. Some of the cowboys laughed raucously, and I knew why. Clum had told me about the pretty young showgirl who had been Behan's mistress until she met Wyatt. There would come a time when she and Wyatt would wed, and have a long marriage. On top of that, there was talk that Wyatt might run against Behan for sheriff in the next election.

I remembered Wyatt from years ago at Tom Speer's Bench in Kansas City. He wouldn't remember me. All I'd been was just another gawker at all the well-known gun experts who gathered there to compare firearms and techniques.

No trouble started at the Oriental that evening, but it was brewing. By that fall, Behan would have tried unsuccessfully to implicate Holliday in a botched stagecoach holdup where two people got killed. Soon after that, there was a rumor that Wyatt had offered Ike Clanton the reward for the bandits if Ike would set things up so Wyatt could arrest them, which would have solidified his bid for sheriff.

Ike accused Wyatt of deliberately spreading that story although, from what I observed during those days, Ike was the only one who talked about it, especially when he was in his cups. As it turned out, it didn't matter. The men Ike was allegedly supposed to finger got wiped out in a shooting scrape elsewhere. But all of that heightened the bad blood between the Earps and Clantons.

It came to a head on October 26, in what came to be known, mistakenly, as the gunfight at the O.K. Corral.

I had no idea how famous the coming events were going to be, even though I knew that Virgil Earp had clobbered and arrested Ike during one of Ike's drinking sprees earlier that day. And then Wyatt had a run-in with one of the McLaury brothers, Tom, who was part of the Clanton entourage. Only when some of the cowboy faction got together later in the day did they meet the three Earp brothers and Holliday in the streets of Tombstone, resulting in a kind of shootout which rarely happened actually but would provide the pattern for hundreds of movie versions to come.

I happened to be near the stable by the O.K. Corral getting some grain for Star, who couldn't forage for himself as he would do when traveling. When I heard a step behind me, I assumed it was one of the stable hands. The next thing I felt was a hand over my mouth and more hands forcing my arms behind me.

I struggled, but I'd been taken totally by surprise. Someone forced a tobacco-stained bandana into my mouth and tied it. Others wrapped ropes around my wrists and ankles. When they'd finished, they dragged me to the back of the stable and dumped me on the floor.

I managed to squirm around to see who they were, and found myself looking into the cold eyes of Cord McCluer. So much for my wonderful disguise.

The sight of him caused me to jerk spasmodically, but there was no give in the ropes. McCluer stood over me with his sawed-off shotgun. I wondered why he hadn't used it.

"I told you we'd meet again," he hissed. "Watch him, son. I'm going to slip into the photo gallery and be ready to blast those lawdogs when they come by."

When he moved away, I saw that Alias—or whatever name McCluer's son was using now—had been standing behind him. The younger McCluer had a shiny pearl-handled revolver slung low on his right hip, and the same cold eyes I'd just seen seconds earlier. Like father, like son.

"Did you really think I wouldn't know you?" he chided me, after his father had moved out. "I've had my eye out ever since I first saw you back in New York. You had my father's gun then, remember?" He patted the pistol at his side. "Don't worry, you won't have to wait long. We're gonna give the Clantons and McLaurys a little help in settling with the Earps. Wouldn't want to alert them with an early gunshot." He moved his left hand over to where a pitchfork leaned against an empty stall behind him. "Of course, there are more quiet ways I could use."

He reached over slowly and picked up the pitchfork in both hands. But he hesitated.

"Guess I'd better see how things are shaping up outside, first," he said. "If I hear any threshing around by you, I'll come right back and pin your hide to the floor."

I exhaled when he moved to the door. I hadn't realized I'd been holding my breath.

But I didn't follow his orders. As noiselessly as I could, I moved myself along the floor to the nearest wall. When I backed up against it, I was able to squirm up to my feet, using the wall for support. Alias must not have heard me. At least he didn't come running back to stick me. I pulled at the ropes that bound my wrists behind me, but they stayed good and tight. I couldn't move away from the wall because my feet were tied together, too.

I could hear Star moving restlessly in his stall to my right, no doubt upset with me for not having delivered his grain. Then, I remembered his one bad habit, and was glad for the first time in my life that he was a cribber.

I barely managed to hop over to where he was, and stuck my hands over the front of his stall. Come on, boy, I thought. You want to chew something? Try these ropes.

He didn't need much encouragement, once I got my wrists close to his nose. Unfortunately, a horse's teeth are more blunt than sharp. I had to hand it to Star, though. When I didn't pull away and he realized I wasn't going to fuss at him over his chewing, he became persistent, nipping my hands once or twice. He never did quite manage to chew through the ropes, but he loosened the knots enough so I could finish the job.

As soon as I got my wrists free, I slid down and started working on my feet. Kid McCluer still hadn't come back. By the time he did, I was waiting to the side of the stable door.

He turned toward me as I jumped, and both of our hands gripped the pitchfork he was still holding. We struggled in silence—he, I guess, because he didn't want to alert the Earps, and me, because I didn't want his father coming back. He was stronger and more wiry than his father, and I wasn't at all sure he wouldn't get that pitchfork loose.

It was Ginny who saved me—not in person, but because, in the midst of our struggle, I remembered her lying on our floor, the blood on her dress, carrying our child...

A fury rose within me, and I heaved upward with all my strength, ripping the pitchfork out of his hands and swinging its handle against his head as hard as I could. He fell to the floor of the stable, shook his head, and went for that fancy gun of his.

The only weapon I had was his pitchfork, and I used it. Two of the prongs went into his gun hand and through it, pinning it to the floor. He gave a high-pitched scream, like a woman's, and then he fainted from either shock or pain.

By then, I didn't much care which. I left the pitchfork where it was, impaling his hand against the dirt floor. I even gave it another healthy push to make sure it was well anchored. Pretty brutal, I know, but I didn't care. And I figured Letty would be pleased.

I bent down and grabbed his fancy pistol. I seemed to be collecting lots of sidearms from the McCluers over the years. Then I tried to remember where Tombstone's photo gallery was located in relation to the stable where I was.

I'm not sure why it became known as the fight at the O.K. Corral, because that's not where it happened. As I emerged from the stable and into the corral area, I could see the backs of Ike and Billy Clanton, Frank and Tom McLaury, and another young cowboy named Billy Claiborne, who I'd seen around and who liked to refer to himself as Billy the Kid now that Bonney was three months gone. They were several blocks away from me, rounding a corner onto Fremont Street by Bauer's Butcher Shop. Holding the revolver I'd appropriated, I started to follow them, but then decided to slip down an alley behind the butcher shop where I might head them off.

I slowed down and moved more carefully past the shop and an assay office, towards Fly's Photo Gallery. That must be where Cord McCluer was waiting in ambush.

Fly's boarding house sat just in front of the photo shop, both on Fremont Street. The cowboys took up positions between the boarding house and another building, and I could see them passing a bottle back and forth. And then, farther down the street, I made out four men coming around the corner, all wearing dark coats, moving inexorably toward the cowboy faction. It wasn't hard to recognize Virgil, Wyatt and Morgan Earp, and Doc Holliday. I backed up against the corner of the photo gallery, out of sight of both groups.

As I watched, Sheriff Behan came running ahead of the Earps toward the cowboys. He stopped and began talking earnestly to them. I couldn't hear what they were saying, but I saw Ike motion toward the photo gallery with a confident smirk. Behan started to look, then caught himself and nodded. He took off his hat and mopped his balding head, then turned away and began walking back toward the Earps.

According to the testimony from the Earps at their trial afterward, Behan told them he had disarmed the cowboys. If so, I'm not sure where he was carrying their confiscated weapons. Billy Clanton, who towered over his older brother, Ike, still had a pistol in plain sight. So did Frank McLaury. I noticed Billy "the Kid" Claiborne drifting away from the others, as though having second thoughts.

By then, the Earps and Holliday had shoved past Behan and were marching toward the remaining four cowboys. Virgil Earp was holding a walking stick in his hand, rather than a pistol. He and Wyatt were in front, with Holliday and Morgan lagging a bit behind.

I moved to the back of the gallery and found a door. I tried it. Unlocked. I eased it open and slipped inside, the pistol in my hand.

The place seemed empty. I heard no sound at all. And then I spotted the skinny form of Cord McCluer, his back to me, crouched just below an open window with his sawed-off shotgun at the ready, waiting for the Earps to walk past.

I blinked my eyes to get rid of a momentary sense of seeing double—McCluer, the remorseless paid killer, and, through the window, Doc Holliday, just about as skinny and also carrying a sawed-off shotgun, looking almost like a mirror image.

The sound of the pistol when I cocked it seemed loud in the room. McCluer recognized it for exactly what it was and stiffened.

"Don't move," I told him in a low voice.

Although the later testimony would be that the cowboys went for their guns first, it seemed to me that Doc Holliday got off the opening shot. The cowboys may have been counting on McCluer to start blasting first and were over-confident. And Holliday, like McCluer, didn't believe in second chances.

In the flurry of shots exchanged outside, McCluer may have thought I'd be distracted enough for him to swing around with his shotgun and nail me. But I was ready for that. I fired as he spun, and then cocked and fired again.

"Look out, boys," I heard someone yell outside. "You're getting it from the rear."

I decided it was time to vacate the premises, before the Earps or Holliday started shooting into the building. I backed quickly out the door. Then I bumped into someone. I was shocked to see it was Ike Clanton. He brushed past me and kept running up the alley. I guessed he had also decided to get out.

Instinctively, I raised the pistol at his retreating form. He glanced back at me. "No!" he yelled. "I'm not armed." I thumbed back the hammer and aimed at him. As sure as I was that I'd recognized Ike as one of the shooters back in Utah, I just wasn't sure enough to fire at an unarmed man who was fleeing.

I uncocked the weapon and stuck in under my coat. Then I walked around to where the fight had ended.

Tom McLaury lay dead with a rifle beside him. I noticed an empty scabbard on the restless horse standing nearby. Billy Clanton was sitting with his back against a wall, but he was not moving. Frank McLaury lay dead in the street.

Virgil Earp was kneeling with blood seeping from the calf of one leg. Morgan was on the ground, clutching a bloody shoulder. Wyatt and Holliday were the only ones still on their feet. They were looking around for more potential enemies.

Other folks had started to gather by now, everybody trying to recap the sequence of events to someone else. You've probably read lots of accounts of the fight, but the fact is that nobody seemed to know who'd shot who, who fired first, or much of anything else. Of course, that never stopped the gunfight from being the prototype western movie showdown for all time, to the point where lots of folks today think such gunfights happened with regularity.

By the time I got back to the corral and inside the stable, Kid McCluer was gone. Only the bloody pitchfork remained. I felt sure, with that mangled hand, he would no longer be following in his father's footsteps. I'd have to be satisfied with that being my revenge on him. Well, that, and just having killed his father.

# THIRTY-TWO

That gunfight—which became the archetype for so many movie shootouts—
lasted maybe thirty seconds. It might well have been forgotten within a
few days, except for the newspaper rivalry in Tombstone.

At the Epitaph, John Clum published news stories stressing the virtues
of the Earps and said they had rid the community of a band of rustlers and
trouble-makers. At the Nugget, Harry Woods published alternate versions of
the shootout, claiming the cowhands had been unarmed and murdered in the
streets of by the Earps and Holliday.

This journalistic feud continued for months, and some of the rival accounts
got picked up by other publications across the country. I had actually done
some of the writing for Clum's paper, and those pieces probably got more
national exposure than anything I wrote in my dime novel days.

Alias had disappeared. I never saw him again. From time to time, I would
hear rumors about a drunk with a crippled hand begging for drinks in some
distant saloon, and cursing someone he referred to as Double-Six. I figured

I knew who it was, and thought it fitting that my brother was getting some measure of revenge, with Alias thinking Jackson had been the one who ruined him.

I did see Ringo and Clanton afterward, along with maybe twenty other horsemen. I was accompanying Mr. Clum at the time on a business trip to Bisbee that December, and they took some potshots at the stagecoach in which we were passengers. I still think it was an effort by the gang to eliminate Clum, or maybe me, or maybe both of us. But they missed. However, the presence of Clanton and Ringo in the bunch made me think there might well be a connection to the colonel again.

The attack was duly reported to Sheriff Behan, who did not bother to form a posse to pursue the band of gunmen. And I had finally decided there was no way I could ever manage to rid the country of all the colonel's hired assassins. I decided it was time for another approach.

I rode Star on another long journey filled with campouts and occasional overnights at settlements, back to Utah. I had a vague plan that I hoped would keep Ginny safe, once and for all, from any future attacks on me. It would require something I had never considered before. But I decided that, if cold-blooded murder was what it took, that was what I would do.

The same month I left Tombstone, some men ambushed Virgil Earp in the night, leaving him crippled. Three months later, in March, 1882, Morgan Earp was fatally shot in the back through the window of a pool hall.

Wyatt and Doc Holliday put together a posse of their own, and set out to hunt down the killers. They never caught up with Ike Clanton. Like his father, he was eventually shot down while rustling. Somebody else brought down Ringo in mid-1882, but neither Wyatt, Doc nor anyone else ever claimed credit. Doc himself lived on until 1887 when his consumption finally caught up with him. Despite all his years of living on the edge, he died of natural causes.

I had been keeping Leland Stanford, soon to be a U.S. senator, advised of all that had happened. I did not tell him about my plans to return to Virginia, to Shenandoah County, after all these years. Stanford and his wife had suffered a loss of their own, one with which I could identify: their 16-year-old son had died of typhoid. In 1885, the same year he became a senator, he and his wife endowed a university named for their son.

After I'd enjoyed home in Utah for a bit, I didn't tell Ginny where I was going next, either. How could I tell her I was setting out to commit murder? Not that the colonel didn't have it coming. I was convinced—heck, I'm still convinced—of his involvement in the deaths of two presidents, and of at least financial support of terrorism tactics that Quantrill and Bloody Bill Anderson had taught their followers, to try and hurt the country, to create distrust in the safety of its banks and to sabotage its rail transportation. Not to mention his attempts on my life, and what had been done to my brother and Ginny. No, his death would not weigh heavily on my conscience at all.

I paid my own rail fare east, not wanting to connect Stanford with what I planned to do by using his pass. I wasn't sure just how I would do it, but there was not a doubt in my mind that I would put an end to Colonel Sutherland soon after I arrived.

As it turned out, I was several days too late.

Sutherland was dead by the time my train crossed into Virginia, although I didn't find that out until after I'd arrived. I set about making my systematic inquiries, and found I hadn't lost my talent for getting people to talk to me.

Sutherland had been a widower for several years and, just recently, married a much younger woman. It was she who had shot him. And she was pleading self-defense.

Out of curiosity, I sat myself in the back of the county courtroom to watch her arraignment. And when I got a look at her, I knew I would be staying around for the trial.

The years had not been kind to Callie St. Clair, but she was still attractive.

Later in the day, I went to the county jail to see if I could visit her. I said I was a friend of her family. After a little argument and a search to make sure I wasn't carrying any weapons, they let me in.

Callie didn't even look up until the cell door clanked shut behind me. Then it seemed to take a minute to register. "Johnny," she finally said. "Johnny Six."

It didn't take long for me to get her story. It turned out her plans had been much the same as mine.

As I said, she was still attractive enough to get the colonel to court her, and then to marry her, all to get her to a place where she could be alone with him with none of his usual bodyguards.

"My chance came last week, in the house, and I took it," she told me with utter calm. "He was the one behind Jackson's death, Johnny. We both know that, even if there's no way to prove it."

I nodded. "Him," I said. "And Sean."

"Sean's handling the colonel's business interests out west somewhere," she said. "I don't believe he even made it back here for the funeral. Although I don't really know. Or care."

"I care, Callie," I said. "And I'm going to get you the best legal representation I can."

She stared at me. "Why would you do that?"

I could have told her that, if she hadn't taken matters into her own hands, it would probably be me in jail facing a murder charge. "Let's say for Jackson."

"Thank you, Johnny," she said, touching me on the arm. "But I don't imagine I'll be inheriting any of the colonel's fortune to spend on lawyers."

"That's okay. I've got money in a bank right here in this town." I smiled as I remembered the money had come from the late Colonel Sutherland. "I'm sure Jackson would think this is a perfect use for it."

It was not easy to find someone willing to go up against the Sutherland power and influence, but an up-and-coming lawyer named Grabill finally agreed to take the case. He exceeded my expectations. Although the marriage had been quite brief, he managed to elicit testimony from some servants in the Sutherland mansion showing a pattern of cruelty and abuse by the colonel toward his new wife. He got them to talk about nastiness that Callie hadn't even told me. It wasn't until a few years ago that I got that kind of treatment into a movie script, *Arizona Ranger,* over at RKO. I'm sure Sean recognized what I had Steve Brodie's character doing.

But Callie was still convicted of manslaughter. Even the claim of self-defense couldn't overcome the male prerogative no doubt held by the jurors that a man had a right to treat his wife as he saw fit. Still, Grabill got the sentence down to the one-year minimum. Better than life, or hanging. When I made one last visit to her cell to tell her goodbye, she insisted on passing along a souvenir from her personal articles held as evidence during the trial.

When I left Virginia this time, I thought all of my lifetime battles were finally behind me. I was wrong, of course. My future battles would be very different, but they would continue—right up to now.

A lot had been going on out west in the meantime. A guy named Bob Ford—soon to be immortalized in song and story as the dirty little coward who shot "Mr. Howard"—had indeed laid Jesse James in his grave, back-shooting him even as Jesse was supposedly planning a new series of bank robberies.

A year later, in 1883, Bill Cody went back into show business with the first of his many "Wild West" extravaganzas. He brought along a cute little gal named Annie Oakley as the show's resident sharpshooter in 1884. In another coup, he added Sitting Bull, the former leader of the Hunkpapa Sioux that had helped wipe out Custer. And he added me in 1886 to help write a script that had Buffalo Bill rushing to save Custer at the Little Big Horn but arriving too late. That stuff turned out to be good practice for what I ended up doing in Hollywood.

We'd lost Ginny's mother in the intervening years. After that, there was really nothing to keep us in Utah, so we left the real west to join Buffalo Bill's fanciful version. His shows went all over the country, and even to Europe where we did a special show for Queen Victoria herself. That was where little Annie Oakley shot a cigar out of the mouth of German Emperor Wilhelm II. Some thirty years later, she said that, if she had known Wilhelm would be among those responsible for World War I, she might have adjusted her aim.

Back home, the North American railroads adopted four time zones we still have. The end of 1886 saw the start of the most devastating winter anyone could remember, sweeping across the Great Plains from Canada to Texas. It marked the end of the cattle boom, and an end to the open range method of raising cattle.

Ginny and I were back in the states on April 22, 1889, in time to watch part of the Oklahoma land rush for what had been Indian Territory lands, declared open by President Benjamin Harrison. Star and Curly were no longer up to being in such a race, but we did get ourselves a small piece of land where my two horses spent the rest of their lives happily grazing. They had even mellowed enough to do it in the same field.

Sitting Bull had left Cody's show, too, and then had been accused of supporting the so-called Ghost Dance in 1890, which some Indians believed would rid them of the white man, bring back the buffalo, and restore their old way of life. It was pure delusion, even more than the scenarios I'd helped create for Cody's entertainments. Sitting Bull was killed by some Indian Police, in spite of an attempt by Cody to intercede on his behalf.

The Dalton gang was about all that was left of the infamous robber bands. They over-did it when they tried to take two banks at once in Coffeyville, Kansas, in the fall of 1892. All but one of the band got killed, and the survivor was sentenced to life in prison. Near the turn of the century, train robbery got fashionable again with a gang led by Butch Cassidy and the Sundance Kid, all of which was continuing grist for my pulp writing. In fact, I had some input in a fictional version of Butch and his Hole-in-the-Wall gang as part of a radio show that put WXYZ on the broadcasting map in Detroit. We changed his last name and make him a lot worse than he was.

I lost my mentor and friend in 1893 when Leland Stanford died, in Palo Alto, California. He was still serving in the Senate. Among all those whose paths I'd crossed in my lifetime, he probably came closest to understanding the internal threat to the country that the Sutherlands had posed.

A New Englander named Percival Lowell came west and built an astronomical observatory near Flagstaff, Arizona, in 1894. Soon afterward, he claimed to be able to see a network of canals on Mars. Maybe he did. It was just a few years ago that the Air Force reported one of those flying saucers crashing near Roswell, Billy the Kid's old stomping grounds.

It was in 1898 that Teddy Roosevelt led his Rough Riders up Kettle Kill in Cuba in the Spanish-American War. We mentioned that in *Arizona Ranger*, as well as one of Billy Elliott's "Red Ryder" movies. And we appropriated the Rough Riders name for a series of movies with Buck Jones and Tim McCoy, in their last roles, with Raymond Hatton making it a threesome with his old-timer character. Just between us, Hatton was almost the youngest of the three.

That was the same year Thomas Edison did a short film which maybe could be called the first western, *Cripple Creek Barroom*. The Lumiere brothers in Paris had already started showing simple movie scenes, an entertainment that soon spread through Europe. Then Edison came up with a way to project the moving pictures onto a screen in a New York City music hall and, by 1899, George Melies in Europe was doing short films as actual stories.

All that led to a fellow named Edwin Porter directing an eleven-minute film called *The Great Train Robbery,* in 1903. The actor who became "Broncho Billy" Anderson was in it. Maybe Tom London was, too. Tom's still making movies. When someone asked him how many he'd done, he said that would be like asking him how many times he'd changed his socks.

The early films were made in New York and New Jersey, until the Nestor Company built a studio in the part of Los Angeles that became Hollywood. Out here, filming could take advantage of the climate, great scenery and lots of daylight most of the year. By the mid-1920s, Columbia, Fox, M-G-M, Paramount, United Artists, Universal and Warners all had studios out here.

It was in 1900 that I lost Ginny.

Despite the injury that kept us from having children, we'd enjoyed a good life and a pretty adventuresome one. I always figured Ginny would outlive me, and made sure I kept plenty of writing money in the bank for her. Now I wish I'd lavished it on her when she was alive. One day, she was her usual self, flitting around one of our homes and talking about how happy we'd been over the years, and the next, she was gone. A stroke, they said.

I felt like a lost little boy again.

Eventually, I packed up and followed the growing number of out-of-work cowboys migrating here to Hollywood to put their skills to work in front of movie cameras. Some became actors, some did stunt work, but I was a little long in the tooth for that. So I started doing some script-writing, or more like script-doctoring, giving advice on how to make a story more realistic.

I wasn't the only one. Wyatt Earp came out to Hollywood, too, and made his suggestions on making films like *My Darling Clementine* more authentic. So did Bill Tilghman, Frank James, Cole Younger, and Emmet Dalton, who didn't spend life in prison, after all.

It was during those years that I crossed paths once again with Sean Sutherland. We were still on the opposite sides of things, but now our duels were being played out on movie screens.

# INTERMISSION

*The direct approach hadn't worked. Clay McCluer didn't want to risk wearing a white coat again to try and slip into the old man's room. True, he hadn't been caught, but repeating a plan could be dangerous. He had to finish the job he'd started on Gower Street, when he'd only managed to wound the target.*

*McCluer had checked out windows in every building that bordered on Jonathan Six's hospital room. He actually found three that could offer a shot into the room's window, but none of them were at the right angle to see the patient's bed.*

*However, Six might soon reach the point where he could leave the bed and walk about the room. Sooner or later, he would pass close enough to the window to show up in a telescopic sight.*

*But the old man was not willing to wait. There was too much that Six could tell people about him, he said. And that might affect his recent arrangements with some Puerto Rican dissidents to pull off something that he had been working on for a long time.*

*The Old Man's plan actually scared McCluer. He didn't want to know any more about it than he'd already learned.*

*And McCluer didn't want to wait, either. In particular, he did not want Mr. Sutherland to give this assignment to anyone else. He hadn't managed a killing shot when Six had been set up for him during that fracas on Gower, but that hadn't been his fault. Who could have foreseen that Six had made so many friends among those actors and stunt men when he worked on their movies?*

*Well, he would not miss a second time. He had grown up hearing constantly* from his late crippled father how Johnny Six had killed his grandfather back in 1881. His father could never handle a gun again, but young Clay Junior could and did.

He had been an apt pupil. Maybe it was in the genes. His grandfather had been one of the best. And the young McCluer had honed his skills well enough to find a permanent place on Old Man Sutherland's payroll.

His father finally kicked off from too much rotgut, but Clay McCluer was on the payroll by then. Sean Sutherland's empire ranged from movie enterprises to gambling houses, and a good number of covert political activities that McCluer didn't really want to know about. If those politicians on the House Un-American Activities Committee only knew about them, they wouldn't be wasting their time on Hollywood writers.

Clay had lived up to whatever recommendation his father had made on his behalf. Until now, he had a perfect record for hits assigned by the Old Man. And now, for the hit he'd been waiting for most of his life, the Old Man might be questioning his competence.

"I'm going to make sure there are no mistakes this time, young McCluer," he had told Clay, with no apparent realization of how he was parroting the most frequent line ever uttered by the brains heavy in movies. "I'm handling this myself."

He had made clandestine arrangements to get McCluer admitted as an overnight patient under a false name. McCluer didn't even know what ailment he was supposed to have. All that was important was that he now lay on a bed in the room next to where Jonathan Six was recuperating. The connecting doorway was locked, but he knew he would have no trouble with that when the time came.

# THIRTY-THREE

*Roy Rogers: "Well, gang, if we were makin' a picture,*
*right here's where somebody'd holler 'Action!'"*
Bells of Rosarita *(1945)*

Nancy, I've got to admit your new husband has been very patient with me, especially making you take down my story these past weeks. Well, you'll be glad to know I'll finish it up today. Yes, that's right, don't faint. After today, you'll know everything I know, and your husband will have a written account if the authorities can do anything about it.

In fact, I hope it reaches the ears of the Secret Service in Washington. If Sean Sutherland realizes he's reaching the end of the trail, he might just try to arrange yet another presidential assassination. Yes, I'm serious. It could happen any time.

All right. We're up to when I moved here and became a "script doctor." I wish now I'd tried to persuade old Wyatt Earp to let me do his life story. Stuart Lake ended up interviewing him before he passed on, and Lake's book about Wyatt has been the bible for more western movie scenarios than any one source I can think of. Just read *Wyatt Earp, Frontier Marshal* some time. You'll see bits of stuff that turned up in movies from George O'Brien to Randolph Scott. I've even heard that Mr. Lake may become a consultant on a TV series about Wyatt.

You know, Josie, Wyatt's widow, tried to get that book quashed. She said

Lake made up most of it, once Wyatt was no longer around. She did force a title change, from *Wyatt Earp, Gunfighter*. She always insisted her husband had been a businessman. She wasn't nice about it. Someone who knew Josie and Wyatt said nothing would ever convince him Wyatt was a killer, seeing as how he'd lived with Josie for fifty years without killing her.

The only other book deal I might have considered would have been about Tim Kellerher. You haven't heard of him? He was chief special agent for the Union Pacific, and the lawman who should have gotten credit for breaking up the Wild Bunch. Frank Spearman wrote a novel based on him, *Whispering Smith*. There have been a bunch of pictures based on it, the last one with Alan Ladd a couple years ago.

I got to see my old employer, Mr. Clum, at Wyatt's funeral back in '29. He was one of the pallbearers, along with Bill Hart and Tom Mix. Josie lived until 1944, always threatening to sue movie-makers over scripts she felt didn't portray Wyatt in the right way—even when the script changed his name, like *In Early Arizona*, *Marshal of Mesa City*, and *Law and Order*, to name a few. That actor, Ronald Reagan, is doing a remake of *Law and Order* lined up for next year over at Universal-International.

While I was running around from one studio to another doing my uncredited script stuff, I ran into objections that I made my heroes too heroic, always fighting fair, letting the bad guy draw first, all that. They had a point. The real-life counterparts of the movie heroes drank, swore, smoked, womanized and shot first if they could. But these little B-movies were aimed mostly at youngsters. I figured these old west figures should set some ethical standards. Herbert Yates, over at Republic, agrees. He has it in his contract that his western stars can't smoke or misbehave in public. Even John Wayne had to sign it.

It must've griped Sean Sutherland something awful. I knew he was orchestrating the opposition. He wanted to make the historic bad guys the heroes. We've talked about some of the cleaned-up versions of Jesse James and Billy the Kid. You can bet he had some influence there. Even the guy who's doing the Lone Ranger on TV played Jesse as a good guy in a couple of serials.

So Sean knew I was out there, even if he couldn't find me. I managed to stay below the radar. I did show up on sets of movies occasionally, and sometimes stopped by Gower Gulch to pal around with friends. I thought those places were safe.

You see, Sean does more than use movies to propagandize youngsters. That's just mischief. Like his father, Sean still hates this country. I'm sure he colluded with the Axis powers during the last war. He'd collude with North Korea now if he could find a way.

He and I have played a cat-and-mouse game all over Los Angeles for decades now, and not just by influencing cowboy movies. Luckily for me, I got along with a lot of the stars and extras and stunt doubles while I was working on their pictures. They kind of looked out for me.

Rick will tell you, Nancy, it's not unusual for fights to happen around Gower Gulch. Sean's people were never very popular with the working stiffs on the little pictures, so I figured I was safe there. Wrong.

I wasn't totally naïve about it. I went armed. With all the costumes folks were wearing around Gower Street and Sunset Boulevard, my gun belt with Kid McCluer's old revolver never looked out of place.

But there was something different about the corner last time. It wasn't unusual for guys to hang around the Columbia Drug store on that corner looking for a day's work as members of a posse or outlaw gang, but today there were more western stars milling around than I'd ever seen at one time. True, some had gotten their start there, but they had contracts now. They didn't need to be there looking for work.

A short bouncy stuntman from Republic walked by me. "Watch yourself, Mr. Six," he whispered. "We've heard somebody was hiring some roughnecks to take you out."

Minutes later, an actor in an all-black western outfit ambled by. "Mr. Six, you should get out of here. There's a rumor there's going to be trouble."

The grapevine was active. I took note of my surroundings. A good number of the stars had formed kind of a protective wall around me, and even some of the actors who played heavies were there.

Then a group of men I hadn't seen before began trying to shove through their ranks. And they were coming in my direction.

That's when I knew Sean Sutherland had finally tired of our little game. Maybe I was getting too close to his activities outside of our movie-scripting rivalry. I had been a fool not to take more precautions, and it looked like I was going to pay for it.

"Get out of the way, you drug-store cowboys," one of the men said, trying to push past them. If he had been a regular at this watering hole, he'd have known that was the wrong thing to say.

One of the actors whose career had taken him to Columbia and Republic and who was now at Monogram, pushed the man in the face. Surprised, the man stumbled to the sidewalk. "Now then," said the actor, "beat it."

The man lunged to his feet. "Clear these guys out of the way," he said to his group.

"Kind of high-handed, aren't you?" said the man in black.

The bigger man took a swing at him, but the actor dodged easily.

"Well, fellows, if this was a picture, here's where somebody'd holler 'Action,'" said the king of the singing cowboys.

And all hell broke loose.

To my right, Columbia's last cowboy star was battling back to back with the lanky stuntman who usually doubled for him, hammering several of the newcomers. A former Alabama football star turned Monogram cowboy star punched one of them in the stomach, then placed his left hand behind the man's head and drove his right fist into it. Another Republic singing cowboy had twisted his antagonist's arm behind his back and punched him in the stomach, then spun him around and knocked him down.

The blows didn't sound as loud and meaty as the sound-effects punches you hear in movies, but they did the job. The guys after me were outnumbered. I found myself worrying about these actors risking bruises and black eyes that would mess up their shooting schedules, but I was almighty grateful.

The stuntman who had been the first to warn me took a running leap across several battlers and came down on top of two of the men, knocking them both to the ground. He sprang back up while they were still fumbling around, looked at me and grinned. "That would have killed an ordinary man," he said.

Two of my attackers managed to break through the line and were almost on top of me, when two bullwhips wrapped themselves around their necks and jerked them back. The guy in black and a star from Monogram were on the other ends.

And then something smashed into the window beside me. At the same time, I heard a shot. Everyone prudently dove for cover after that, and I pulled out my own pistol.

Since everybody else was on the ground or hiding behind something, it didn't take long to spot him. He was waving what looked like an automatic back and forth, trying to line up another shot. I shot first.

He gripped his shoulder and the pistol spun out of his hand. I felt like congratulating myself, but it really hadn't been that good a shot. I'd been aiming for his head.

And then I heard another shot, farther away, and found myself flat on the sidewalk. That was the last I knew until I woke up here.

# CURTAIN

Clay McCluer held the pistol with its silencer straight down beside him in his left hand, while his right worked the door key which the Old Man had obtained for him. A quick twist, and the door was unlocked. Switching the automatic to his right hand, he opened the door and stepped through.

He stopped in surprise. His target was there on the bed, as planned, but he wasn't alone. A pretty young woman was seated by him, a stenographer's pad on her lap.

Well, that was too bad for her. He didn't want any witnesses.

"I thought I'd put you down for good over at Gower Gulch," McCluer said. "This time I'll be sure."

With his free hand, he reached toward the young woman and picked up the tablet. He stuck it in his belt under his coat.

"First things first," he told them, as they stared back at him. "The Old Man will want this."

Six and the young woman continued watching him in silence. McCluer eased around them, located a "No Visitors" sign on the table by the room's other door, and opened it just long enough to hook the sign to the doorknob outside.

"Now it's just us," he said. "You've had this coming for a long time, Mr. Six. Seventy years or more, you've had it coming. This is for my grandfather, and my father..."

"I thought you looked familiar," said the man on the bed. "Your name must be McCluer."

"Yeah. The last of the McCluers. Just like you're the last of the Sixes."

"I've been telling this lady a good deal about your grandfather these past few weeks," the patient said. "I guess the last time I saw your father was in Tombstone, if he was the one who called himself Alias."

"Good guess. I'm glad you know who you're getting this from."

"You mean this is revenge? The set-up at Gower, the thugs you hired to come after me? Nothing but that?"

"A little more than that," McCluer said. "I'm getting paid for this, which makes it even sweeter. You know too much about the Old Man. As for the doll—she may know your story, but she won't spread it around, either."

Nancy spoke up. "I've been taking down his story for several weeks. The police have my notes."

McCluer patted his coats. "They don't have these. And these are probably the ones that tie everything up."

Nancy raised her eyebrows. "You mean what he's been saying about Sean Sutherland are true?"

McCluer gave a sharp laugh. "Didn't you believe him? If the FBI hadn't tumbled to his work during the war, he'd have been landing squads of German saboteurs by submarine right here in California. And right now he's paving the way for some Puerto Rican nationalists get a shot at the president while he's in Blair House…"

He was talking too much. These two were much too calm. He backed up a step toward the door into the adjoining room, and raised his pistol.

Before he could shoot, the room's closet door swing open and two armed men jumped out. But McCluer's instincts had prepared him. He grabbed the woman by the arm and jerked her from her chair.

"Put your guns down," he said, pulling her closer with his free arm. "Or she gets it."

"Take it easy, McCluer," said the taller of the two men. McCluer recognized him. He'd been in the elevator with the woman when he'd made his first run at Six. "You don't want to hurt anybody. You can't get out, we've got men all over …"

*The silencer on the end of his pistol pressed against Nancy's neck. "Drop them. Now."*

*"Do it, Ed," the taller man said. They lowered their arms, and let their pistols fall with dull thumps to the floor.*

*"Now, move over by the door. If anyone fires through it, they'll hit you, not me."*

*"McCluer, you're making it harder for yourself," the taller man said. But he looked panicky. This girl must be special to him. Good. She would be his ticket out of here. "We've got everything you said on tape," the man added.*

*McCluer began to realize what he had walked into. "How'd you know...?*

*"I remembered you in that doctor's getup, and later pretending to be a patient. We looked through mug shots, and there you were. Never convicted, but often arrested. So if you want to take it out on somebody..."*

*"Rick, you know better," the stenographer spoke up. "I was the one who recognized him."*

*"Nancy, shut up!"*

*"McCluer," said the man on the bed, "haven't you forgotten who you came after? Not these folks. If you waste shots on them, you'll have a buildup of gases in that silencer that could blow up your gun. Maybe your hand, too."*

*The pistol swung toward Jonathan Six, then back to Nancy, as McCluer's face hardened.*

*"If that happens," Six went on relentlessly, "it'll be just like what happened to your father, won't it? That seemed a fit punishment for him..."*

*With a snarl, McCluer shoved Nancy away and spun toward the bed. One shot made a snapping sound in the crowded room.*

*The rage on McCluer's face turned to shock, then became no expression at all. He fell forward, spilling onto the front of the bed. Then he slid onto the floor.*

*Six pulled back a sheet which now had a blackened hole, exposing a shiny two-shot derringer. He handed it to Rick.*

*"Callie St. Clair's last gift to me," he said.*

Rick and Nancy sat quietly in a hospital waiting room, until it would become their turns to give statements to other detectives now handling the shooting. Six had no doubt saved his life, or Nancy's, or maybe both. But it had ended their plan to take McCluer alive and get him to testify against Sutherland. Again, Old Man Sutherland remained above the law, as Six had warned. Even the tape would be of limited value without McCluer.

Nancy finally spoke. "It's hard to believe we've spent our entire married life on this case, you know?" They both smiled, but then Nancy turned serious. "Is it over, Rick? Will it ever be over?"

"I don't know," he admitted. "They might not believe his story. And Sutherland's had a lot of years to build his power base."

"You believe Mr. Six, don't you?" Nancy asked. Rick nodded. "So do I. Think how it must be for him. We've spent weeks on this, but he's spent a lifetime." She paused. "What if we took his story to the papers?"

"We'd get sued," Rick said.

The door opened and one of Rick's colleagues came in. "Hey Rick, Nancy. We need to talk to Mr. Six now."

"He's not here." Rick stood up, suddenly worried again. "They transferred him to another room after the shooting. Isn't he there?"

"The staff says no. If he's not with you…"

Rick and the other man hurried out, and joined the other officers who were questioning hospital employees. Could another Sutherland man have gained access to this floor and snatched Six?

It took about half an hour before they found a nurse who remembered seeing a man wearing a surgical mask getting on an elevator. She had wondered at the time who he was, since she didn't recognize him as any of the doctors on duty.

"Was he old? Young? Tall? Short?" Rick demanded.

*"It's hard to say. He had a hat and overcoat, and that surgical mask."*

*It might have been Six himself, Rick thought. Was he going into hiding to avoid Sutherland's minions?*

*"I don't think it was a doctor," Rick told the other detectives.*

*"It wasn't?" said the nurse. "Then—who was that masked man?"*

Clipping from the *Los Angeles Daily Sentinel,* Nov. 10, 1950

RECLUSIVE MILLIONAIRE DIES IN MYSTERIOUS SHOOTING
By Grace Koppelman

LOS ANGELES—Police identified the victim of an apparent shooting Thursday night as Sean Davis Sutherland, a reclusive business executive and movie producer.

The shooting apparently occurred sometime Thursday in Sutherland's Beverly Hills mansion, according to detectives at the scene. Dr. Armand Schwartz, the medical examiner, said Sutherland died from a single gunshot wound to the chest.

Sutherland's roots go back to a prominent Virginia family whose fortunes began in the late 19th century. He dabbled in film production, owned several gambling casinos in Las Vegas, Nev., and is said to have had other businesses with assets totaling into the millions of dollars. But little is known about his personal life.

Even his age is a matter of conjecture. A brief biological sketch obtained from one of his companies several years ago listed it as 70, but some of his employees, speaking off the record, thought that number was far too low even then.

A source close to the investigation said authorities had been seeking grand jury indictments against Sutherland, but would not specify their nature. There was speculation that the death was a suicide, prompted by the potential indictments.

But other sources say a security guard at the home had been knocked unconscious by someone wielding a blunt instrument, possibly a handgun, before Sutherland's body was found.

It is known that detectives recovered a matched pair of Colt revolvers in the study where the body was found, along with a gun belt with two holsters on a table in the middle of the room. One pistol was in Sutherland's hand. The other was on the table near the gun belt.

One shot had been fired from each pistol. One bullet was found lodged in the study wall across from where Sutherland lay. The bullet from the other pistol, pending ballistics tests, is believed to have inflicted the fatal wound.

A detective speaking on condition of anonymity said one theory is that the guns were placed on the table between Sutherland and the hypothetical intruder.

"It looked like a scenario from some movie shoot-'em-up," the detective said, "where two combatants place guns on a table and then grab for them at the same time. That very scene was enacted between Vaughn Monroe and Ward Bond in a picture I saw last winter."

However, no charges have been filed and the intruder, if there was one, remains unidentified.

This is the second "wild west" style incident in Hollywood this year. A shooting fracas at Gower and Sunset several weeks ago left two men wounded. Details on that incident have also been sketchy. There has been speculation of a cover-up because prominent movie stars were said to be involved.

That investigation was led by Detective Rick Martin, who was unavailable for comment. He and his recent bride, the former Nancy Hamilton, were at an undisclosed location on their honeymoon.

# THE END